FRENCH LEAVE

Recent Titles by Suzanne Goodwin

JOURNEY FROM YESTERDAY
A RISING STAR
THE RISING STORM
STARSTRUCK
WHILE THE MUSIC LASTS

FRENCH LEAVE

Suzanne Goodwin

F

This first world edition published in Great Britain 2001 by
SEVERN HOUSE PUBLISHERS LTD of
9–15 High Street, Sutton, Surrey SM1 1DF.
This first world edition published in the USA 2001 by
SEVERN HOUSE PUBLISHERS INC., of
595 Madison Avenue, New York, NY 10022.

British Library Cataloguing in Publication Data

Goodwin, Suzanne
French leave
1. France – History – German occupation, 1940–1945
2. Love stories
I. Title
823.9'14 [F]

ISBN 0-7278-5691-X

Typeset by Hewer Text Ltd.,
Edinburgh, Scotland.
printed and bound in Great Britain by
MPG Books Ltd, Bodmin, Cornwall.

Part One

Jill

1944

One

It was pelting with rain when Jill joined the Red Cross ambulance nurses, who had gone up on deck to watch the approach of the low coastline. The sea was rough. The crossing had been made in a battered grey-painted steamer which years ago had ferried holidaymakers to the sands of Boulogne. Now it was stripped of past glories, a dirty British coaster.

A high wind blew, the dark sea heaved. The ship was still at a distance from the shore.

A good many of the troops grouped and crowded on deck were green in the face. Some were bringing up their boots (as the Red Cross lieutenant said) in the lavatories. The moment the voyage began and the ship emerged from the shelter of Dover harbour walls, Jill felt very sick. A sailor going by, carrying a slopping tray of tea, saw her colour and said matily, "Best keep your eye on the horizon."

"Sorry?"

"On the horizon," he called over his shoulder. "Old Navy trick. Don't look at the sea, look at what stays level. All right?"

Jill, sickness worsening, supported herself on a chair and tried to do as he'd said. Through rain-lashed portholes she saw the horizon, a long straight line which did not heave or fall. Up rose the ship. Down it fell. Up. Down. The movements sickening. But the horizon didn't move, there it remained, level and straight. Very slowly, Jill's nausea wore off.

The Red Cross girls, plus Jill and another interpreter who had joined the group at Victoria, were silent as the ship slowly made its way towards the harbour walls. It was extraordinary to think this was actually France. Not one of the girls except Jill had set foot in Europe in their lives. They had grown up on an island cut off from the Continent as if from Mars; there was something awesome about actually seeing it now. The battle of France was being fought in this country, this very minute. Less than a month ago the town they were approaching had been bristling with German soldiers, German guns. Boulogne had been liberated. Paris had been liberated, but the enemy still fought on.

In England the newspapers published pictures of victory day after day. The troops necklaced in flowers, girls stretching out their arms to kiss them. Flying flags. And faces filled with joy as if angels had come swooping down from Paradise. There were the tanks that rolled down the long tree-edged roads of Normandy and symbolised freedom. That vision had been in the thoughts of the girls until the ship docked in the French harbour.

The process was long and laborious. It was over an hour before the first troops began to disembark.

"Women," remarked the Red Cross lieutenant, a smart sharp young woman, "are very low priority." They had been ordered to wait their turn and they stood on deck watching soldier after soldier marching down the gangplank, packs on their shoulders, rifles slung. A good many of them were still ashen.

"Poor lads," murmured one of the girls, who was tall and soft-hearted.

"Seasick, you mean?" said the lieutenant. "That'll wear off in half an hour. They've got more than that ahead of them, Alison."

Alison looked crushed, which was the response the lieutenant had intended.

French Leave

Thick clouds hung low and the station roofs were rent with enormous holes through which the dark sky showed – it was almost the colour of broken slates. There was a burnt-out lorry near one blackened wall. As the girls were finally ordered to move, the rain grew heavier. On the platform two sergeants moved up and down ranks of miserable, sodden soldiers standing at attention near a very long, battered-looking train. The sergeants, checking the men present, reminded Jill of dogs she'd seen in Wales rounding up sheep. The soldiers looked so tired and wet. Was this a noble invading army?

One of the sergeants marched up to the girls, who had no umbrellas and were huddled in a little group. The glass on the station roof had gone years ago – there were only rusty girders now – and the rain poured in.

"You don't need to check we are all present and correct, Sergeant," said the Red Cross lieutenant. She looked him in the eye. He was big and burly and no match for her. "There are six of us and we are here, as you see; there are also two interpreters. Now. Do you think we might get into the train and stop getting unnecessarily drenched?"

"Not ready to entrain yet, Ma'am."

"You may not be. We are. Come along, girls, look slippy."

Before the sergeant had time to do more than begin, "Look here, Ma'am . . .", eight young women ran across the platform and scrambled into the train.

"Ugh. It is filthy." The lieutenant looked up and down a corridor gritty with coal dust. "Wait a moment. I will see if there's anything better."

She returned almost immediately.

"There are the remnants of first class carriages further along. The officers have bagged three. I've requisitioned one."

Entrained, as the sergeant would call it, Jill and the rest sat down in a once first class compartment. The Red Cross girls chatted, mostly shop. The other interpreter whom Jill had scarcely seen on board, said, "Name's Waters. Rosalind. Known as Roz."

"Jill Sinclair."

"Hello. Didn't see you on the crossing. Where did you get to?"

"Staring at the horizon."

"Like that, was it? Cigarette?"

"Thanks, but I don't."

"Good-oh," said Roz. The corners of her eyes creased, the laughter lines were heavy. She was the oldest member of the group. Late thirties, with masculine features, coarse skin and clever eyes flecked with flaws like those sometimes seen in porcelain. Her brownish hair was frizzy, her manner as confident as that of the Red Cross lieutenant.

"I'm always pleased when somebody I'm with doesn't smoke. And the lieutenant," said Roz, giving the young woman in the corner of the compartment an approving look, "has forbidden me to offer my cigs to her lot. Selfish, you get, when you smoke. My mother told me she felt the same about fresh walnuts when she was pregnant. There was a tree in the garden and every time anybody went out and helped themselves to nuts which had fallen on the grass (it was September, like now), she thought 'that's one less for me'."

She smoked pensively.

"Are you over the sickness?"

"I feel OK."

"Your colour's come back," she said, looking at Jill critically. "Have you noticed the Brigade doesn't know what to do with us? That's why they packed us in with the Red Cross. Relieved to make us part and parcel of the Florence Nightingales."

The lieutenant heard that.

"You aren't with us for long. We're only going to Paris. Didn't I hear somebody say you're travelling on with the Brigade?"

"Yes. Much further."

It was Jill who spoke and everybody looked at her. She felt forced to say, "I used to live in France."

The statement was received in total silence.

She added weakly, "My father brought our family back to England when I was fifteen."

"Did you like it in France?" asked the gentle Alison.

Rescuing Jill from admitting that she did, Roz Waters said, "Ah. We're starting. About time."

The train shuddered. Went backwards. Clanked, blew steam, and finally began to move.

The lieutenant pulled down the rucksack she'd placed on the half-rotting shelf of netted string above her head. She unfastened the pack and handed out leaflets.

"Now, girls, I think you should all read these carefully. Six points. But they must be kept in our heads and remembered the entire time."

The girls obediently took the leaflets and bent their heads to read them. (Roz looked as if she'd like to read one from curiosity.) The lieutenant had the girls well in hand.

Roz caught Jill's eye.

"Shall we go into the corridor? Then I can smoke with a clear conscience."

Standing together by the rain-splashed windows, they watched fields going by in the long lightless day. The unrelenting rain continued to fall on meadows, ploughed fields and long stretches of what looked like land abandoned to weeds. The train went through several deserted stations. Jill noticed that the names of the stations were still there . . . Abbeville . . . Poix . . . unlike England where the places you passed on a journey were anonymous. The signs in England had been taken down during the invasion scare – every name on every station, every signpost, had been removed – a simple idea to confuse enemy troops parachuted or marching into a strange land.

Roz and Jill looked out at the panorama in silence. At one place they saw the hulks of three or four partially destroyed tanks. An air of desolation seemed to lie across the country and seep through the windows like a curse.

"Roz. Why did you say the Brigade doesn't know what to do with us?"

"We're a problem. Lavatories. Washing. Two females close to too many men. What my French teacher at school used to call *les grosses pattes des hommes*."

"You sound as if you approve of your teacher's description."

"Maybe I do."

"Don't you like the opposite sex?" Jill spoke in a voice of such surprise that Roz laughed.

"A few. Not the leering hundreds. Neither can you, surely?"

The train was unheated, their breath a steam, but daylight hadn't quite gone. It was only early autumn. Supposed to be. Jill stared out at the drowned and dreary country. France. Where she had lived so happily as a child – François's country.

In the French HQ in Kensington, where she'd worked for months, Jill had talked to soldiers or officers about their return to France. "We will get there. The General is determined." They spoke of him with mockery and reverence, the General was an invisible presence anywhere a few Free Frenchman had gathered. Jill had lived among patriots. And here, at least, outside the windows was the land from which they had escaped so they could fight for it. "For Her," they would say. France was female.

Roz leaned her back against the glass door of the train

compartment in silence, smoking another of her hoarded cigarettes. Her thoughts apparently interested her – she showed no desire to rejoin the Red Cross girls or to talk seriously to Jill. The girls in the compartment finished their study and began to doze. The lieutenant worked at papers spread on her knee, now and again biting the end of her pencil like a schoolgirl.

Jill was reminded briefly of the officer she'd worked for at French HQ. He used to bend over papers like that . . . overworked, bureaucratic, maddening, loyal Captain Gautier. He was faraway now. She began to wonder where Peter had got to. Since she'd driven with him to Victoria in an army car at an unearthly hour that morning, he had disappeared. She hadn't seen him once on the ship, crammed as it had been with troops. She supposed the officers had been too busy to bother with a mere interpreter. But Peter was her passport, the only reason she could perhaps get to Bourg; she was eager to keep close to him. Anyway, she liked him.

The train drew to a halt some time after a dull, late sunset. Roz suggested they go back into the compartment.

"The only thing to do on journeys like this is to persuade yourself to sleep."

She slid open the door. The compartment was as peaceful as a school dormitory. Even the lieutenant had dropped off. Jill and Roz slipped into their seats.

It grew dark and the train jolted to a start again. Dim stations went by. Then long periods of blackness. And then – Jill woke up and couldn't believe her eyes – they were approaching the outskirts of a city and the streets were lit. Actually lit. It was a sight she had not seen for five years. And the suburban houses had windows which shone as the train went by.

"My God!" Roz had also woken up.

"I suppose they know we won't bomb them.'

"All I can say to that is lucky bastards."

"We're coming into Paris," said the lieutenant, waking, looking out, and immediately in command. "Girls, wakey, wakey, we'll soon be there. Alison, brighten up. You look as if you are still in dreamland. Brighten up."

After more halts and slowings-down and the noise of raised voices along the corridor, the train limped into a huge vaulted station. The lieutenant bustled, as neat and bright as she'd been at six that morning. She mustered her charges, checked their luggage and asked in motherly tones if they were hungry.

Alison sighed, "Starving." The others agreed.

"I'll see what can be rustled up." Jill thought nobody would dare refuse the formidable young woman hot drinks, sandwiches, even chocolate. She nodded at Jill and Roz like a hostess bidding her guests goodnight after a successful party.

"This is us. Goodbye."

"Loads of luck," added Alison. Chattering like starlings, the group left the train; the last thing Jill heard from them was the lieutenant's voice.

"No, Sergeant. We will not wait. My orders are to go straight to the Acting Transport Officer, Eastern Section, who will have organised our transport."

One section of the masses of soldiers who had filled the train began to shuffle out on to the platform, where they were lined up by their sergeants and marched away. Their boots made a thundering regular noise until it slowly died into silence.

Roz began to arrange her few possessions in the newly vacated compartment.

"Now is the time to have another zizz," she said, having only woken a quarter of an hour earlier. She pulled her thick uniform coat over her and, with enviable talent, went straight back to sleep.

But Jill, very cold, sat wide awake in the unlit compartment. The door opened suddenly.

"Found you at last!"

The young man who came into the compartment was tall, with a round boyish face and indeterminate brown hair. The only unusual thing about him was his blue eyes. He wore khaki with the panache of a man who wears nothing else, and three pips on his shoulder – a Captain.

Peter Whittaker glanced at Roz asleep in the corner, closed the door and sat down beside Jill, taking her hands. He whispered, "Jiminy, you're freezing. I began to think you'd fallen into the Channel. Where did you get to? I looked all over when we were on board ship."

"I was told to join the Red Cross. Roz, that's her asleep, was with them as well. I just sat by a porthole feeling sick."

"Poor you. I'd have given you a tot of brandy. I never thought to look for you among the Red Cross. They were only travelling as far as Paris. Have they gone?"

"A few minutes ago."

"I didn't see them." He lit his lighter and held it up so that he could make out her face in the small flame.

"Hellish dark, isn't it? Look, come along down to our compartment. We've got a bit of light."

"Are you sure I should?"

"Why not? The Colonel knows about you. I told him about your terrific French and he said we're going to need that." He snapped the lighter shut, murmuring, "Got to save fuel". Then he lit it again.

"Believe it or not, Jill, there isn't an officer in the entire brigade, not a sergeant, not a nothing, who can speak the lingo."

"There's always school French."

"Funny joke. French was everyone's most hated subject – wasn't it like that with you?"

"Not really."

In the wavering light he touched her hand again, said "Still freezing?" and gave his disturbing, boyish smile.

"Poor love, you are cold. Oh, just remembered. My flask. Have a swig."

He produced a silver flask; it had been used for men out hunting and was curved to fit against the hip. He uncorked it and offered it to her, carefully holding the lighter in his other hand.

Jill took a gulp. The brandy went through her like fire.

"Come and meet my Colonel. Don't bother about your sleeping friend – he'll meet her later. Anyone who manages to sleep on this lark should be encouraged."

The train had moved out of the station at last and Jill followed Peter down what seemed endless corridors, passing carriages filled with troops. All she saw was the blur of khaki in the obscurity, clouds of cigarette smoke and faces in the faint light from a platform as the train passed yet another empty station. And, now and then, there was the spurt of a lit match.

Peter finally led her down a corridor which was carpeted and into a compartment where, despite the cold, a certain comfort reigned. Three officers sat round a table drinking from cups which steamed in the damp air. Hip flasks stood about, a plate of biscuits and two cigarette lighters, upended on saucers and burning like candles.

A man, with a face so thin that the flesh across the bones resembled tensed silk, glanced up.

"Peter. So here she is."

"Colonel. This is Sinclair, known to her friends as Jill."

"Hello, Jill."

The Colonel put out his hand. Across it, as if drawn in red ink, was a livid crimson scar shaped like the warning notices on telegraph poles, a jagged lightning flash.

"Peter was directed to find you. He assured me you were to

be found but we didn't believe him. You look – and feel," he still retained her hand, "like ice. Sit down. What you need is this."

It was a thick cup with the Wagon-Lits sign on it. The steaming liquid pretending to be coffee was liberally dosed with more brandy from one of the flasks.

"Thank you very much, Colonel!" said Jill, drinking the hot intoxicating brew. What a pity Roz wasn't here, she'd love it.

The Colonel introduced her to the other officers, one schoolmasterish, red-headed and freckled, the other dark and lazy looking. All four men, including Peter, sat looking at her as if she were a puppy they'd befriended.

Exchanging small talk for a while, the Colonel remarked on the rough sea, the lack of light, "Fortunately Guy's laid in a canful of petrol for lighter fuel – only lasts an hour then out it goes." When he laughed the noise was like a scatter of machine gun fire in an old Great War movie.

Jill was intimidated by Colonel Fisher. Fame hung round him. When they were in London, Peter had told her about him, he had been wounded in a hand-to-hand battle in the desert, "Blighters tried to steal his supplies. They didn't know who they were up against". She told herself not to be too impressed; after all the Colonel was in charge of men doing a job which was not dangerous, except for what Peter called the "odd bomb". The men in the RASC weren't part of the fighting machine, although that machine depended heavily upon them. The Brigade's job was supplies. Ammunition. Food. The components to keep an army on the move. So why, thought Jill, sipping the scalding stuff, did Fisher have so strong an effect? It was his appearance and manner. His voice was abrupt. When he smiled in that taut face it was a grimace, his teeth were too big for his head, that bony head with cropped hair, the forehead deeply lined, chin pushed out as if expecting a blow he'd counter with a knife thrust.

He finished off his so-called coffee and the two officers, David and Guy, stood up, muttered politely to Jill, and left on what they called their rounds.

The Colonel leaned back against the age-blackened upholstery.

"So you actually speak French?"

Jill said she did.

"How good?"

"Very good. I've heard her, sir," from Peter.

Fisher shot him a look. "Let the girl speak for herself."

"I lived with my family in France for six years. I went to school there, in Bourg-en-Bresse."

"Why did the family leave?"

Was it an accusation?

"My father ran a hotel. Les Lys. Three stars in the *Michelin Guide*."

"Translate."

"*The Michelin Guide*, sir . . ." put in Peter, rather pleased with himself, "everybody on the Continent used it. It told you about the good hotels you could go to, where to find them, whether they were comfortable and so on. And awarded stars for the best."

"Like those?" said the Colonel, pointing to the officer's pips on Peter's shoulders.

The feeble joke was greeted with sycophantic laughter from Peter.

"So your father was a successful hotelier," continued the Colonel.

"Very," said Jill. And was given a look of mockery. She continued – apparently this was expected since neither man said anything – to describe Les Lys, Bourg, and to tell how her father had decided to sell up and leave France at the outbreak of war.

"He got an awful price for the hotel."

Did she expect a tongue click of sympathy? The Colonel absently sloshed more brandy into his own Wagons-Lit mug.

"So let's hear some French, shall we?"

Somewhere, usually concealed but popping up when she was with men who admired and indulged her, there was a show-off in Jill. Sitting with Peter and his bizarre commanding officer, she launched into a fanciful speech in French, describing the ancient city of Bourg-en-Bresse. A beautiful city, with churches from the fourteenth century, the river Saône flowing through it, and – perhaps the most memorable building of all – the church at Brou with the tomb of Philibert le Bel. Carved round the tomb and also along the top of the church's ceilings, and circling the baptismal font, was a phrase accompanying the princely crest. "Fortune. Infortune. *Forte Une.*"

"It was," said Jill, "a French pun."

The Colonel, sipping now and again, listened in silence. When she finished, earning a glowing look from Peter, Fisher said, "Very pretty. Didn't understand a word. Peter, did you?"

"Bits and pieces, sir."

"God be thanked for that. I may well need those bits and pieces if our second interpreter is up to her neck in other work. So, young lady . . ."

It was a dismissal.

Jill thanked him for the drink, stood up and gave a sketchy salute to which he replied with an even sketchier one. He picked up some documents, reminding her for a moment of the Red Cross lieutenant. He called, as Peter ushered her out, "Get some sleep. We need all the sleep we can get."

It was a recurring theme on this journey. What was waiting for them?

When she and Peter arrived back at her compartment in the dark, they looked through the glass and saw Roz hadn't budged.

For a moment Peter did not slide open the door.

"This journey's going to be hellish long."

"Am I allowed to ask where we're going?"

"On and on. The Yanks are in Paris, praise be. We're needed a good way from there."

"I shall possess my soul in patience, then." It was a phrase of her mother's.

"You do that."

He didn't say that the train on which they were travelling into the night carried freight more precious than gold bullion. That it was a target if ever there was one and could very well be blown to bits. Trains in a country at war were prime military targets. The Resistance knew that, and so did the Nazis.

Peter was responsible for Jill being there and although her presence gave him, now and then, a moment of joy, he had begun to wish he'd never agreed to help her. When he'd broached the subject with the Colonel, the addition of an interpreter to the Brigade had been welcomed, and simple to arrange.

As they stood together and the train gathered speed, they rocked to and fro and once he was thrown against her. Catching her from falling, diffident in the way of the brave, he kissed her.

She returned the kiss like a child. Her response hurt him.

"See you in the morning," he whispered. "We'll manage another drink, I shouldn't wonder."

She liked Peter Whittaker. Was truly fond of him. Well aware that he, who never said so, was in love with her. She'd met him in Chelsea two years ago when she had been working at the War Office and billeted with a Colonel's widow, Clarissa Whittaker. She had thought Clarissa Whittaker pretty dire, an astounding snob, a cold fish. But Peter was another story. And it had been Peter who had, wondrously to

Jill, managed to get her transferred to the RASC. To what in the dim past people had called La Belle France . . .

When Peter had shut the compartment door, she curled up in a corner. On went the train . . . into what? The enemy was in retreat but not withdrawing in good order. The German army had broken into groups, parts had surrendered, other fragments still fought, like their once-allies the Russians at Stalingrad, street by street, house by house.

Jill and Roz slept to the sound of guns. And woke, tired and dirtier, to the same distant sound of guns and the splashing rain. Jill looked out of the windows. How France had changed. She thought of her years of childhood – girlhood. She remembered Bourg in glowing colours, picnics, parties under the trees or on the river. The disciplined convent smelling of beeswax, the sound of nuns' voices in class teaching the prayers Jill still used sometimes. She thought of her mother's garden which Lucy Sinclair, Jill's mother, had planted with dahlias as large as dinner plates.

And the talk. So much talk. Voices laughing and exclaiming and arguing, for nobody agreed with anybody. It was that sound most of all, expressive, lilting, euphonious, which had never quite left her inner ear.

The train hurried through the empty fields, the grey seemingly deserted villages where not a soul could be seen, just narrow empty streets as if the place had been visited by the plague. The towns had their names in the stations and along the roads: Auxerre, Ses Eglises, Son Université, Son Ambiance.

And then she began to notice other things. Road signs in German. Barbed wire entanglements squashed flat, apparently by tanks. Once, when the train stopped outside a station, Roz gestured at a number of wooden crosses by the roadside. They were so close that Jill could read the names scrawled in pencil.

"Resistants," Roz said. "The Germans often executed near

stations, so plenty of people could see what had been done and learn their lesson. See? The Cross of Lorraine."

The morning crawled. True to his promise, Peter sent a corporal with a tin tray of what could be called breakfast. Two hot drinks (more water than coffee), some nearly inedible bread and squares of dusty chocolate. "I must say," said Roz, cradling the hot drink and looking over at Jill, "travelling with you has its compensations. Do you always collect useful admirers?"

"Always."

"Bully for you."

Time was even slower after the short pause for breakfast. Neither of the girls dared to wash. The lavatory, used by so many soldiers, was an experience they could only just get themselves to bear when, as Roz said, "Nature Called." For the rest of the time they simply sat – neither of them with any kind of book – and watched through the smeared windows the panorama of a conquered country.

How dirty everything was. The platforms. The houses with unwashed curtains lank in windows, a few vehicles, buses, one or two vans drove by. Most of all, they looked out at the people. It was as if they were coming to a place which had once been as radiant as Eden, painted by the Impressionists with water lilies and picnics on misty rivers, with budding trees arching over lazy women, but where now a sorcerer had pronounced a malediction. Once the train halted on the outskirts of a village and three workmen went by. They looked indifferently at the train, their faces pinched and bitter.

"Oh, what's happened to them?" Jill suddenly cried.

"It's obvious, isn't it?"

"But the war's nearly over, they're free."

"You're a romantic," said Roz, taking out a cigarette. "Hasn't anybody told you how dangerous that is?"

* * *

The interminable hours on the train stretched into two miserable, cold and endless days which finally came to an end. Roz called it, "the worst journey in the world." When the train drew up at a vast shadowed station it turned out to be Lyon. There was the same scramble and sorting out of the troops, the same barking sergeant, shuffling boots, general movement; and a sense of relief as pervasive as scent. Scores of army trucks were lined up outside the station on the cobbled road.

Peter appeared from a group of officers and hurried over.

"I'm taking you to your lodgings."

"What does that mean?" demanded Roz. "Aren't we going with the rest of you?"

"Apparently not." He studied a scrap of paper. "It's fixed for you to go to the rue de Grand Sermon. Not far. I can't lay on transport. We'd better grab a taxi."

Roz sniffed.

"Don't tell us. There's no room for us. Must get rid of those two women."

Jill wondered why she seemed annoyed. Maybe the digs would be more comfortable than army barracks and they might even be cleaner. Peter looked for a taxi without success. Finally he said he would take them on foot. It was not far. He had a map and they set off down a long cobbled street.

Quiet. Ill-lit. Miserable. Jill had been to Lyon with her father once on a feast day. Not like this. Not like this.

"It's rot," grumbled Roz, trudging beside Jill. "You behave as if the British troops go in for rape. Pillage, yes, but rape is a bit far-fetched."

"Only obeying orders, Second Officer," was Peter's mild reply.

"My name's Roz and Jill informs me you're a mate of hers."

"I like to think so."

"And you pulled a few strings to get her over here."

Peter wished Jill hadn't told this gruff woman any such thing. Studying his scrumpled and out-of-date street map, he stopped at a row of houses.

"I should have thought," drawled Roz, still in a thoroughly bad temper, "you could have pulled one more string and managed to get us into barracks. We wouldn't take up much room, for God's sake. At least we'd be conveniently placed to get on with the bloody job."

Peter rang the bell. The house was one of a row of nineteenth century houses with balconies and shutters: dusty, the stucco cracked, a rent in the marble step. After a pause while the trio waited in silence, there was a click and the front door opened.

Peter ushered them inside. As they entered a voice shouted, "*Je suis au premier*."

"Yes, well, you'll manage much better without me stammering through intros. Here are your papers. All in order. I must scarper. Jill, I'll be in touch. I'm sure my lot will be needing you and Roz all the time. Have a good night's rest."

He gave them a salute and left them in a dark hallway.

"We'll go up," Roz said, looking towards the staircase. "I ask myself what's in store for us? Nothing good, you can bet your boots."

They climbed the stairs in silence. The voice shouted.

"*Ici. Dans le salon*."

Roz looked at Jill and raised her eyebrows.

A pair of painted double doors stood open, they went together into a very large room.

It had been furnished a hundred years ago and not a tabouret, screen, fan pinned to the wall or glass-fronted cupboard of china had been altered. Sitting on a throne-like chair of plush and chipped gilt was a gaunt woman in black.

Long black skirts. An ebony walking stick, propped against the chair arm.

"Hello," she said in English. "You both look as if you could use a drink."

The accent was American.

"I'm Philomène and it's fixed for me to put you up, OK? I know your names and your job. Have you had anything to eat? By the way, don't expect me to hop about after you like a two-year-old. I have a wooden leg."

She tapped one of her legs concealed in the long black skirt. It made a solid sound.

"Everybody believes I lost it in a little argument with the Gestapo. I let 'em think it. As a matter of fact some idiot surgeon in the States chopped it off. Later another sawbones assured me it hadn't been necessary. But I'm sure smart on my crutches."

She had no intention of showing them how smart on her crutches she was. She did not attempt to run around after her visitors. Instead, she sat upright on her chipped throne and rapped out instructions. The kitchen was that way, to the left. Philomène, raising her loud voice as they obediently went into the kitchen, told them where to find bread in what she called the crock, and some ham from the Marché Noir. It was under a cover of netting. And so on . . .

She shouted to them what food to take, where to find trays, glasses. She commanded them to "bring the eats" into the salon and sit with her.

"Things I want to hear . . ."

Roz led the way, both girls carrying trays loaded with good food. Jill was amazed at such plenty.

Philomène told them to draw up their chairs and put their feet on footstools, kicking two towards them.

"Now. The journey. Begin at Victoria."

She listened in silence, thirsty for facts. She could be any age, fifty, sixty. Jill, looking at her, thought there were traces of lost beauty. Her nose was straight and handsome, her high cheekbones could have come from Red Indian ancestors. She had wonderful American teeth. Iron grey, luxuriant hair was scraped away from her face and coiled in a bun low on her neck. Not a crumb of make-up. Her eyebrows were grey and frizzy, her slanting hazel eyes were underlined with the worst bags Jill had ever seen. Philomène looked as if she hadn't slept for six months.

When Roz and Jill between them ended the story, Philomène felt for her stick, placed it upright in front of her and leaned on it.

"You did well. No night attacks. No explosion. Your train had a charmed journey. I asked myself what the Milice thought they were doing letting all that ammunition through Auxerre."

She gave a slow smile, showing the perfect teeth, looking from one girl to the other.

"By God, you don't know what the Milice is, do you? Holy Moses. Doesn't seem possible."

Jill began, "Madame . . ."

An impatient gesture from a large hand.

"Philomène, for Pete's sake."

"Thank you. The fact is, Philomène, we don't know a thing. About France now."

"Not briefed then?"

"The Army didn't think it necessary," said Roz, dryly.

"So it seems. Ignorance is dangerous."

"We're only interpreters, Madame, I mean Philomène."

"Only! Yeah, well, we'll let that pass for the moment. Go on eating. Try the ham with the mustard, it's quite something. While you eat, I'll do the talking."

The meal was as strange as the journey from England had been. Philomène set out to instruct them. She spoke in her matter-of-fact American voice, talking of horrors as a journalist might have done. Philomène, born in Chatham, New Jersey, had been living in Lyon long before the war began. She was a neutral journalist and had been allowed by the Germans to file stories to Washington. Stories so bland and feeble that she said she had been ashamed to mail them.

She married a Frenchman in the 1930s, he was killed in one of the first battles on the Belgian border. It was then that she'd decided not to return to the States.

"You might say I'd begun to see the French point of view. After all, I married this country. And God, was I sorry for them."

And so, in the flat she and her husband had borrowed from his mother, long since dead, Philomène had remained alone since 1939.

"I guess you could say I've been a kind of courier." Neither girl asked if she was talking about the Resistance. Looking at them she said, "Sure. I began working for them. The Resistance. They were at each other's throats most of the time; holy God, the French are quarrelsome. But for the present I'm here to tell you what the Milice are."

The story was hideous and made worse by her cool rendition.

"Milice. You haven't heard the word? You," she said, looking at Jill, "worked for the de Gaulle lot in London, I hear. I guess they preferred not to talk about the bastards in front of an Englishwoman. The French are ashamed of them."

She rubbed her nose.

"You both speak pretty good French."

"Not bad," said Roz. "I was a governess in the Midi before the war."

"I know. Golfe Juan. And you . . ." looking at Jill.

"I lived in Bourg-en-Bresse."

"Sure. Les Lys belonged to your father. You wouldn't like it now. The Nazis used it as an office."

She had a habit of tapping her stick against her wooden leg. How children would laugh at that, thought Jill. Were there any children around? She had not seen one.

"You'll run up against the Milice or rather you may see them running as like as not. They are, or were, a paramilitary body of fascist Frenchmen, guys who joined the enemy and have been working for them. Conservative Roman Catholics. Veterans of the 1914–18 war. Aristos. After the Germans came, there were a lot of classy guys in the Milice. Pre-revolutionary titles, Marquises, Comtes. Some of the families split down the middle, Milice on one side, Resistants on the other. I knew a father and brother who were denounced and tortured by another member of the same family. How the Milice are loathed. That's the trouble."

"But shouldn't they be?" burst out Jill.

Philomène, as if Jill hadn't interrupted, went on, "Murderers create murderers. The Resistants were a haphazard, badly-organised lot until last year; they got caught too often, tortured until they gave the names of their friends. A few died like Jean Moulin or Odette, betraying nothing. But gradually they became a hardened secret underground organisation and I'm telling you now they're good."

But she made a gesture of disgust.

"Their newspapers have begun printing the names of Miliciens. Men condemned to death by secret court martials. They get sent small coffins through the post. Or nooses. You have to understand this because it is all around us now. Lyon seethes with it and you'll not be able to escape coming up against it. There's nowhere for the Milice to go now. If they're caught, they're dead; so for every man killed by the Resistance, the Milice counter with a murder of their own. Or more than one. Innocent people get caught, tortured. So do the guilty. There are bodies on the road every night, pinned with papers saying "Death to collaborators" or simply the name of some dead brother, husband, lover. This is a civil war you two girls have come to join."

Roz spoke suddenly. "There's a thing called justice."

Philomène raised plucked eyebrows. "I guess so. But the vice is catching. The desire to kill. I have seen many good men change."

A spasm went through Jill's heart. Was François dead then? Tortured by the Gestapo or this Milice who sounded almost worse – his own countrymen. Jill thought – why did I come?

Philomène turned Red Indian eyes on her. "Lyon is marginally better than it was. Let's say a month ago. The fear of the Germans returning and the Milice with them is beginning to go. The people smell liberty. But the danger isn't over yet . . ." She tapped her stick against the macabre wooden leg. "Of course everybody knows the enemy's in retreat. The General's latest is to call on all Frenchmen everywhere to rise up. But . . ."

"But won't they?" Roz was very curious.

"My guess is no. Of course they want the Allied victory. With their souls, that is. But at no risk to themselves. Who can blame them?"

Jill told nobody, not Roz with whom she soon had a camaraderie, not Philomène who impressed and rather scared her, least of all Peter, the reason she'd begged to come to this vanquished country.

Sometimes in bed in Philomène's flat or patiently translating floods of French in the icy cold depot on the outskirts of the city, she had a sense of total unreality. Love, the emotion said to be the greatest in human life, had nothing to do with anything. She had been a minuscule part of a fighting machine in London and had simply moved into another part of the machine, this time in France with harder work and longer hours.

During the months of autumn turning into winter, she talked French for eighteen hours a day. She dreamed in that language. She sat on upturned packing cases, scribbling lists of supplies with hands like blocks of ice. She had never been so cold in her life. It was seldom that Peter could get away from organising supply trains and lorries. Occasionally he had to cope with the horror of a Milice undercover attack. Bodies, mutilated bodies, were found. And every time she heard that, Jill thought of women in the silent shut-up houses, grieving for the victim, guilty or innocent. The wind blew in the deserted streets. The river was swollen with rain as winter approached. The snow began.

Occasionally there was a respite. Philomène told them about a black market restaurant on the left bank of the Rhône. Chez Thérèse was something remarkable, a place where members of the Resistance actually sat in the same room with ex-Vichy policemen. It was as if some kind of dishonourable bargain was temporarily struck. Everybody drank too much and the restaurant with its old red banquettes and marble tables was blessedly, steamily, hot.

"I'm told you're a worker in a million," said Peter one night, as he and Jill sat eating an appetising, almost unbelievable, coq au vin. He refilled her glass with the usual red wine which set the teeth on edge. The place was noisy, there was laughter which Jill thought sounded slightly frantic. The girls wore no make-up, their clothes were shabby, their faces blushed from the heat, wine and food. Outside lay snow. It was along the window ledges still pure, and in the streets, black.

Jill traced her finger in a drop of wine on the marble. Peter looked at her, thinking her lovelier because she was tired.

"Roz said she's heard rumours."

"I'll bet she has."

"Why not? Everybody talks."

"Too much for safety. And what does she say, that friend of yours? Which reminds me, she did some good work on the transport yesterday. I must tell her."

"Oh do. She said there's going to be a German offensive."

Jill had lowered her voice, it was scarcely louder than a sigh.

"Perhaps."

"Here!"

"I see you've been too busy to read the newspapers. The nearest organised German forces are round Colmar, at least 150 miles away." He dropped his own voice. "But in the north . . ."

"Hitler's last throw."

"And we'll beat him."

"Please God."

"What about a pudding?" was the unexpected reply. "I saw an apple flan as I came in."

After he kissed her goodnight on the stairs of Philomène's flat and whispered his special word "darlingest", Jill climbed the stairs to her room. She ached with tiredness. She undressed and lay down in bed. And quite suddenly, for no reason, she remembered François so intensely that he could have been in bed with her. She wanted him so much that she almost groaned out loud. He was the one. The man who had taken her virginity and her imagination, stirred and satisfied her so that she had understood every love poem in his language and hers. The Greeks said man was made when two creatures in one body were split in half. And all your life you looked for the missing piece of bone and flesh. That was why she had to come to France. How much closer was she to finding him?

All she'd done so far was to condemn herself to grinding, hard, dirty work. She sat, as Roz did, in freezing warehouses or stations or in the open air. There was never enough water to wash, a bath once a week was a luxury.

The first impression she'd had from the train window was right. The pictures in English papers of laughing people embracing the soldiers, of flowers, of euphoria, were all lies. she had come to a land which resembled a kind of hell. The people, undernourished for years, were haggard and thin; the mood of Lyon, the once-beautiful city overlooking the rushing river, was vengeful and tight-closed.

Now and then Philomène told her of the bodies found on the snowy roads. Messages pinned on them. "Terror for terror". Hatred was in the air, in the voices, in the coarse and brutal manner in which she and Roz were treated by the French. When men talked of the Nazis they showed their teeth like dogs.

Her reason for being here faded while she worked, frozen-fingered, and trailed home in the dimly lit streets to Philomène from whom she was given no sympathy for exhaustion, dirt and depression. A little respect if she was lucky.

I came for you, François. What have I done to find you?

Two

Eight months before, a lifetime from the diminished and icy work in just-liberated France, Jill's boss at the War Office had invited her to the Colonel's sherry party for some French VIPs. When the visitors from French HQ in Kensington arrived, Jill had politely chatted to them. Most of the French officers couldn't speak a word of English.

The Free French in London resented the British. Their General cut up rusty with everybody, starting at the top with Churchill. But they were not averse to a bit of help; grinding their teeth, they demanded it. And Jill Sinclair had been the help in question when it turned out that she spoke good French.

Two days later, after an air raid which sent everybody trooping to the shelters in the bowels of the earth, Jill was sent for by her boss.

She brought her notebook, but he waved it away.

"Apparently the raid was merely over the Thames estuary. A beautiful clear night," said the Major chattily. He added "You're quite a linguist, Sinclair."

For some reason, Jill felt the remark was not good news.

"I have been talking to Captain Gautier. You remember him from the other evening? A little man. Very polite," said the Major humorously. He added without further delay that she was to be transferred.

"To work for the French."

Jill's jaw dropped.

"Yes, it is quite a surprise," said the Major, who was wiry and brisk and matter-of-fact. He was sorry to see the good-looking young women go. But there it was. "The thing is, their Colonel heard you talking French and Gautier did too. It seems the French are desperate for girls who speak their language."

He toyed with the idea of a joke; but no, it wouldn't do.

"You're to be at Free French HQ in Kensington at 1400 hours. Here is the chit to sign. So. It's goodbye."

He held out his hand and shook hers.

Jill saluted. Quite furious.

Her beautiful and fluent French was something she'd never had to use until now . . .

Jill's father had moved to France when she was a child. Clement Sinclair had French blood and flair and left England with his family while the Depression was still on. He daringly bought a run-down hotel in Bourg-en-Bresse. Jill, uprooted, was sent to the local Convent and to her parents' amusement turned quickly into a chatty French schoolgirl. Clement and Lucy, his shy wife, set about making their hotel a success. It was, until just before the outbreak of war. Clement then made another of his decisions. He sold the hotel and packed his family back to Newcastle-upon-Tyne. His and Lucy's relatives, roots and loyalties were still there. And Clement, who had been in the Great War, came back to England this time with relief.

When she was called up, Jill at first had a dull time in a Northumberland barracks, but luck and a high-up friend of her father's helped to transfer her a few months later to the War Office. She'd enjoyed that. Her boss was cheery and the men in uniform seemed to spoil her. It made it all the worse when, like a parcel, she was handed over to Free French HQ – she'd heard about them.

Arriving, as per orders, at French HQ she made her way up an overgrown drive to a battered rambling old private house in a large unkempt garden. It must have been rather beautiful five or six years before; but now the garden was wild except where somebody had planted a row of cabbages.

The entrance hall was presided over by two lipsticked and disobliging French girls who looked at her with dislike. She was directed down a narrow corridor with cardboard walls, into a pokey office.

Captain Gautier, with a very different expression from the one he'd worn at the party, told her she was five minutes late.

"It was the bus, mon Capitaine." Really, thought Jill, I'm only on loan.

Not acknowledging her excuse or the self-confident English smile on her face, he handed her a twenty-page report. Every word was in bureaucratic and – to Jill – near incomprehensible French. Would she type two copies. Top copies. No carbons were permitted.

Jill worked all that afternoon in a corner allotted to her, at a dusky desk pushed against another cardboard wall. The office was a small segment of what had been somebody's drawing-room. The real walls had been of patterned wallpaper, colourful pheasants and formal trees. A partition had been cut neatly through the design and Jill faced the birds' tails and rumps and a flowering tree sawn in half.

Captain Gautier kept hurrying out. Unlike her Major in the War Office, he never said where he was going or how long he would be. Each time he came back, it was with more work for Jill.

She felt sulky.

At nineteen, Jill was a mixture of girl and woman; she was pleasure-loving, bending towards enjoyment like a plant towards the light. Meeting her, men fell in love with appalling ease, and Jill, with what they considered more appalling ease, refused to go to bed with any of them. The passionate embraces, the chagrin (sometimes), the disappointment (often) did not change her mind. In a world gone sex mad, there were some girls who didn't. She was one.

Now in 1944 in the thick of things, she was too young to suffer from the war exhaustion which had come over other Londoners. They had been brave last time and somehow couldn't summon up the same emotion, the same buzz, all over again. But Jill felt courageous and clever. The idea of danger had a tang to it. Or had done until now when, surveying her new boss, her heart sank down into her polished Army shoes. She was trained in the British army's dictum that a desk with nothing on it was a sign of efficiency and filing cabinets must be kept up to the minute. Captain Gautier sat among papers, documents and notes as thick as autumn leaves all over the place. When somebody telephoned he reached for anything, a chart, the back of a letter. Or little squares of paper he pulled out from some secret stores – they were the most plentiful.

She tried to work. The next day she arrived with bright intentions but her temper deteriorated when her boss slammed an enormous pile of graph paper on to her desk without a *s'il vous plaît* and barked, "For Schedules."

Jill said nothing. She kept remembering the courtesy of War Office Majors, the quizzical flirtatiousness of a Colonel or two. There had been one officer who used to say "thanks most awfully" when she typed his short memos. All that was now replaced by a French bully drowning in bureaucracy and pulling her down with him. To make Jill's mood worse, he refused to allow her to go to the canteen for lunch.

"*Il faut travailler.*"

"But . . ."

"You may have *le sandvich.*"

It had to be admitted that the sandvich, brought by another

sulky-looking French girl – this one in a white overall – who dumped a tray down on Jill's desk and flounced out, was not the usual disgusting British version. Even here, even now, the French managed to provide fresh bread, greyish but slightly warm and delicious. As for the spam, it was spread with mustard which tasted of wine.

Such pleasures did not banish Jill's bad temper. When the Captain found ten mistakes in one of her documents, her look would have killed him stone dead if he hadn't been checking her work to spot more. And he had the gall to slap more work on her desk before he marched out.

Stretching out a hand to pick up the new sheets of martyrdom, Jill dropped the lot. They slithered right across the dusty parquet floor.

"*Merde, merde, merde*," burst out Jill, kneeling down among the scattered and now disordered sheets.

The flimsy door reopened. She expected an angry "What did you say?" and a reprimand. All she saw was a pair of polished black shoes, too narrow to be Gautier's. Still on her knees and crossly scrabbling at the papers, she did not bother to look up, but snapped in French.

"The captain is not here."

"Evidently. But you are, *belle Anglaise*."

Startled, she looked up to see a young man standing in the doorway. He gave her a confident smile. He was olive-skinned, dark-haired, not much taller than she was. His face was narrow, with high actorish cheekbones, his black hair waved slightly, his nose was thin and so was his wide mouth. She'd never seen such black eyes, they shone like treacle.

"I think we know each other."

Jill had a strange feeling just then. Was this the way animals felt? Dogs? She did recognise him.

"If I say Bourg-en-Bresse, will that ring a bell? You are *la petite St Clair*, are you not? My name is Ghilain."

"François!"

He put out his hand, pulled her to her feet, formally shook her hand and laughed.

Jill continued to gape.

"But how did you know it was me? I was only fifteen."

"Attractive fifteen."

He had the swagger she'd noticed in every Frenchman in the building except Gautier.

"You didn't give me a look," she was still amazed.

"Alas, I 'ave no time to do so now . . ."

Oh, those dropped 'h's.

"I must go," he said, "Or trouble. The General's minuscule army 'as the passion for courts martial. They might," he continued flirtatiously, "court-martial *you*."

"Handcuffed in front of a French judge," said Jill, giggling.

"There speaks the Englishwoman. I came to introduce myself. Also to ask you to have supper. I am off duty tonight. Will you come? Are you engaged? Married? No, no ring. 'Ave you, of course you 'ave, a dozen men paying court to you."

She liked that bit. She did have a date with a lieutenant in the War Office, now mentally postponed. She looked at the man tidying the retrieved papers.

"I'd like to have supper with you."

"Excellent. The Brevet? Do you know it? It is near the Metro in South Kensington."

"Yes, I know it." She had been there scores of times.

"Excellent," he repeated. "So tonight, then. I 'ope there is not a raid. Shall you come if there is?"

"Why not?"

"*Femme du courage*," he said.

London was full of clubs. Jill knew a dozen. Clubs for the RAF, for the three services together, for visiting troops . . . Norwegians, South Africans. There was a remarkable number of Polish clubs, with names like Polski or White Eagle.

The Americans had taken over a hotel near Harrods and would sit on the steps outside it, like people at a supper dance in the *Tatler*. There was Rainbow Corner and the Stage Door Canteen. Despite different languages, a different smell, the atmosphere of the clubs was oddly similar. Crowded and sexy even in the middle of the day.

"Do not get run over crossing the road," said François.

Jill promised not to.

The Brevet had been a store for books in peacetime, two floors up from a modest, not very successful bookshop. The building was next door to a grocer's which had had a direct hit, and was now a weedy hole in the ground. The old bookshop and store, damaged and cracked, had strangely survived. Its owner, an elderly Czech, was fond of saying that lightning and the Nazis did not strike twice. The building was unrepaired; there were jagged cracks in every well. The club had become a favourite meeting place and was always packed.

The air raid warning had wailed an hour ago, there was the usual rumble and thunder of guns but no sound of bombs, when Jill went up the stairs. Above her, she heard a piano.

The room was lofty, the windows were draped with thick blackout curtains and lines of candles burned along trestle tables. The light was shadowy and dim, the music was sexy and sad, the pianist old, he took no notice of anybody. There wasn't even a drink on the top of the piano.

Jill saw François the moment she came in. He was at the bar, one foot on the rail, talking to another man in Free French uniform. Her stomach dropped as it used to do when she suffered from those schoolgirl crushes in Bourg-en-Bresse. Don't be a bloody fool, Sinclair, she told herself.

Seeing her, François came over. He kissed her hand.

"You're late."

"Aren't I just."

"But alive. I did begin to wonder."

"The bus conductor said they're over the estuary again."

He looked at her fixedly for a moment and Jill looked back at him. He was more handsome than she'd thought him yesterday. Nice and thin. 'Free French' said the shoulder flash. She'd never liked the sign before.

"You are brave, Jill St Clair. You should have the *Légion d'honneur*."

"Yes, please. Will you arrange it?"

He put his arm round her shoulders and they walked to a table not far from the pianist. She recognised the tune.

"I never slept a wink last night

Because we had that silly fight."

She knew the words and sang the song to the end. François watched her with the indulgence of a man sexually attracted to the singer. When she finished, "Very pretty. Now. A drink? Only Algerian, alas."

"I love Algerian."

"Impossible."

François beckoned the barman and he came over carrying a bottle and slopped red wine into tumblers. François sipped and grimaced.

"Vinegar."

Seeing Jill drink hers with enjoyment, it occurred to him that this girl had never known anything better.

They began to talk. But they had scarcely shared the past. Jill almost never thought about Bourg-en-Bresse and since the fall of France – to Jill an age ago – her parents rarely spoke of their time there. It was too tragic and they were too busy, like everybody else in embattled England. But, in this young man's company now, Jill did remember Les Lys, its elegance, its foreign smell of coffee and Gitanes, and she remembered the times she'd seen François there.

She was enjoying herself in the company of this attractive man and it showed in her vivacious face and in her eyes. But, far more than just taking a natural pleasure in her company, the usual question loomed in François Ghilain's thoughts. Would he manage to get her into bed?

He had had two affairs since he had come to England (heroically, he always said) some months ago. The real French heroes had come in 1940 or 1941 but things had been difficult for the son of Bourg's collaborating mayor. It had taken François a long time to get away from the city. He had been working for his father at the Mairie, up to his neck in Vichy orders and counter-orders, in trouble with the Germans and far more trouble with the French military police. These, called the Milice, were loathed by every patriot in France. People hated them and were terrified of them, the Milice's reputation for murder, torture and betrayal was far worse than that of the occupying Germans.

Now, he was in London at last. Drinking Algerian wine with an alluring girl he'd known when she was a child.

So. Were they going to bed?

The question disturbed him, particularly when they danced. As for Jill, she was hazy with pleasure.

François was not like the other admirers of which Jill had had scores in the two years since she began to be beautiful. Like all young women in wartime Britain, she had had boyfriends of every nationality: serious Norwegians, sexy Americans, fascinating and dangerous Poles. There was a certain similarity in the way the men of different nationalities behaved. They were warm, flattering. They said she was lovely (she thought so too). They talked of the countries they had left and about the progress of the war. They wooed her. Eventually without success. But this Frenchman paid no compliments and Jill's girlish remarks were greeted with laughter.

But the question was there tonight for them both; it was in their eyes and the accidental touch of hands on the table.

Glancing idly across the candle-lit room, to her dismay Jill saw her new boss. Gautier had spotted them and was walking over purposefully.

She was curious. Was he going to behave out of character and exchange a bantering word with his secretary? When he came closer she saw that the idea was preposterous.

If it was possible to look more exhausted than when she had left him in the office a few hours ago, Alain Gautier managed it. The dust of fatigue was smeared under his eyes, he was so pale that she felt in the wrong for enjoying herself. Document-mad, the man was working for duty's sake. For France.

Ignoring her, he spoke to François.

"Enfin, I discover you, Lieutenant. I have spent much time during the Alert telephoning from the shelter. You should have left information as to where you could be found."

"Has the All Clear gone?" enquired François.

Gautier answered that of course it had, how otherwise would he be there?

"Lieutenant. You must return to HQ, at once."

François raised his eyebrows. He had stood up politely, now he sat down.

"I am not on duty, Captain."

"We are all on duty. Always. You must return."

"Tonight?"

"At once. The task of tracing you could have been, with forethought on your part, avoided. I am only here," added Gautier, perhaps struck by the frivolity of the venue where he was issuing orders, "because I was informed by a fellow officer that there was a good chance you would be here. You have been seen twice in this place."

A gendarme now, thought Jill.

He looked round with a frown, adding that the job of finding the Lieutenant had not been made easier by the bad lighting.

Jill managed to stay serious while her boss, avoiding her

eyes, stood on the other side of the table. Did he expect François to salute and march out at the double?

François had not caught the urgency. He replied that he would be at HQ as soon as possible. His manner appeared to pacify Gautier who, finally acknowledging Jill's presence with a short "M'selle" and a nod, left them.

They watched the disapproving back until he'd gone. François began to swear in French. She didn't recognise the words, but the general sense was obscene.

"What a peculiar time for you to be sent for, François."

"True," he said indifferently. "The Free French are peculiar, you must have noticed it. And you are enslaved in the bureau of that peculiar man. Alas, we must part. I will get you a taxi but can't travel with you. As you said in the office this morning, '*Merde, merde, merde.*'"

He gave her a look, lowering his eyelids so that for a moment he seemed half asleep. But Jill was slinging her gas mask over her shoulder and did not see. The pianist began "All the Things You Are".

"The promised kiss of springtime," sang Jill, as they went down the stairs. She was rewarded by a guffaw from her companion who said something about accursed English sentimentality.

The stars overhead were enormous. The All Clear still held. François stood dangerously in the middle of the unlit road until he flagged her a taxi.

Opening its door with a flourish, he stopped her from climbing in by giving her a violent kiss.

"That must last us for the present."

He was still in the road as the taxi drove away.

Jill was typing a six page letter, at intervals studying her French shorthand with dismay, when Captain Gautier picked up the telephone. But instead of a flood of talk (invariably about mislaid documents) all he said was, "Yes," and slammed down the receiver.

"Sinclair."

"*Mon Capitaine*?"

"You are to go to Reception."

"Is someone asking for me, sir?"

"It is not acceptable in the French service to ask questions. Orders are obeyed."

Coo, thought Jill.

"Take your cap and gas mask, Sinclair," he shouted after her.

She did as he bade her and went out, saying in revenge over her shoulder, "I am making no progress with your work."

The entrance hall of French HQ, unlike the chopped-in-half sawn-down middle rooms of what had once been a handsome house, retained its shape, wallpaper, style even. There were black and white marble tiles, rarely washed, and knobbly gold and brown wallpaper like tooled Italian leather. A chair from forgotten peacetime, with a blue velvet seat and a carved back, stood under a space where a painting had hung. Jill often looked at the space and invented portraits or landscapes . . .

The desk for the two French girls on duty consisted of two splintery tables pulled together.

The girls were gossiping. They always did and had the attractive habit (Jill had noticed the same thing about the staff in Harrods) of looking outraged if you wanted to know, or in Harrods' case to buy, something.

Both girls treated her with de Gaulle-like dislike. Their appearance was alike, shiny hair, dark as a blackbird's wing, flashing eyes and faces you saw on French stamps. Narrow. Handsome. The sort of women you'd imagine advancing at you with scythes.

Yvette Longjumeau, the senior of the two, said in bad

English – she never used French to Jill and pretended not to understand when Jill spoke in French,

"Your driver is 'ere."

"M'selle," said a man in uniform, who had been hanging about. He was short but huge, like a boxer or a wrestler, with a neck so thick it was the same width as his face. He gave an exaggerated salute.

"You go with 'im," said Yvette.

Jill was damned if she would ask why or where and followed the man out into the foggy morning. He opened the door of a car parked in the drive.

They travelled through Kensington, passing empty houses next to bombed gaps which resembled extracted teeth. Somebody's home had been there. Other houses half-existed, a third floor strangely balanced in mid-air, with the remains of a bed, or a wreck of a chair. Ruined walls retained flower-patterned wallpaper.

"*Voilà, Mademoiselle*."

The driver slowed up.

He caught her eye in the car mirror – he had insisted she should sit in the back – and gave her a matey wink. If ever a man repudiated discipline and gave the unmissable impression that uniform was ridiculous, it was this man. He followed the wink with a flattering grin.

Jill looked up at the early Victorian house where she'd been deposited. There was a flight of steps and a black front door, the brass knocker well polished. The street was tree-lined, residential, respectable. No bomb damage so far.

"Are you sure this is where I'm supposed to be?"

The driver was running his engine, about to leave.

"*Je suis certain*," he said, revving loudly. Not a boxer. A racing driver. With another wink, he roared away down the empty street.

A middle-aged woman answered the door. Handsome and

dignified, she made a slight inclination of her well-shaped head. She had beautiful dark coiled hair and, on her white silk blouse, a brooch of the Cross of Lorraine. Such small pieces of jewellery had become fashionable for women who had French connections.

"Miss Sinclair? Do come in."

Jill was ushered into a chilly but rich-looking house and taken into a drawing-room where a very small coal fire burned. Bare hazel twigs were arranged in a large cut glass vase. The place was lined, floor to ceiling, with books.

"Would you like some coffee? I am sure he won't keep you waiting long."

Jill was dying to ask who *he* was, but instead she politely refused the coffee; for a moment her hostess looked relieved. Perhaps her supply of coffee was at its lowest ebb.

Jill was more and more convinced that she should not be here at all. Somebody had made a mistake in the far-from-efficient French HQ. All the more reason for not swigging the lady's coffee. It'll be that idiot Gautier's fault, she thought.

Shaking a cushion for her, gesturing towards *The Times* which lay folded on a low table, the nameless lady left. Jill dragged her chair nearer to the tiny fire which just about warmed her khaki-stockinged legs.

A ringing pause.

Then the sound of a car broke the hush of the London morning. She longed to jump up and look out of the window but she knew she shouldn't. Unprofessional. Nosy. The air of mystery had begun to have an effect; she was nervous.

There was a mutter of voices, her hostess's high-class tones and somebody with a French accent. It couldn't be . . .

François Ghilain walked in.

"I am sure you will not need to wait long," repeated the lady. And left them.

"François! What on earth . . ."

He put his fingers to his lips.

"Don't speak for a moment. How beautiful you look this morning."

"François!"

He spoke in a whisper. "I have arranged this well, have I not?"

"Arranged what? *Why am I here*?"

His complacent face annoyed her.

"Did Alain Gautier not tell you? You are to be my interpreter."

"Your what!?!"

"Do stop exclaiming like that, charming Jill, you will give the game away. You don't want them to suspect, do you? Not after the trouble I've taken. You are my interpreter for this morning. Your French is so good, it is, in fact, essential. What is complicated about that?"

"François, I'm a secretary. Interpreters are in a totally different section, some quite high up, you have to go before Boards and things . . . what's the idea of all this?"

She looked, she was, exasperated. He sat down beside her on a low stool and patted her knee. She pushed his hand away.

"Last night after I left you too soon (did you get home safely? Of course, you did), I happened to catch sight of the female who was to be my interpreter this morning. A gorgon. Enormous. Fierce. I was terrified."

She did not join the smile.

"You'll get us into trouble."

"Somehow, I do not think so."

He pulled out a squashed blue packet of Gauloises, looked at it, then put it back into his breast pocket.

"We'll get court-martialled," said Jill wildly.

"I see you have already caught the mania from Gautier. These courts martial. They come to nothing. They are filed, but does he put them in the right boxes? Calm down, my child.

When I have had my interview, at which you will brilliantly translate and interpret every subtle point, I will take you to lunch. I thought Chez Prunier."

She said helplessly, "I give up."

"*A la bonne heure*."

The door opened and a burly man in dark clothes came into the room.

"I see you are both here. Do sit down," he said to François, who'd sprung up like a boy.

The man took a high-backed chair facing them.

All three were silent for a moment. He could have been anything from fifty to seventy, swarthy, spectacled, round-headed, with a jowly face, thick glasses and a precise folded mouth. His nose was an aristocratic beak. He wore a Guards tie and on one of his pudgy hands, a heavy gold signet ring. Something in his manner reminded Jill of high-ranking officers in the War Office.

"So you are my interpreter this morning, young lady."

"Yes, sir."

"Good-oh. I'm afraid my French is not as sharp as it used to be. You have your security papers, of course."

He put out his ringed hand.

Jill blushed.

"No sir, I . . ."

"What's that?"

The mouth became so thin that his lips disappeared. Stammering, trying not to implicate François, she managed, "Captain Gautier told me I was wanted. I work for him at French HQ."

"Let me get this straight. You are not an interpreter."

He looked at her so fixedly through his thick spectacles that she felt frightened and answered like a schoolgirl.

"I lived in France for six years and can easily . . ."

She was interrupted by a short noise which was scarcely a laugh.

"Might I make a guess," said François, coming to the rescue, as well he might, thought Jill, out of her depth and going down for the third time.

"I can only imagine that the interpreter allotted to us, Monsieur, has reported sick. I think I heard something to that effect. Sinclair must be the replacement."

The nameless man said nothing.

"I am certain she could do a good job. I have heard her speaking French and Captain Gautier is very enthusiastic about her work." François was gambling on the fact that their host had never set eyes on Gautier.

At François's suggestion of using Jill, the man made a gesture as if brushing away a fly. He replied in passable French with an accent Jill thought deliberately anglicised. "Since we have no interpreter, I think I can make myself understood. Time is short, Lieutenant, I cannot wait while French HQ goes into this matter. We must do the best we can." Then in English. "We will not use your services, Miss Sinclair. You'd better wait."

Perhaps Gautier would be commanded to fix a court martial after all.

He motioned François to follow him and opened double doors which cut the drawing-room into two. He closed the doors.

Jill sat alone for an hour, hearing muffled indistinguishable voices. She was alarmed and bored, half expecting their hostess to reappear and say she had been sent for – a prisoner in some Army vehicle! At last François and his elderly companion returned. The man gave Jill a very cold nod when she saluted. He walked out without another word and through the window she saw him leave the house and get into a staff car of the kind reserved for officers of field rank.

The car drove away.

"Some transport," remarked François, joining her at the window.

The tone of his voice made her look round quickly. He did not sound quite the confident man of last night and earlier this morning. She had the sensation that he was scarcely conscious she was there. He finally said, with an effort.

"Doubtless Gautier thinks you are still interpreting away. Shall we lunch?"

He was back to normal by the time they reached St James's and the lunch which followed was the longest of Jill's life. Her feeling alternated – guilt at the thought of Gautier without her to type and be snapped at, joy at her companion. It was far too late when the meal ended to go back to Kensington and François was on duty at six. She went home in a slow bus and a dream.

Next day, and for the rest of the week, François took to appearing unexpectedly in her office. He always arrived a minute after Gautier had gone out.

Does he keep watch, thought Jill, followed by the conscientious – hasn't he any work to do?

François, coming into the office, cleared one of the littered chairs, dropping files and documents unceremoniously on the floor. Jill tried to go on working.

But every time she glanced up, there was François, legs stretched out, the picture of tender attention.

"François, I beg, do go."

"You are very cruel today."

"Don't flirt. Just leave me in peace."

"Why must I do that?"

"Because," she blurted out, "because I can't concentrate when you are here."

"That is what I 'ope."

Never an "h" in François's English or for that matter in the entire French headquarters.

She stared at him over the ancient and enormous type-writer, feeling helpless.

"It is nearly midday. I take you to lunch."

"You know that's impossible."

Exaggerated surprise.

"I did not mean to Chez Prunier, *ma pauvre*. I mean, allow me to accompany you to the canteen."

"Captain Gautier prefers me to have what he calls a sanvich."

"Oh does he? Come along, we will see what Marie-France can produce for us."

Jill, guilty and willing, allowed him to bustle her down the narrow passages into the loud and steamy canteen where at least a hundred Frenchmen in uniform, and very few girls, were queuing or eating. François moved fast to grab a table just as some officers stood up to go. He corralled one of the sulky girls in white overalls and began to talk to her. Jill knew the girl, who was often as rude to her as only a Frenchwoman, thought Jill, knew how to be. She was now transformed. All smiles and eyelashes, hurrying off to do his bidding.

When it came, the food was some kind of meat, some kind of carrots, all delicious.

"How do you do it?"

"I do not cook, my friend."

"Don't be annoying. I mean how do you manage to get that girl . . ."

"Marie-France?"

"To bring you this. I've never eaten anything like it before."

"Of course not. It is a way I have."

He had lots of ways. He had, for instance, not kissed her since the other night. Yet somehow gave the sensation, almost the certainty, that they had passionately embraced. It was a way he had.

"I can't wait for coffee, François. I've already been twenty-five minutes."

"Poor you," said François, ordering his own from the slavish Marie-France.

Jill picked up her gas mask and slung it, in the familiar gesture, over her shoulder. Suddenly she detested her bondage to Gautier. Duty, an accusing ghost, gibbered at her.

"Have you so much to do, then?" asked François, getting to his feet politely. But he intended to stay and in the tail of her eye Jill could see Marie-France hovering in hope.

"Captain G works me like a pack mule. Someone once told me that in Spain they pile stuff on the poor creatures so heavily that their legs buckle and they lie down and die."

"Propaganda. The Spanish are greatly charitable to their animals."

She gave a hoot of disbelief.

"What about bullfighting?"

"You English. The sentimental nation again. Bullfighting is an art, I see it many times in Pamplona."

"I must go. I'm late. And you have a hard heart."

"While yours," he said with satisfaction, "is butter."

It was finally arranged on one of his unheralded office visits that he should take her to dinner. He was not on duty that night.

"Not to Chez Prunier. That was last time. Let us go again to Brevet Club. We will pray Gautier does not track us there. Eight? Suppose there is a raid?"

"I will come anyway."

"Bravo."

It did not occur to her that everybody at the club, or François, or she herself, could be killed. She still found the air raids exciting. And nobody she knew had been hit . . .

Dressed in her best civilian dress (it had been her mother's) and pearls (also her mother's) Jill was five minutes early. No raid either. She came by Underground, walked the five minutes to the club and was delighted in the gloom to make out François's thin figure by the entrance.

He took her arm and led her up the stairs and into the candle-lit restaurant. For one innocent moment she gave him a grin of sheer pleasure.

Until she saw his expression.

"What's happened?"

"Thank God you're punctual, women never are, I thought it could be an hour – *ma chère* Jill, what I have to say is hateful. I am so angry. I cannot spend the evening with you. Not tonight, or for the next fourteen days. I am posted."

She was so disappointed that she felt sick.

"The stupid mysteries. How they enjoy them. I am simply told to go," he said irritably. "But they say I will be back by the end of the month."

He took the hand hanging listlessly by her side and said, the lines of his cheeks angular as he smiled, "Can you stay faithful until then?"

"Not sure."

"No illicit sex with Captain Gautier. I see how he looks at you sometimes."

She couldn't help laughing.

He still retained her hand.

"*Ma belle*," he said. "I am only here because I make a tremendous drama about not being able to get in touch with the person I am meeting. I say she has high connections in the English army. They do not believe a word but they know how *ennuyeux* I can be, so my Colonel gives me an hour. Thank God you are punctual," he repeated.

She gripped his hand for a moment to show him she could take whatever it was. She gave the resolute, even ghastly smile you were supposed to give. The role, the face, were false and he knew it.

He went out with her into the dark street to find a taxi which came nosing up. As she climbed in, he pulled her into his arms.

"See you February twenty-eight, *sans faute*. Don't you dare to forget me."

"How could I?"

"Yes, it would be difficult."

Three

February was bitterly cold, and when the fog lifted, the Blitz began again. "A short sharp blitz" was how it was described in the newspapers. Rumour had it that Churchill remarked cheerfully it was quite like old times; a comment resented by the Londoners who until now had made him a hero.

The spirit of adventure which Jill had been too young to feel, but had heard so much about, disappeared from London. Victory was on the horizon and people no longer felt heroic. For some Germanic reason, the enemy planes, buzzing like venomous bees, never stayed much after midnight, and were followed by the All Clear. Instead of going to bed in relief, a good many people in London now developed the odd habit of emerging from their burrows – shelters, Undergrounds, below-ground flats – and setting out to watch the spectacle of fires. Whether because a fire is exciting or to get a selfish comfort in gaping at other people's homes in flames, it was hard to say.

Pouring rain dispersed the fog – the damp seemed to eat through Jill's uniform. Her khaki-stockinged legs were freezing. The air became clear as the last vestiges of fog disappeared, but the rain beating down on bomb dust turned the streets into a sticky mess. The gutters were awash with black soup, and indoors people's shoes left marks as if dipped in soot.

Jill was late for work because her mother had telephoned to be sure she was safe. She was hurrying through the gates of the French HQ when a man appeared from nowhere and caught her arm.

"*Toi*!" he said. Then "Sh. Don't say a word."

"François . . ."

"Sh," he repeated and pulled her not down the drive towards the house where windows shone in the dark morning, but into the garden. The air was sharp.

"Oh François, it's so good to see you, but . . ."

He took no notice, busy pushing her ahead of him towards what had been a formal hedge of box trees. They had grown wild and tall and shaggy. Behind their wet shelter, hidden from the house, he took her in his arms and embraced her.

Jill returned the kiss with passion, locking her arms round his neck and closing her eyes. When they drew apart she pressed her cheek against his chest. His battledress was coarse and scratchy, she pressed against it as if it were velvet. Looking up, she was vaguely conscious that the French flash was missing from his shoulders. He returned the look with a sexy one of his own.

"François. I must go."

"No, *ma belle*. That is what you will not do. I have exactly four days and you must get away from here."

"*I can't*."

He had expected the horrified whisper and rubbed his chin, then undid the buttoned breast pocket of his uniform and took out a packet of cigarettes, automatically offering it to her which she just as automatically refused. He lit the cigarette, sheltering his hand more or less from the falling rain.

The smell of Gauloises was strong.

"You have to get away, *coquine*."

"That's impossible."

"Impossible to be ill? Surely not. The officer in my section has just had *la grippe*. Very ill he was. A high fever, a burning face. You have caught the same kind of thing, yes? Some French pig came into your office and breathed his germs all over you."

Jill was frightened at the enormity of the idea.

François looked at her with amusement.

He reminded her of an old poster in Bourg-en-Bresse, advertising a French night club singer at a Café Chantant. The same lazy confidence. The same I'm-so-tired-of-life. The same cigarette.

"Dutiful woman. Patriot. It is terrible you have caught such bad flu."

"I can't."

The rain was heavier, they stood there, already drenched. François took hold of her hands, both his and hers were wet.

"Listen to me, coquine." Did she imagine his voice slightly shook. "I have four days and after that God knows. Perhaps we will not see each other again. It is possible. Perhaps I will be dead and you hit by a bomb. Such things happen, do they not?"

"Yes, but . . ."

"But not to you because you are nearly twenty and immortal. True."

He brushed aside a raindrop which coursed down her face like a tear. "What we are talking about is something which at this moment means everything to me. Jill Sinclair, I want you. I must have you. And I think you want me. Four days is not a crime, though Gautier would say it is. Absent without leave. Men have been shot for it. Do you think the French Army shoots girls?"

"I wish you'd be serious."

Her teeth were chattering in her head. She didn't know how cold and wet she was.

"I am very serious. I have never been more so. Four days. We will go to Brighton."

"Brighton!"

She had begun to cry.

He ignored that. "They tell me in peacetime Brighton was not bad. A resort, is that it? Like Cannes or Juan. I have booked two rooms. Now, attention. What you have to do is to go into the Captain's office at once and tell him, behold, you are very ill, could not get through on the telephone, should not be here, and must go immediately home. Tell him you know you are infectious. Add that you will get a medical certificate. No, no," a wet finger on her wet mouth. "That can be arranged later. Off with you to break the bad news. What is your address?"

"In Chelsea. Twenty-seven Markham Square."

"Is there a concierge there?"

Jill laughed, still crying. "The person who owns the house is always out during the day. WVS . . ."

"Out? Good. Write down you unpronouncable address for me."

The pencil marks ran with rain as she wrote. He dabbed the paper against his sleeve and pocketed it.

"I will be there in one hour. Before I come, have a hot bath. It would be a comedy if my four days were spent with you having *la grippe*."

She felt like a criminal. She was about to break every solemn wartime principle. With guilt heavy inside her, she went into headquarters where men and women in uniform hurried by, intent on the work which must win a war. She reported to Captain Gautier.

Unlike a good many of the people she passed in the corridor, he did not notice she was sopping wet. She had taken off her cap and the edges of her hair stuck to her forehead. She looked ghastly from shock and fear.

"Very well, go home but it is most inconvenient. However it

would be worse if I caught your germs, Sinclair. Not so close, please. Yes, you had better go."

At home, after a shivering bus journey which seemed to last forever, Jill had a five inch bath in near-scalding water. She changed into her only civilian suit. It was fine turquoise and brown tweed and her mother had given her one of her own silk blouses. My going away clothes, she thought. It was the first joke she had made to herself for weeks. She was at her dressing table, trying to do something with her damp hair, when the front door bell imperiously rang.

She rushed and threw open the door.

Kissing her, holding her against him so that she was forced to go backwards, he moved into the corridor and carried her up the stairs.

"Delight begins now," he said, setting her down. Then picked her up again.

"Where is your bedroom? Ah yes, I recognize the hideous uniform on the bed."

Even after five years of war the train from Victoria to Brighton only took an hour. François did not use his army pass but bought two first class tickets. The empty compartment was none too clean and humbly showed its past luxury by the worn patterned plush. The early afternoon was quiet, the crowds who came to work in London, returning at night before the raids, were still in offices and factories.

"Sit by me," he said, as the train began to move.

She leaned against him, watching the misty suburbs go by, rows of leafless tress, washing in back gardens. Why did people hang out their sheets when the air sprinkled them with smuts?

She felt sleepy and weak, as if every bone in her body had melted. So that was sex, was it? She had the dreamy idea that the whole world had been in on the secret all the time. And only today had she been told.

François kissed the palm of her hand.

"You never told me you were *vierge*."

"It isn't something one announces, François. How do you do. My name is Sinclair and I am a virgin."

"You're a miracle of nature. They used to say that in the *Michelin Guide* about the caves outside Bourg. *Quelle miracle de la nature*. Worth a detour. That's you."

"More than a detour, I hope."

"Of course. Three stars. Worth the journey."

"Really?"

"Really," he said, imitating her. They were speaking English, though during their lovemaking the little he had said had been in French.

She looked at him lazily, her guilt at the crime of desertion forgotten, never to return. She felt like a miser in a fairy tale gloating over a cellar full of gold sovereigns. But Jill's gold was time.

When François told her he'd booked rooms at the Grand Hotel she laughed and said that was because he had believed its name. As it happened, the hotel did retain a trace of old grandeur. Thick red carpets. Marble pillars. But it faced long beaches guarded by eight foot high rolls of rusted barbed wire. There were concrete walls, sentry posts. And an inescapable feeling that the town sat there waiting to be attacked from the sea.

Jill hadn't seen the sea for almost five years. When they had unpacked – their possessions took less than half a drawer apiece – Jill suggested they should go for a walk.

François raised his eyebrows but acquiesced and they went out into the wind. The Channel was rough, the waves crashed and showed yellowish teeth, hissing backwards, thundering down on to the pebbles. There wasn't a soul about, they seemed to be the only people on the promenade and in the world. François bent his head, but Jill couldn't stop turning to look at the sea.

"I believe you actually like it," he shouted over the noise. Jill touched her face and licked her fingers salty with spray.

"Of course I do, it's wonderful. You must feel the same?"

"Of course I do not, my poor friend. It is ugly and dangerous. What is more I am dying of cold. Let us go back and have some English tea."

"I can't believe everyone doesn't love the sea," shouted Jill, allowing herself unwillingly to be turned back.

"Now you have met the man who does not. Come along, come along. We will ask for toast."

"OK. But do breathe in the ozone, it is good for us."

He began to shake with laughter.

Sex. Their time together was all sex. He wanted her over and over again, taught her, loved and excited her. Learning so much about his body and hers, she found she did not know the man. After that first time when he had been willing to reminisce, he never spoke about France. Once, when she tried to, he said, "What is happening there is not for you to hear."

"Is it so bad then?"

"Worse."

François had refused more sea walks and they were lying on her bed after lunch. He propped himself up with one of her pillows.

She knew, just then, that she was on dangerous ground and questions could make him angry. She couldn't bear that. A few minutes before, they had finished making love. She simply wanted to listen to his accented voice, lie beside him naked. She said like a child, "Do you know what I would like to hear about, darling François. How you got here to England."

She saw by his expression that danger had passed.

"You don't want to hear that old story again."

"You never really told it. You said about three sentences that night at the Brevet before Captain Gautier hove into view and ruined everything."

"So he did. Do you think he's watching the post for your doctor's certificate?"

"Don't change the subject. Tell me the story. I long to hear it."

"It is scarcely worth such interest, *ma belle*. I was at the Mairie coping with documents which poured in like the deluge. Far worse than you have to manage, I must tell you. And then there were the people. The Bressois who wanted something, to complain about if they dared, poor things, or get permits I could not issue . . . all those crowds . . . they began to queue up outside the Mairie at five in the morning. So . . ."

"So?"

He thought for a while.

"So there were some old friends of mine who did not enjoy the way things were at Bourg. I was useful to them for a while. No," putting his finger on her mouth. "No questions. As I say, I was useful. And then I wasn't. In fact the contrary, and it was decided the sooner I got out the better. So I stole a motorcycle. The machine belonged to the Wehrmacht, a magnificent thing, it went like the wind. It had to."

Jill waited. He said no more.

Then turned to look at her.

"Poor little love. You need a hero."

"I've got one."

He really laughed.

"No such thing. My story is no different from other Frenchmen you have seen appear in Kensington, found on beaches in Kent. The motorcycle was recognised and I had to abandon it. I slept in ditches, that is the usual story, isn't it? Finally, I crossed the Spanish border on foot, a twisting goat track through the mountains above the village of Le Perthus. Then I had to walk one hundred and fifty kilometres to Barcelona. That part of the story is heroic. I had such blisters.

Blood in my sandals. In Barcelona somebody gave me a ticket to Madrid."

She knew the somebody was a woman and said nothing.

"I got to Santander. To a ship sailing to join a convoy. I was lucky. They signed me on as a pantry boy."

"Tell me about that."

"I hate to remember it. My duties were to clean the ship which was filthy. The Spanish are not fond of soap, they scarcely supply it in the ships' stores. Or didn't on the *San Cristobal.* I had to scrub the decks only with water. You see? Your lover is no hero."

"I think you are."

"I am afraid you are a romantic. That is dangerous. Of course I am not a hero, *ma belle.* I am a practical man. It is practical to wish our country free of the Nazis. Practical to be useful, if that is possible, to the General. Compared to many men I knew at Bourg, I have done little enough. My poor best, you would say in English."

"Escaping isn't a poor best. It's a best best."

"Poor little love."

They lay for hours on the bed in her room. He always visited hers, she was never invited to come to his and once when she suggested it, he refused. At night after supper and a dance or two in the cavernous ballroom where many electric bulbs were missing from the chandeliers, they went decorously to their separate rooms.

Then François in a dressing gown, a towel round his neck, would knock at her door. Bliss, thought Jill, every time.

Now he leaned on his elbow and studied her face.

"We will have less romance, *s'il te plaît.*"

"I adore you."

"So you do."

"What about you?"

"Of course I am your slave."

It was all she was given on that or any other day.

The miser's gold began to melt. Three days. Two. They went to Hollywood films in the big cinema in West Street. The place was packed with Brighton people. François said they were "as guilty of romance" as was Jill herself. She was pleased when after a torrid movie featuring one of the biggest Hollywood stars he told her she was sexier.

"They are physically invented," he said. "You can see if you look at the breasts."

After the first afternoon, a sea fog descended on the town and continued for the rest of the time they were there. They went for walks but François refused to go to the front. "The sea does not attract," he said, leading her away from the expanse of mist which was the hidden ocean. They explored the Lanes where he bought Jill a last century mahogany box "for all my letters" he said, laughing. He also picked out a necklace of beads which suited her, but said they were certainly not amber. "They are pretty anyway. We will have them."

Jill was sure he was wrong when she fingered the silky surface of the beads, but did not argue. He would never change his mind. She had seen from early on that he was a man convinced, never swerving, that he was always right. It was relaxing to know that and his mistake about the amber privately amused her.

François discovered a restaurant in one of the cobbled back streets where real fish was served, not the smelly stuff sold to patient queues.

"One detects the black market," he murmured to Jill as they ate Dover sole.

"François, sh! That's treason."

"You, *coquine*, are a prig."

They drank Algerian wine and during the meal François made a solemn vow that when peace broke out he would never take another cork out of another bottle which came from his country's Algerian empire.

"I like it."

"That is because you have no taste."

Jill tried not to sleep too long or too late but it was difficult; tired out as she was by his energetic, breath-taking sex. She detested thinking that, drifting into sleep, she was going to waste seven hours of his company. At night he stayed in bed with her, only leaving before six in the morning while the hotel still slept.

In the night she sometimes woke to feel for his hand or touch his naked thigh and though asleep he always reacted. After her awkward beginnings, he taught her all kinds of ways to make love. He said she had a "natural talent".

As the misty days went by and the nights came darkly down, they heard enemy planes droning through their dreams, on what could be the fatal journey to London.

Once she said sleepily, "The RAF will shoot them down." She did not see the look of pity he gave her.

Made love to, admired and what he called "bercée", she changed as many wartime girls had done. Jill did not dye her hair silver blonde and become the mistress in men's fantasies, but the insouciant girl was gone, she grew alluring and heavy-eyed. François, smoking and watching her, thought Cleopatra must have been like Jill. Older, of course.

Despite her worrying happiness, Jill gave herself a careful alibi. She telephoned Captain Gautier, choosing a time when he would be at his most harrassed, mid-morning, and using a dying duck voice said her flu was worse. Temperature high. That sort of thing.

François, listening with a delighted face, mouthed, "Offer to come in today."

Jill did. To the angry, snappish and alarmed, "Kindly stay away until you are recovered, Sinclair."

Warming to the task, Jill said she would telephone him twice daily with medical reports.

"Kindly do not waste my time, Sinclair. Concentrate on your recovery. You are needed here. But not when you are highly infectious."

Jill had a surge of grateful joy at being given what she wanted.

"If your fever is gone in three days, I will expect you back on Tuesday morning."

It was the day François was to go. It hurt her to agree.

"Remember not to telephone again. Just be at your desk when you are normal," said Gautier. Jill, joy evaporating, did not even think that funny.

The final evening came at last. Fog still veiled the sea, the town, the narrow streets; it hung from high buildings and clung to the curtains in the ballroom. François agreed for once to Jill's earnest entreaty, they would go for a final walk along the deserted promenade.

"Maybe I shall like it this time, as I cannot see the sea."

They walked in silence. Around them was eerie quiet, a white mist like cotton wool. There was no sign of the sea but they could hear the long sigh and sucking of pebbles. Jill, her heart giving her excruciating pain, thought this is what it's like to be dead.

The Grand Hotel made one gesture to wartime gaiety which Jill was too sentimental to laugh over and François too French to ignore. An elderly lady played the piano during dinner and later moved into the ballroom and played there for the few dancers. She always wore the same dress, beaded black velvet. François said it was forty years old at least. He was also convinced that she wore a wig, which Jill denied. Her back was bent with arthritis and she played wrong notes in a sprightly way, her repertoires exclusively from 1930s musical films and plays. She would slip from Fred Astaire's "I've Just

Got An Invitation Through The Mail" to the Jessie Matthews' "May I Have The Next Romance With You?"

Every evening both in the dining-room and later in the ballroom the management placed a glass of sherry on top of the piano. François said it was refilled too often and that explained the wrong notes.

Listening to "Smoke Gets In Your Eyes" during the meal, François and Jill were as quiet as when they had walked by the invisible sea. Eating his ice cream (*Dieu*, what is it made of?) François remarked casually that he was due in London early the next morning.

"Yes. I must be early too" she said.

"We will take the London train together. Then at Victoria – you to beloved Captain Gautier. Me to somewhere else."

When he smiled, the creases in his thin cheeks broke into angles.

"You will have made a miracle recovery. *Voilà, mon Capitaine*, I am myself again. The fever left me and here I am ready to type your unending documents until the General leaves for France. How grateful Gautier will be to see your pretty face again, let alone the use of your willing fingers."

"Tonight I'm going to be Scarlett O'Hara. I'll think about it tomorrow."

"Sometimes I do not understand a word you say."

It was often like that. His references were not hers, his experience miles, kilometres apart. He had been in France when the government collapsed, when panic spread like fire, when the river of refugees flowed out from Paris and a second river as thick and desolate began to flow northwards, the mass of people passing each other and going nowhere. François had seen the Germans march in to Bourg. He knew the shock and rage and fear, the curfews, hunger, enemy troops pitiless in the street. And no future.

Jill could not share such things even in her imagination. She had grown into womanhood in an embattled island, fed on meagre rations, encouragement and patriotic propaganda. "*Your* courage, *your* cheerfulness, *your* resolution will bring us victory." She knew about the war effort and the glorious fact of being nearly twenty years old.

They made love often that last day. Three times. Four. Neither could eat any dinner, to the sad frown of the elderly waiter who placed stringy chops and grey potatoes in front of them with an artist's flourish. They did not drink either.

"We do not need it," François said.

They travelled up in the lift and walked down the long passages to Jill's dull bedroom. Its high window was draped in dusty satin curtains covered with blackout cotton. François locked the door and Jill pulled off her dress and ran to him naked.

"You cling like a limpet," he said, laughing. "I like it. Cling away."

And as he had done the first time in Markham Square he picked her up and threw her down on the bed.

The fog vanished. During breakfast they saw from the huge windows crisscrossed with paper strips that the sea was rough again. Big waves crashed. There was a wind.

"Look at the sea, François. It's exciting."

He made a face at her.

The taxi ride to the station was too short. And then there they were on a platform crowded with people waiting for the early London train. It was bitterly cold and passengers wound their scarves closer round their necks, reading half-folded newspapers. Everybody looked small. Diminished. I suppose my eyes are doing that, she thought.

The train pulled slowly in at last. Very late. There was a stampede to the open doors and, although they had first class tickets, they had to stand in the corridor.

Jill was close to François, as close as she could be and, at times when the train swerved or half stopped, she was thrown against him. François steadied her and smiled. But absently. A British officer, blonde and tough looking, was nearby. François spoke to him.

"If you pay for a ticket, do you not have a right to a seat?"

"Shouldn't think so. It's damned clever of them to lay on trains at all."

François winked at Jill who, torn between approval of the officer and passion, looked prim.

During the journey he placed his hands on either side of the compartment's door behind them so Jill was imprisoned from the worst jolts. To the unconcealed disapproval of the officer, he gave her a kiss.

At last the train slowed down and stopped at East Croydon where a huge crowd poured out on to the platform, but before Jill and François could even stretch or try to get a seat, a further thicker crowd clambered and jostled on to the train. Jill was no longer protected inside François's arms, there wasn't room. They were crushed together, from breast bone to knee.

At last. Victoria.

And another rush and shove and many English "Sorry"s and angry looks from people with suitcases or army packs who had to squeeze past them. In the briefest time, scarcely two minutes, the train was deserted.

For a moment François did not move. He looked down at her, slightly narrowing his eyes the way her father used to do when he took photographs. Jill was white in the face. The curly hair along her forehead was damp. He saw, with a stab of the heart, that she was sweating.

"I have to go, *coquine*. I'm afraid I cannot see you into a taxi. I have scarcely time," glancing at his watch, "to go where I am supposed to be."

"I shall take a bus. And go home and change."

"Back into the hideous uniform, mm? Gautier will be keenly waiting for the medical certificate."

It had been a running joke for the four days. But when he said it, she could hear that the remark was automatic. His thoughts, his eyes, were elsewhere.

He made a move and they left the train at last; they were almost alone on the long empty platform.

He put his arms round her and kissed her. She shut her eyes. But the embrace was not long or tender, his mouth was closed and, when she opened her eyes, he was looking over her shoulder.

"Oh my darling."

"Off you go."

The words she had sworn she wouldn't say, had bitten back, burst out. And the moment she said them she hated herself.

"Shall I see you again?"

"*C'est possible*," he said with a grin and then again, "Off you go, *coquine*."

Four

Silence arched over Lyon. When Jill woke and looked out of the window, the snow was thicker than ever. It had snowed all night long and the window sill was inches deep; everywhere – street, roofs – was eye-blindingly white. The snow, it seemed, had stopped now but occasional flakes came floating down as if to say – don't think we have left you. The silence was uncanny and as she dressed Jill shivered.

In Philomène's kitchen, she found her hostess propped against the antique cooker, quietly cursing.

"No gas. The damned snow, we're not used to it here. Try upstairs, Jill. Ask Madame Massard if you can heat some water on her electric. She uses a stove she puts flat on its back."

Jill, who knew nobody except Philomène in the building, toiled up the stairs. The once rich carpet got worse as she climbed higher. More holes.

She knocked on a varnished door exactly like Philomène's; it opened a crack. A high voice squeaked, "*Oui*?"

Jill explained her errand.

"Ah. From *Madame au Premier*," said a little person opening the door. "*Entrez, entrez*. Yes, I am heating some water myself."

She was no bigger than a little girl of perhaps seven years old, very thin, wearing at least a dozen bead necklaces and bracelets. Her grey hair was tied with a ribbon. She ushered Jill into a sitting-room, the twin of Philomène's, high-ceilinged, net-curtained, faded and poor-looking, and taken over by gigantic French provincial furniture. The great dark pieces had a hostile air. Lace mats were scattered about. Tarnished silver coffee pots.

In the centre of the room, a very large ungainly electric fire, dating back to the early 1930s, had been placed on its back. It glowed red and a saucepan small enough for its doll-owner was simmering. Madame Massard, piping like a tiny bird, fetched a bigger saucepan filled with water and somehow managed to fit it next to her own. She switched on a second bar of the fire.

"For myself, Mademoiselle, only one is needed."

"That is very good of you, Madame, but the one bar for us both is surely sufficient."

"Ah. *C'est vrai*," The little creature hastily switched off the second bar and remained on her knees, watching the water meant for Jill. It was a long way from boiling.

She turned and gave a most beautiful smile. She was the first French person, man, woman or child, who had smiled at Jill since she had set foot in France. The English troops laughed. Peter grinned. Roz chuckled now and then and Philomène might give an ironic half-smile. But Madame Massard's was a raying look like a blessing. Her pale face, covered with a network of lines like crushed tissue paper, shone with exquisite benevolence.

"You are *l'Anglaise*."

"There are two of us, Madame. Staying with Madame au Premier."

"I hear your voices on the stairs sometimes. I like the English language. I hear it on the wireless. The BBC."

"You can listen in safety now."

The little lady shrugged, playing with her necklaces.

"I have listened for a long time. The wireless under the cushions on the divan and turned very soft. A peep. A tiny sound. But it comes from London."

"Wasn't that very dangerous?"

"Evidently. But since Jean-Marc was taken, what else had I? He went to Germany as a worker. Not from choice. Never from choice. Dragged away and put on a train."

She spoke matter-of-factly, still playing with the necklaces. A pause. Jill's saucepan began to bubble.

Jill said gently that she hoped Madame would have good news one day soon.

"Oh no. My poor Jean-Marc is dead. He was always delicate. The bad chest, you know? *Dieu*, always ill in weather like this. He is dead. I pray for his soul. And imagine, Mademoiselle, I would not tell this to anybody but an Englishwoman, I pray also for the enemies who killed him. *Quelle affaire*. To pray for those you hate." She carefully switched off the fire and handed Jill the saucepan. "It is an exercise. One must keep healthy and exercise is necessary."

She gave, again, the extraordinary smile.

Jill thanked her and went downstairs with the water.

"Swell," said Philomène. "And how is little Saint Massard? She will be canonised; I shall personally see to it."

She took the saucepan, mixed dried milk and what passed for coffee. Ground acorns? Dandelion roots?

Jill murmured that Madame Massard seemed very nice.

Philomène raised her eyebrows.

"A saint, as I say. Who was it who said that the saintly ones are those who have to live with saints? Muriél is a sore trial when she calls in here for a quick pray."

She and Jill sat down to the hot but disgusting brew which passed for breakfast, joined by a yawning Roz.

The heavy snow continued. The Nazi *communiqués* were threatening. The people in Lyon went to work or to queue for food and said little; when Jill and Roz returned at night to the flat, Philomène was as silent as the French.

Roz had more to do with the Resistance than Jill had and none of her news was good.

"The Milice are getting worse," she said, appearing in Jill's room one night. In the last few days they had had no chance to talk.

Despite Nazi victories in the Ardennes, she told Jill, the enemy now knew they were going to lose and the Milice were desperate. It was a murderous orgy. Over a hundred men shot near Paris in a forest; in reprisal the Resistance had gunned down more.

Roz quoted one of the resistant newspapers. "Kill Germans to purify our land. Kill them to be free. Exterminate the Milice, strike them down like vermin." She sat on Jill's bed and pulled the quilt she'd brought with her round her shoulders. Jill did the same, the stained voluminous quilts kept the cold at bay.

Roz was talking again. "Some of the people the Resistance execute are innocent. Christ, Jill, why did we come to this country?"

"Why did *you* come, Roz?"

It was something Jill had often wondered. Laconic, short-tempered, efficient, grudging of her real self, why had Roz volunteered? She would have guessed it was going to be rough. Jill, with her outdated ideas of France had not had the wit to do so. But Roz was a realist. And couldn't have come for love.

They sat like snowmen wrapped in their goose-feather quilts at either end of the carved bed. The dim light scarcely lit their faces – Philomène's bulbs were twenty-five watt and would have been less if lower power ones were manufactured.

"I was browned off with being a driver. I wanted a bit of action."

"I don't think that's true."

"You're in the intuitive mood, I see. People should look out when that happens. OK. So it isn't why I came."

"Why then?"

Roz lit an inevitable cigarette.

She looked straight at Jill.

"Revenge," she said. "Melodramatic, isn't it? True, though. I had this notion that if I got into what they call the theatre of war, sooner or later I could have a go."

"Kill somebody."

"Yes. I wanted to revenge a friend of mine. She was killed in the first blitz in 1940. I was at work and our flat had a direct hit. When I got home, nothing. They found one of her shoes. Corny stuff, isn't it? But she was mine and they killed her and that's why I'm here."

She stared up at the stucco ceiling.

"That desire to kill somebody. A belief, you know, that it's justice. The debt paid. No such thing. I loathe what's happening here. During the last five years the brave ones in this country have learned to kill, to sabotage, to derail trains, to disobey what they were told was the law. Who gave them the order to assassinate? The General. The best men have learned to commit terrible crimes against other human beings – and to despise those weaker than themselves who do not."

"Many of those they killed are murderers."

"Yes, yes, but it won't do. It's filthy. It's human, understandable. And filthy. it leaves no escape from the slaughter."

"What will you do now?" Jill said, after a silence.

"Stay. Be useful. And get the hell out of it when I'm told. In the meantime I notice you haven't told me why *you* volunteered to come to this literally God-forsaken spot."

Jill had a moment of wavering. Should she tell Roz? Even to her own prejudiced eyes, the reason she was in France was naive. Pathetic, really. Roz's way of speaking about her love was the right way. It was hard and downbeat and truthful. But what of my grand passion? Jill thought. I suppose I am absurd, coming to work in a country of misery without a hope of finding him. She drew a breath and tried to use Roz's tone of voice, "Well, when I was at the War Office I got transferred to the Free French, which I must say maddened me. But . . ."

It was there, she told Roz, that she had met a man she'd known when she was a schoolgirl in Bourg-en-Bresse.

"And – and in London we fell for each other."

Roz raised her eyebrows, interested. Said nothing.

"He got posted, Roz. He was not allowed to tell me where, he simply vanished the way people did – do – sometimes. Later I tried to find out where he'd been sent. Hopeless. But then . . ."

"Yes?"

"I had a letter from him. From France."

"That's impossible!"

"It is, isn't it? It was marked *Censored* and covered with all kinds of official stampings like the ones I saw sometimes at French HQ. It was months old. François said that now he could write to me and the Americans were in Paris and – and he hadn't forgotten," she lamely ended. A pause, then she added, "But I knew he was in Bourg."

"How the hell did you know that?"

"He put a heart round the letter 'B'."

It was in Roz's personality to laugh. She didn't. She said dryly, "Don't tell me. You fixed to come out here by using the unfortunate Peter Whittaker."

"Yes. I told you, I was billeted on his mother in Chelsea."

"You don't like her much."

"She's awful. But Peter's . . ."

"I know, I know," Roz was still dry, "I've seen him with you often enough."

"I scraped through my interpreter's tests," said Jill, sighing, "the written stuff, I mean. OK for the oral."

"I'll say."

A pause.

"When I suggested to Peter he could pull a string or two with the RASC he was terrific."

"You surprise me."

Another of the pauses.

Roz said curiously, "Did you mention Bourg at all?"

"Not really. Of course he knew I used to live there. I'd told him all about my father's hotel and being at school and he did say sooner or later we might land up in the town. He was rather sweet. Kept saying 'I hope it won't upset you. Seeing it now, when everything's different and very rough.' He just thought I was keen to get to France."

Roz said briefly,

"Poor guy."

"He's OK," said Jill.

"I take it you know the Colonel has decreed you and I are to move on together. He says we're a good team."

"We are."

"And you know where we're going, with Peter Whittaker's lot, the day after tomorrow?"

"Yes, Roz. To Bourg." said Jill, calmly enough.

Roz made her swear not to tell anybody that they both knew about the posting. Roz's own informant was a young private who had taken a shine to her and had been on duty in the office when the orders were prepared. Everything worth knowing, much that shouldn't be, spread in a regiment.

"You can bet your bottom dollar Peter Whittaker will turn up and break the news. Don't you dare not to look surprised."

Sure enough, the next evening at Philomène's, when the three women were having cups of tea and sawdust-dry cake, Peter appeared. He hadn't seen Jill for days: trouble with supplies sent to the war zone, some of which had been stolen. He arrived covered in snow and stood in the hallway thumping his shoulders and leaving trails of melting flakes. When he kissed Jill, his lips were cold.

Philomène in her throne-like chair welcomed him with more enthusiasm than she ever gave Jill and Roz.

"Peter Whittaker. Have you brought any brandy?"

"Of course."

Philomène watched while he poured out. Jill and Roz refused a glass, not because they wouldn't have enjoyed the stuff but because of the greedy eye of their hostess.

Philomène sipped.

"Marché Noir. I know the taste. Why have you called by?"

"To break the news that we're moving on," Peter spoke in his brisk, boyish way.

"To Bourg-en-Bresse, then on to Besançon. Your Colonel has heard the rumours of German troops behind the lines."

Peter said nothing, his face expressionless. Philomène looked irritated.

"Brother, haven't you got it yet that I know what happens? I'm still," she banged her wooden leg viciously with her stick, "useful to some people. I know your lines of communication are in trouble. Or will be soon as damn it. You're off to do some mopping up. About time. And you're taking these young women with you."

"Us?" exclaimed Roz on cue, opening her eyes. She did it rather well and Jill had the uncomfortable feeling that comes when you see lies effortlessly succeed.

"Yes, we will need both of you," said Peter.

"I'm glad to be included," said Roz dryly. "Not surprised about Jill though, since she lived in Bourg for years and must know every soul in the place."

Philomène became even more disagreeable, remarking sarcastically that she had clearly got it wrong. Jill must have been a popular hostess in Bourg, not a child getting a convent education.

It took Peter the rest of the brandy to get her back into a good mood. "Philomène, the Colonel is always saying you're vital to our work . . ." Things like that.

"I'm glad he knows I do my job. I may be a cripple but it would be nice to be treated as if I have two legs and some brains."

When she stumped off to bed and Roz had gone too, Peter and Jill lingered by the door.

"Do you mind leaving Lyon and your friend Philomène and this rickety old place?" he murmured tenderly. Jill muttered a reply between kisses.

"Bourg," he said. "Your old home. I guess it's going to be a shock for you."

"I am sure it will. But I am glad to go."

"Brave girl," he said with another kiss, totally undeserved.

It was late afternoon and dark when the convoy of lorries halted in Bourg-en-Bresse. The barracks consisted of a series of dingy last-century buildings set round a number of exercise yards, one leading into another. Dim lights, those twenty-five watt bulbs of Free France, burned in only two of the barrack windows.

Jill and Roz, stiff from long hours of sitting in a lorry crowded to bursting with soldiers, some over six feet tall, climbed out on to the cobbles.

"Hey!"

It was a yell from a soldier in the lorry ahead as he and two others leapt down and began to run after a figure suddenly lit by the lorry's headlights.

An NCO, a big man made bigger by the light and dark, came up.

"Sergeant says you ladies speak French. Join us, will you?"

Jill and Roz followed him across the yard. The two soldiers had captured the fugitive – he was half their size, a shrunken figure in bedraggled clothes. The Resistance armband pulled up above his elbow had once been white. I suppose anybody could get hold of one of those, thought Jill.

"Must your men treat him so roughly, Sergeant? He's scarcely a giant," said Roz.

"Might be armed, Miss."

"OK. Sorry I spoke."

"Will you ask him where the French troops are. And where's the barracks commander?"

When Jill began to speak in French, the prisoner's face changed. He ceased to look like somebody who had lost his mind. She saw instead an expression she had never seen before – and she thought, is that what hatred looks like?

"The troops are gone. Disbanded. Gone."

"And the commander?"

"Dead."

"In the fighting before the Germans went north?"

The man spat.

"His body is down the well. Do not drink that water."

Jill, feeling shaky, translated and the NCO sharply told his men to take the prisoner away.

"That's a lovely start, isn't it?" said Roz. "We'd best rescue our kit bags before they're driven off into the middle of nowhere."

They returned to their lorry and were dragging out their bags when Peter appeared.

"Six lorries and you girls in the seventh. Evening, Roz. Got to take Jill away for a sec. The Colonel wants a word."

The yards were alive with khaki figures and lorries, noisy with shouts of command and, now and again, a hoot of laughter. Jill knew the mettle of RASC cooks; there was already a smell of cooking in the air.

Peter took her across a further yard where a few months ago sullen Vichy troops, hating the guts of their officers, had incompetently mustered.

Lights began to spring up in a long row of windows and, when Jill and Peter arrived at the first door, a lance corporal on guard gave them the salute of his life.

The building was as cold as out of doors and as dimly lit as Philomène's bedrooms. Jill guessed that where the Colonel worked there'd be more light. Drink perhaps. Nothing as feminine as heat.

Peter took her down corridors of slippery lino into one of the larger rooms. The Colonel and the two officers, Guy and David, were squatting on top of an outsized table which occupied most of the space. No fire. But a corporal was busy taking out electric bulbs and replacing them with stronger ones. As he did this, it gave a curious effect like a scene on stage; dim squares of the room sprang into raw light. The job finished, he saluted and left.

The Colonel regarded Jill.

"There you are. Have a corner of the table. We haven't located chairs yet."

She climbed up to perch on the slippery table. The Colonel swung his legs and his boots winked.

"Hope you can help. We've been trying to locate the French officer who commanded this dump."

"He's dead, sir."

She wasn't sure what she expected. She half hoped, with the satisfaction of possessing a startling fact, that he would react. He raised his eyebrows slightly higher than Philomène used to do. People here relied on eyebrows.

"And where did you hear this interesting news?"

She explained, but he was not satisfied and rattled out questions she couldn't answer. He pressed his lips together thoughtfully, reminding her, with that big nose and alarming mouth, of a vulture. Better looking, though.

"Peter, go and find the man young Jill was talking to. Yes, yes, I know your French is good, my child. But we need more than one version, even if a second and third merely verify the first. Not that we necessarily believe a dam' thing . . ."

Peter disappeared and silence descended on the Colonel and the two respectful officers. The Colonel rubbed his hands together making a sound like sandpaper.

"That bulb looks as if it's about to go out," he said to Guy. "Get it seen to."

Guy left the room.

Colonel Fisher turned to David and gave him a task as well – something about field telephones.

This left the Colonel and Jill alone. A thrill of expectation went through her and for a mad moment she wondered if he was going to tell her something about François. The idea was idiotic. She saw that at once.

He fixed her with a glance, a glare, really. She knew this was a technique to unnerve. Bugger it, she thought, you're frightening all right but I refuse to oblige. She gave him a questioning smile.

Up went the eyebrows.

"I trust you are treating this job seriously."

"Of course, Colonel. I know its importance."

"Your importance, you mean?" he sounded like a schoolmaster. "Not as important as all that. But I don't want a young woman (this goes for your colleague as well, you can tell her so) who can't knuckle down to the essentials."

Knuckle down to whatever he wanted. Fair enough.

He rubbed his hands again. He wore a heavy signet ring on one bony finger. It was engraved with an elaborate crest.

"I don't question that story of yours. I daresay my predecessor's body was pitched into a well. As the prisoner helpfully pointed out, we'd better discover which well pretty smartly or the MO will have his hands full. There's mayhem about. It was bad in Lyon, it's worse here. What I wish to say to you, Jill, is that you are not to believe any gory story told you by the French until it's been checked and double-checked. And remember, only report what you hear if it affects our job. The task of the Corps, as I trust Peter has repeatedly told you, is this . . ." He banged on the table with the palm of his hand. "Deliver what's needed when it's needed, at the right time and to the right people."

Jill nodded respectfully. Indeed, Peter had said this to her, but about his own work and its urgencies.

"There'll be a good many stories about, mobs murdering each other, horrors – and the implication that *we* are here to clear everything up. This country's in bad trouble. But believe nothing at face value and remember every man jack will tell you he's a freedom fighter. Some of the worst collabos are now posing as heroes. Before they get their throats cut. Remember that too."

Jill nodded again. But she didn't understand why he should waste his time telling *her* all this – warning *her* about what they were up against. She was a cog in the oiled RASC machine, with its huge tasks of keeping the allies on the move. Why her? And then she thought – of course. It's my French. He is speaking to one of the people in the brigade who holds a key.

He did not dismiss her but continued to swing his legs. He looked as tough as a nutcracker. She had noticed the scar on his hand, but not, until now, another scar high on his forehead near his hairline. Unconsciously pushing back his Army cap, he revealed it, silvery and thick, cutting right through one of his eyebrows.

Glancing up, he caught her observant look and she had the grace to blush. He sounded, after that, slightly more friendly.

"They don't like us, Jill. Noticed that?"

"Yes, Colonel, now and then."

"Now and then," he repeated with a barking laugh. "The indig pop can't stand the sight of us. We shame them by our presence here. By fighting for them. Everybody ends up by hating their liberators. Of course, they want us. And as I said, can't stick us."

"But the Free French . . ."

"Need us the most. What they want, in actual fact, is our victory which they'll help with in their little way," he spoke derisively, "And then they'll claim the glory. Like our friend the General in Paris. The French are a pain in the arse, I do beg your pardon. And the Americans don't help by throwing cigarettes at them as if they were chucking crusts at monkeys in the zoo . . . What am I doing, saying all this stuff to you, child? What you need to remember (and tell that pal of yours who looks like a Guide Mistress) is that Bourg-en-Bresse is a minefield, so step carefully. Well, well," he said with a look which skewered her to the wall. "Back to your job. Dismissed."

Jill slid off the table and gave her best salute. He replied with a flip of one hand, and shouted "Guard!" so loudly that she jumped out of her skin.

The tables in the canteen looked as if they'd been used for target practice. The place was loud with English talk and smelled of Woodbines. Roz was at a table with an officer who was making her laugh. Thin. Bony. Very Irish. With a black moustache.

"Jill. Come and meet Dermot Brady. Dermot – Jill. Get her a drink, do."

Dermot smiled and went to the counter. Roz looked over in his direction.

"I knew he was in our outfit but I'd no idea he'd materialise in Bourg. We go back a long time. Oxford together."

"Sorry I couldn't do any better," said Dermot, returning with a glass of wine. Jill sipped and listened while the two friends exchanged wisecracks of the kind she'd never been good at. It was obvious they liked each other, but without a nuance of sex. Jill thought of Roz's lover killed in the blitz.

The canteen was curiously familiar; it could have been whirled by flying carpet straight from Lyon and before that from Aldershot. Dermot looked over at her.

"What did our revered Colonel want you for, Jill?" He finished off his drink as if it were vodka. "Top secret?"

"Only to check the story about the dead commandant."

"Ding Dong Bell. Pussy's in the Well. That crack about bodies in the drinking water was rather smart, I thought. Troops are now scurrying about like bats in hell, checking. If they find a body (very possible) that'll mean more checking of water supplies. If they find nothing we'll have wasted a hell of a lot of time. How the locals do hate our guts," he finished, echoing Colonel Fisher.

But there proved to be little need during the next few days for the Colonel's warnings about minefields, real or psychological. Roz and Jill scarcely left barracks. They worked in an office, typing page upon page of army instructions, breathed on by waiting corporals who needed the documents yesterday. They translated edicts as long as the Bible, issued by Bourg's Town Hall. As Roz said, nothing written in French was ever brief.

The worst work was when either girl was needed to ask questions and translate replies of men hauled up in front of the officer on duty. The inhabitants of Bourg were sullen and, whenever possible, obstructive. The girls disliked the sessions very much. In the office or guardroom the hours were long. Roz and Jill worked themselves into the ground.

Meals in the canteen – stew extended by rock-hard carrots and frost-bitten potatoes, were washed down by stewed Army tea or, on bright occasions (when Dermot appeared), by brandy. At night the girls were so tired they slept like the dead.

A new operation had begun, the supply of food for "liberated civilians". Roz was loud in demanding that she and Jill should be included in the category.

"Don't we deserve a change from stew, Corporal? I hear the liberated what-have-yous are actually getting *ham.*"

"Ever so sorry, Miss. Haven't set eyes on a bit of ham myself for months." The man ladled out stew into a cracked soup plate. "But I did hear we're to have chicken tomorrow."

"Someone in the division must be going round the farms with a machine gun," said Roz.

The corporal grinned but Jill was too tired.

"Five hundred tons of good food is flown to Paris alone every bloody day of the week," grumbled Roz as they sat down. "I bet the General's guzzling caviar."

Jill was miserable as well as tired and overworked. The idea of François, the memory of his teasing face, the blank look when he made love to her, his smell, the feel of his thin cheek pressed against her, haunted her. She was *here*. She looked for the hundredth time at the now-tattered letter, with the "B" drawn round with an inked heart. How nearer was she to him? Did the resentful, haggard men she was ordered to question know him?

She never ever went into the town

It was Roz who was sent on an errand for the Colonel one wintry afternoon. He'd ordered special posters to be printed and Roz, accompanied by a sergeant, was to go to the Mairie and arrange for the posters to be flyposted all over the city.

It was nearly nine at night when she came back. She'd been drinking in the canteen late with Dermot. Jill had gone to bed early, after washing her hair in half a basin of water. She was sitting up in bed ineffectually trying to dry it with an already wet towel.

"Have mine."

Roz threw hers over and sat down on the end of Jill's bed, lighting a Gitane. "Sure you don't mind?"

"I like the smell."

"I can guess why."

Roz regarded her with grey eyes in a mannish strong-featured face.

"The good sergeant Jackson is coming with me tomorrow morning. We're paying another visit to the Mairie, to check they're doing what they're told. Displaying the Colonel's posters."

"Have you got one? I'd like to see it."

"Sure." Roz pulled a folded sheet of yellow paper from her knapsack. She herself had been told to write the words, they were in slightly academic French.

> CITIZENS. The Allies in Bourg-en-Bresse need YOUR co-operation. There is NO REASON to hide. Reprisals are totally forbidden by the General de Gaulle. France is now FREE. Be courageous. The Allies need your help not by secret courts martial but by CO-OPERATION to bring peace and plenty to your city and your country.

Jill dabbed her hair which had turned into an untidy tangle of curls.

"What does the Colonel want exactly?"

"To stop a civil war. I'm not kidding, Jill."

Silence. Roz smoked for a while.

"You've been very quiet about the real reason you're here. Isn't it time you did something?"

"Christ, Roz!" Jill almost shouted, remembered the thin walls and lowered her voice to an angry hiss. "*Who* do you imagine I've been thinking about day and night since we came here? François. François. It's driving me mad. How can I even get into the town when we don't get leave? I'm so frustrated I could scream."

"I thought you were."

"Well shut up then."

"I have a better idea. Come to the Mairie with me tomorrow."

"I haven't been detailed."

"Easy. I'll say the bureaucratic French is too tough for me and I need help. I'll say all the stuff you did in London is what's needed. Come with me."

"And?"

"You're a bit slow for a quick woman. Hasn't it struck you your boyfriend worked at the Mairie once. Isn't it the place to *ask*?"

Roz's manner, not unlike a hospital sister, was irresistible when she bothered to use it. Next morning, in the freezing half-dawn which was all Bourg managed for daylight, Roz, Jill and the burly sergeant were driven in a jeep to the Mairie. Jill was nervous.

When they arrived, Roz made a show for the sergeant's benefit of taking Jill with her into a big office marked "City Information." The clerk, a ringer for Captain Gautier, was all set to be difficult. It was clear that this put Roz on her mettle. Primed by her, the sergeant painstakingly spread a large street map all over the clerk's desk. Roz had marked it with large red-inked stars.

"Those are the sites where the posters will be displayed, that's correct, isn't it, Monsieur Cézaire?"

The Gautier of Bourg raised objections.

Roz turned with a near-invisible wink to Jill.

"Bother, I left another list in the jeep. Would you be a dear?"

Jill left the echoing room and Roz's enjoyment of the battle. She walked down a long marble-floored corridor; faintly, faintly, she remembered her father speaking about that floor. The Mayor, he said, was always spending the city's money "on glory". There was little of that to be seen now, the floor was muddy, the walls peeled. Near double doors fitted up with cardboard to replace glass panels there was a notice saying "Information." She looked into an office half the size of City Information; a step down on the social scale. A fat man crouched over a desk.

" 'Zelle?"

Using her most colloquial French, Jill said she had an enquiry to make "About the Mayor. Jean Xavier Ghilain."

The name dropped like a stone. The man didn't speak for some time. Jill waited. Then, "There is no Mayor."

"But surely he . . ."

"My name is Gomis," he said as if by rote. "I have work to do. My orders come from your Army."

"But . . ."

"There is no Mayor. The man you speak of is dead."

She felt no surprise.

She still waited.

"It was many months ago. He was killed here in the Mairie. A tragedy," he said tonelessly.

Jill felt a goose walk over her grave.

"For his family, you mean," she bravely said.

"No. For the citizens of Bourg."

"Because he worked well for your city?"

France, a country of shrugs. They meant "I do not know" or "I do not care" or "you are a fool to ask" or "I will not tell you and if I did the answer would be disgusting".

Gomis's shrug was followed by: "Because of the reprisal. Fifty people of Bourg were taken out by the Gestapo into the fields and shot as punishment. It is . . ." he paused. "It is over now."

She hadn't the courage to speak François's name.

When she thanked him, he did not look at her but dipped his pen into the inkwell, the way she used to do at school.

Five

The atmosphere in Bourg began to affect Roz. To oppress her. The trouble was that when there were jobs to be done in the town – ill-nourished, ill-heated and shivering though it was, the city occasionally had surpluses, particularly of wine – Roz was detailed to make the enquiries. A supply officer went in after Roz had confirmed the findings. She disliked these forays even though she was always accompanied by the large and fatherly Sergeant. Her grasp of the French language was not effortless like Jill's, it lacked the slang and ease and made the job all the worse.

Jill had been swallowed up in clerical work when it became obvious to her masters that she was very good at it. Trained by Gautier she was fluent not only at army lingo, but French civil service terminology. And she was (a joke by Dermot Brady) the fastest typist in Europe.

So it was that, after exchanging a look with Jill, Roz set off for yet another expedition into Bourg.

The city was a sort of hell. It lacked spirit and scrubbing soap. Had it really once been prosperous, bustling and full of cheerful people? Roz could not believe it. The streets were almost empty, the people in unheated offices rude, shrunken and not particularly clean. Roz's sheepdog, the Sergeant, found his job depressing too and sometimes persuaded her to go for a coffee if they could find a place which was open. Bar, office or street corner – everywhere was the same.

When Roz had read history at Oxford she'd come across a description of the English after the civil war, "A universal malice and animosity. A savageness which hardened the hearts and bowels of men." She recalled it now. It was a pretty accurate description of the inhabitants of Bourg-en-Bresse. Every man and woman (Roz and the Sergeant rarely saw a child) seemed to have caught a deadly sickness. She wondered if it was infectious.

Her old friend Dermot Brady who had been dealing with the city officials ("what a crew") had met members of the Resistance. A cynic, he was unwillingly impressed. "There are some fellows worth having. Full of energy. An alarming lot. The town hall's afraid of them."

Roz made a mental note of the Resistance HQ. She'd had an idea.

She made up her mind not to tell Jill yet. Since the visit to the Mairie, her friend had been in low spirits and Roz saw that Jill's hopes, which had burned in her although she denied them – romantic, unrealistic and beautiful hopes – seemed to be dying. Roz determined to help. God knows how, she thought.

She and the Sergeant left barracks in the early afternoon at a brisk pace. Jeeps and other army vehicles went by, throwing up scatterings of blackened snow. She and her companion quickened their pace, the air sharp in every breath they took The houses, large and chalet-style, showed no sign of life. If there were people inside, they didn't put on their lights.

Dermot had talked about the Resistants last night. He said they had become the guts of Bourg. Until last year they'd been uncoordinated, even wild, groups of patriots meeting in deadly secrecy. Now in 1944 it had all changed. They had come into the open. They were well-organised and they were ruthless. Their news-sheets (which had been published right through the Occupation) had circulations of a quarter of a million – Dermot thought the papers heroic but ominous. "And the General, I might say, scarcely says a dam' word to commend them."

When the Sergeant and Roz arrived in the city she sent him to collect more forms at the Mairie. He did not look too happy about leaving her, but Roz was firm. Alone, she walked fast until she finally located a once-fashionable street now consisting of boarded-up shops, with a few still open selling frost-bitten vegetables. But there was one window brightly lit, with a Cross of Lorraine daubed in white paint on the glass.

Inside were rows of empty chairs, a ringing telephone and two men who, seeing her uniform, briefly saluted. The telephone still shrilled and the older man, stout and grizzled, picked it up. The younger man, he was the senior, gestured to her politely to sit down.

He had the face of an actor, mobile, bony, with very pale eyes. What was noticeable was his hair combed back dead straight and smeared with something to keep it flat like a cap of patent leather. When he moved the hair remained in place as if stuck by glue.

"Zelle?"

Roz explained that she was trying to trace somebody who used to live in Bourg. "A friend of a friend."

"When did this 'friend' live here, Mademoiselle?"

"Some years ago. Before the war."

He removed his cigarette for a moment. The air was so still that the smoke went straight up to the ceilling.

"*Five* years?"

"Indeed. A very long time," said Roz with irony. The older man had begun to talk loudly on the telephone, berating somebody in peasant French. Roz's man said, "*Doucement*, Anselme," and the man, annoyed, quietened down.

The young man again gestured to Roz to sit down. She drew up a chair on the other side of his desk. The file-filled room had an urgent air. As if the two men had just come rushing in from a battle; she almost expected a stack of rifles in the corner. He smoked for a moment or two.

"This 'friend of a friend' ". He spoke in quotation marks. "Somebody I myself do not know, but the close friend of my colleague in the RASC. We work here at headquarters."

"Evidently."

"We are both interpreters. She lived here before the war. Her father was an hotelier."

He pulled over a pad of paper. "What is the name of this friend?"

"Ghilain."

Both men stared. The one on the telephone stopped talking. Roz's man looked up at a long shelf below the ceiling. It ran from one corner of the room to the other and was crammed with files.

Roz was accustomed to files. The army couldn't move without them. They looked as alike as men in uniform, severe cardboard containers with metal hinges which opened so that documents could be clipped inside in date order.

The Resistance's shelf was filled with an extraordinary collection. Some were newspaper parcels. Some were tied with string and wrapped in sacking. Some were papers pushed into the covers of old books, Roz read *Aesop's Fables* on a blue folder. The files were labelled with scraps of cardboard. 1940. 1941. 1942 . . . Many bore the Cross of Lorraine. What bloodstained information was hidden up there?

Her man lit another cigarette, his fingers were stained with nicotine. "Ghilain is the name of the so-called Mayor. He was executed – let us see, Anselme, when was that?"

"Last Christmas Day."

"So he was. Christmas Day." And what does an Englishwoman in the British Army want with a dead traitor? His death warrant? I daresay we could locate it."

"We are not inquiring about Jean Xavier Ghilain. We are already informed that he is dead," said Roz shortly. "He had a son, François. Who served in the Free French Army in London."

"Then he is with the General in Paris. Why ask us?"

"He is not. He was sent to work for the Allies here in Bourg," said Roz boldly. She saw in the young man's face that François Ghilain meant something, that he knew the name and probably the fate of its owner. And suddenly she recoiled from learning the truth. Nothing in this place was good.

If what Roz now feared was true, Jill must find it out for herself. To help and to wound were often the same thing.

She stood up.

"My regrets for wasting your time, Monsieur."

"I am a lieutenant. Tell your friend we have no trace of any member of that family since the execution of the traitor. Details of that might be given her. If she so wishes."

The Sergeant, blue with cold, was walking up and down outside the Mairie where they had arranged to meet. Roz apologised without explanation and they returned to barracks with the dying day.

That night the two girls shared the usual canteen supper of stew. Roz had splashed out and bought two tumblers of coarse red wine. She gave Jill a carefully edited version of what had happened in the town.

"So the Resistance couldn't help?" said Jill.

"Definitely not. I drew a blank."

Jill was silent and, looking at that expressive face, Roz did wonder if it would be kinder to tell. But tell what exactly? Merely an impression she'd had. Yet she knew it had been more than that. When the young man heard François Ghilain's name he'd *known* François was dead.

But he didn't actually say so, Roz thought, trying to

contradict herself. Nothing's certain unless it's confirmed by a lot of people. The Colonel repeated that often enough.

Jill spoke with an effort.

"Roz, I haven't been to Les Lys. I hadn't the guts to go alone; I suppose you wouldn't come with me, would you? You never know, supposing I met somebody? Like an old friend."

And where, in this place, would we meet one of those? thought Roz, deciding on a third glass of wine so rough it was worse than the coarsest cider.

The girls went out at lunchtime the following day. They were allowed an hour for the meal and cramming slices of bread into uniform pockets, managed to slip out, return a salute at the gate and walk off quickly. Jill used her street map and they located the Avenue du Sphinx.

"There's a bronze sphinx at the corner. Our hotel's almost facing it."

"Coming back to you, is it?" Roz said as they reached the river and Jill turned sharp left.

"Yes . . . the avenue is over there . . ."

In silence they reached the corner of the avenue – it was deep in snow, no ruts from carts or marks from tyres, the pavement a sheet of ice. The avenue was lined on both sides with young chestnut trees, now leafless. It gave Jill a shock to see how much thicker the trunks had grown and she remembered how in autumn the conkers fell in profusion all over the road, splitting into green halves and shining like polished shoes.

They quickened their pace and came at last to the pillars of the hotel entrance. Her father had had those built, topping them with round blue lamps which shone at night like sapphires.

The lamps were gone. The pillars covered in holes as if from bullets or shrapnel. There was no gate and when Jill looked towards the house, she could see nothing but a burned shell.

The bricks were scorched black. The roof was gone. There were gaps where the windows had been. A great jagged hole was all that was left of a double window of the *petit salon*, where her mother often used to stand and watch her skipping outside in the garden.

The fire couldn't have been recent. Large – now leafless – plants were growing from crannies and the split steps were covered in dead moss.

Jill stared. Had she really lived *here* for five years, unbelievably young and lighthearted? In this burnt shell her father had created his successful hotel, had sacked the chef and stolen a better one from a rival, had won a reputation with the discriminating townspeople so it became chic to meet at Les Lys. Her mother was a success too, despite never being able to master the language. She was kind and firm with the staff, deferential to the new (and brilliant) chef, and she tenderly looked after her schoolgirl daughter.

As for her father, he'd settled in Bourg, in the country of his own father's birth, with ease. His French blood woke up. He liked their arguments, their architecture, their wine, the smell of tobacco and coffee which scented the streets. On Sundays he and Lucy and Jill went to Mass at the ancient Church of Notre Dame which had its own scent from incense burning in a silver censer. Clement read *Figaro*, discussed politics. He was all for the Maginot Line. And his good friend was the energetic, plausible Mayor, Jean Xavier Ghilain, whose handsome black-eyed son used to join them at dinner sometimes.

Young Jill had developed a crush on the handsome François, who hadn't taken a blind bit of notice . . .

Everything came back to her with excruciating clarity. Her imagination rushed like a bird through the holes that had been windows into the *petit salon*, stiffly French, its chimney piece of heavy yellow marble, its chiming gilt clock which lost ten minutes a day and the chandelier the maids found such a nuisance to clean . . .

"God almighty," said Roz, standing in the drive and staring. "Did they tell you the hotel had been used by the Wehrmacht?"

"Yes."

"Could have been a mob. Want to go closer?"

"I'd rather not," said Jill and turned her back.

They walked in silence down a road which ran by the river. It was in spate, swirling by in a torrent of grey waves. They stood and watched for a while.

"We said we'd ask," said Jill at last. "We're not due back for twenty minutes. It does seem mad not to talk to somebody."

Roz tried to dissuade her.

"The Mairie. The Free French HQ. Your old home. We may as well face it – François isn't in Bourg."

"But he *was*. Look, see that church? It's in the main *place*, I used to go there a lot. There was a café where everybody met, maybe it's still open. Roz, please?"

How could she refuse? She saw Jill's face brighten when she agreed and they walked towards the town, finally turning into a square – at the far end of which was a very old and ugly church without a spire. In peacetime, Jill said, there'd been a market there every morning. Flowers. Fish. "I used to buy sunflowers for Ma."

Roz muttered something. Her companion reminded her of a girl carrying twigs for water divining. Jill walked across the *place* and lo and behold a café. Open.

"That's it!"

The awning was tattered but Jill said cheerfully, "It hasn't even changed its name – Pierrot and Pierrette."

Poor kid, thought Roz. Oh what the hell. Roz, are you getting soft in your old age?

A balding sallow man, sleeves rolled up, stood behind the bar polishing glasses. He looked at their uniform and not at them.

A waiter came up.

His English was almost incomprehensible as he said his regrets but the tables were all occupied, they would have to share. He was about to speak to a man sitting alone in a corner when Roz said in French, "Thank you but we are not eating. We are here to ask for some information."

The waiter looked flustered and gabbled that they must speak to the patron.

The man at the bar put down a glass and waited for them to approach.

"You ask, Jill," said Roz. "My French gets worse."

"Monsieur, I wish to make an enquiry," Jill was pleasant. "My home used to be in Bourg. My father owned a hotel in the Avenue de Sphinx. Les Lys, perhaps, Monsieur, you know the hotel?"

"I used to."

"My family sold it some years ago and . . ."

"And now it is *foutu*." The choice of word, like the tone, was brutal. Roz pressed Jill's arm to signal – let's go. But Jill continued – she was sick of knowing nothing.

"I was educated at the Holy Trinity across the river."

"I know where the convent is."

"I was there for five years."

No reaction.

"My family made many friends in Bourg," said Jill, and Roz had a stab of heartache listening to Jill's innocent cheeping voice speaking to that bastard.

"I am trying to trace a friend of my family's. We knew him in Bourg. Also in London. His name is François Ghilain."

The man slowly put down a glass.

"I know no such person."

"Surely you could tell me . . ."

"I can tell you nothing. Go and play with your friends the Americans," he said, loudly for the benefit of his customers openly listening.

Somebody sniggered.

"Jill. Let's go."

They went through the swing doors.

It was Roz, not Jill, who saw one of the men near the bar stand up and leave the café unobtrusively. Keeping his distance, he began to follow them.

Six

It was during the Nazi occupation that François Ghilain, who had been missing, presumed dead, quietly reappeared in Bourg. He was received with suspicion. He'd been, he said, in the south trying to sell a family property in Montpellier. His return permit had been difficult to get. Some old friends cut him. But others, hand in glove with the Germans or the Milice or both, were glad to invite him to their houses. The collaborators lived well and made it obvious that they valued François's connection with the Nazis. They asked favours of him.

François's father had been killed a few weeks before François reappeared in Bourg. François asked no questions but the story filtered through to him. It was not a case of a Resistant court martial. Jean Xavier was murdered at the Mairie, his body riddled with bullets, the inevitable word "Traitor" pinned to the body.

Madame Ghilain never knew. She had a series of strokes and by the time her husband was dead she was in a convent, speechless and looking a hundred years old. François visited her three times a week, sat in silence in her bedroom, kissed the lifeless hand and left.

François moved into part of his old home, the rest was used by the Germans as a storeroom. He lived reasonably, his job was a sort of ADC, a go-between and errand boy for Klaus Thiele, one of the Nazi chiefs – a seasoned soldier, at times humane – but a patriot.

François was very thin. His cheekbones stuck out and his eyes, like those of a dog stripped in summer, were too large for his head.

Klaus invited François to dinner occasionally in the rich flat where he lived. It was part of a house built on a hill overlooking the river and had in peacetime belonged to aristocrats. He was waited upon by respectful Army servants and cooked for by a chef commandeered from a once-famous restaurant. When François was a guest, he ate well.

"You will think it perverse of me," remarked Klaus Thiele one night when he'd taken the whim to have his French runaround share his dinner, "but I often ask myself, how you can be willing to work for me?"

"Have you any complaints, Oberintendanturrat?"

Klaus Thiele smiled. He was as blond as a Swede or a Siegfried, his eyelashes nearly white, his shining eyes were bright blue.

"You are most efficient. You could be a German. In peacetime, who knows? You and I might have been friends."

"And in wartime?"

"My dear fellow" said Klaus amiably. "There is something – forgive me – of the horizontal in you. There you are, so to speak, lying on your back willing to oblige me."

"Perhaps I am planning some kind of revenge."

"If we are talking about your father's murder, Ghilain, it was not us, the Germans, who shot him in the back. It was your countrymen."

"It seems so."

Klaus held out his gold-rimmed cup for more coffee. François stood up to pour it from an elaborate silver-plated coffee pot, then sat down again.

"I wonder what you are thinking about."

"Train timetables, Oberintendanturrat."

Both men laughed but it was not a joke. Trains were

dynamited. Derailed. Klaus – and François – had their work cut out to keep the trains moving through Bourg on their way to Paris.

But all that was before the Allies landed in June 1944 and the real war, as Klaus called it, began. The mood in the city burst out at last. There were riots; Klaus was once forced to order his men to open fire on a crowd stoning the barracks. People fell, bleeding, twitching. There was no possibility of knowing who and how many were dead, the crowd snatched up the bodies of fallen comrades and ran, literally vanished. The reason was clear, the rioters' families would be arrested. What followed would have been more vicious if Klaus had not been in charge; he was either merciful or clever enough to know you made things worse by cruelty. But pressure grew from High Command to crush all resistance.

The German army began, gradually at first, to retreat. There was panic in the air, the smell of old scores paid back. François read Resistant newspapers, the Germans had copies daily although they had failed so far to find out where they were printed. The papers carried violent, rallying headlines: "Kill Germans. And kill traitors who denounce, who aid the enemy, kill the policeman who arrests patriots. Strike them down like vermin." There followed printed lists of Miliciens condemned to death at clandestine courts martial. The Germans were the foreign enemy on French soil. The Milice were loathed more – they were French.

It was the Milice chiefs, wild with anger and fear, who carried out the worst reprisals, followed by murders as appalling by members of the Resistance. Both sides were soaked in blood, each crime calling for revenge, each mouthing of justice.

In August Paris fell – or rose – according to your beliefs. Klaus Thiele sent for François.

"I am being called back to Paris, my friend. I leave today."

"But . . ."

"Let us say *near* Paris. The High Command is withdrawing its troops here. We are needed in the north."

"I am sorry."

"As a Frenchman, that is impossible." Klaus stared out at the now familiar view of the river. "It is like the Roman Empire, is it not? They called back their legions when the state began to crack . . ."

He shrugged. It was the only habit he had acquired from living in France.

After saying his farewells, François went to the Mairie. It was closed for the first time since he had been in Bourg. He stood hesitating, then decided to go home. He took side roads in the quietest part of the town. Deep in his own thoughts he heard nothing. No footsteps, no car drawing up. But suddenly strong arms seized him and a gag was forced into his mouth. He struggled violently but he was helpless. His wrists and feet were roped so tightly that the circulation almost stopped.

Dragged by rough hands, stumbling, he was pulled round a corner where a car waited. Two men in the car and two who'd captured him. All were very young and in ordinary clothes, but each wore the white band *France Libre*, pulled up above their elbows. Before he could see more he was blindfolded and thrown into the car. Somebody kicked him in the groin and said "filth".

The car drove for at least half an hour. He had no idea in what direction, only that they were going fast; lying on the floor he was thrown about when the driver slammed on the brakes or swerved at a corner. His captors spoke in muffled voices, he could not hear what they said. The ropes on hands and ankles were painful, the blindfold excruciating. He tried with bound wrists, to shift it. Useless. His head throbbed like an engine.

At last the car slowed down, and entered what must be a drive, stony and uneven. They stopped, the engine was switched off and one of the men dragged him out and threw him, with another kick, on ground covered with sharp granite chips.

The blindfold was wrenched off.

François staggered to his feet. They were outside a large house of the kind sometimes glorified by the name of château. Turrets and narrow windows, a pseudo-Gothic look. The entrance was up a flight of stone steps. Bright moonlight flooded down. Every window of the house was boarded up, the overgrown garden was waist high in summer grass. There was a ringing silence.

The driver of the car who looked scarcely eighteen, with a baby face and cropped hair, studied his watch in the uncertain light.

"We're late. De la Roche won't like that."

There were grunts from the other three. The man who'd kicked him earlier gave François's arm a vicious tug.

"De la Roche is exact," said the driver, angry and nervous.

"How can you hurry when you're looking all over the cursed town for a slippery toad like this one?" growled François's captor. He took hold of François's bound hands and frog-marched him round the side of the château. The moon, with unearthly clarity, shone down on the back of the tall, windowless house. A single black square showed an open door. They entered a lightless stone passage.

"Who goes there?"

A dim bulb swung over the head of a man in uniform.

"Prisoner from Bourg. Orders from Captain de la Roche."

The four men with their prisoner went through double doors. Into what had been a ballroom. The enormous, shattered chamber still retained a line of chandeliers hanging from the lofty ceiling, and walls of mirrors reflected a trestle table and a row of candles in bottles.

François had heard of these so-called courts. Everybody knew they took place, rumours went through Bourg daily of groups of men, God knew who, sitting in judgement on other men bagged like rabbits in the fields or their homes or the street.

What François found extraordinary now was that the Court looked efficient. Six men sat at a table with sheaves of papers in front of them. Wearing Resistance uniforms, they were composed and calm, contrasting with the youthful thugs who had dragged François in front of them.

At the head of the table was the man who was clearly the judge; he had white hair, a hawkish nose and a face which, though grave, had a hint of humanity. The men seated round had the classlessness of the French – they could be bank managers or electricians, dentists or masons. François recognised a dark man on the left, a successful attorney.

Death had never been far from François for many months of his life. It had danced round him in the street, a clown at a fair, or appeared at the end of his bed like an old-fashioned performance of a ghost. "You're next!" said the clown and the phantom.

"Prisoner Ghilain," said the driver, pushing François to the end of the table. He stood facing the court, hands bound – the bonds on his feet had been cut when he was pulled from the car.

"You are accused of supplying information against the Liberation, and causing the death of patriots."

"I am innocent."

"Witness number one," said de la Roche with a gesture to the guard at the door.

A young woman entered the ballroom. She'd worked at the Mairie, her name was Sylvie. She had long hair in a plait over one shoulder, a face like a Madonna. She was terrified.

The officer whose task was to cross-question asked her to

read her statement. Sylvie was given a piece of paper. Her hand shook.

"I many times heard Monsieur . . ."

"The prisoner."

"The prisoner in conversation with men of the Milice. He was often with Major Tilques."

"Chief of police. Yes. Go on."

"Last week I heard Major – I heard Tilques say, 'we have a chance to sweep the traitors out of the district'."

"He spoke of the Resistance?"

A nod from Sylvie. She did not once look in François's direction but stared at the questioner, a big burly man with a country accent.

"You are certain that is what you heard, Mademoiselle?"

"She's speaking the truth," interrupted François. "Of course I agreed with Tilques, I cultivated him, my job was to get information."

"Silence!" from the judge. François's guard lifted his arm to strike him across the face. A snapped order stopped him.

"You will have your chance to speak when the witnesses have given their statements," said de la Roche in a voice of reason.

The trial went on. Two men were brought in, both had worked in the Mairie, both were word perfect, unlike the stammering Sylvie. One of them, André, was a man François liked, short, bow-legged, they often shared jokes.

"I saw the prisoner with Oberintendanturrat Thiele," he said in a loud clear voice. "Many times."

"For God's sake, André, of course you did. I worked for the man."

"If the prisoner is not silent, judgement will immediately be given against him," said de la Roche. "Protestations of innocence are a waste of time. And you have very little."

There followed more statements François did not deny. The

dates were correct, the details too. Yes, he had consulted with Thiele. And he had known of a certain (abortive) raid carried out on a meeting of the Resistance. "About which I warned them. Which was why they left in time."

"Not one of our men received any such communications from the prisoner," said the prosecutor coolly.

"My colleague, with whom I worked closely for many months, will verify everything I say," said François steadily. "I was assigned work here by the SOE. Because of my local connections."

"You mean the traitor, your father."

"Yes, yes, he was a traitor," said François. "I cannot deny it. But I am not. My colleague, my partner if you like, was dropped with me – the RAF brought us from England – in the Forêt de Ceyzériat. Months ago."

The men round the table leaned together and consulted in low voices, now and again looking in his direction. Finally the prosecutor snapped, "We have evidence of one man being dropped in the forest."

"Two. I was with him."

"He did not say so."

"He told nobody. That is his value. There were rumours of an informer in the Resistance and it was important that he did not destroy my cover by talking to the wrong person," said François. Where, oh where, *was* Philippe in this nightmare?

It was the judge who asked, "And do you know his name, this man who was dropped by the Allies?"

"Of course. It is Philippe de Winter."

"Interesting. How do you happen to know his name when he worked in total secrecy?"

François exclaimed loudly, "Because he is my contact. That was why he was sent with me! He's my pianist. My radio operator."

De Winter was a brilliant pianist and a cool steady friend.

"What is the address where he works?" said the prosecutor.

François hesitated.

"The Ferme des 3 Moulins. Ten kilometres outside Bourg, near the village of Ezancourt."

"Does he work alone?"

"No. There are three members of the Resistance with him. Bourget, Esonville, Bura."

"None of whom has ever been heard to speak of you."

"They knew nothing about me."

"Convenient."

There was a pause. De la Roche, not the prosecutor, spoke.

"Your statement is correct as far as it goes. De Winter did indeed live with three of our best men in hiding in the farm. Three hours ago it was surrounded. The Milice went in and all four were killed."

François looked at him with horror. De La Roche continued. "You are the only man who knew of their presence at Ezancourt. The only one who could have betrayed them."

François scarcely heard what came next. The scene became unreal, the men at the table out of focus, Sylvie at the back of the room pressed against the wall as if she were the one to be shot.

As he recovered, a second prisoner was dragged into the ballroom and pushed next to François. It was Doctor Dettmar, a laconic man and a clever doctor who had been a close friend to Klaus. Dettmar exchanged a look with François. It was untouched by hope.

De la Roche was speaking.

"François Ghilain, guilty of treason. Oberleutnant Ernst Dettmar, guilty of murder on evidence given this night at a separate trial. In the name of France, of Free France, you are condemned with justice and will be taken from this place to execution."

As they were marched out of the ballroom, Dettmar said quietly, "I am glad of a companion."

Outside the château, they were pushed into the car which had brought François here. The driver growled, "Let's get rid of the scum fast."

"Execution squad waiting in the usual place," said one of the guards.

The driver drove away into the moonlit forest. Neither prisoner spoke a word. They sat mute on their journey to extinction.

The road was empty and the driver put his foot down, reaching sixty or seventy miles an hour. Suddenly he exclaimed, "*Merde*, what's that noise? What's that car doing?"

François and Dettmar tensed, there was a roar as the other speeding car drove straight at them – the Resistance car with a scream of brakes swerved off the narrow road.

There was a crash like the end of the world.

Seven

"There's a man following us, Roz," whispered Jill. They had reached the corner of the square; the steep road which eventually led to the barracks was deserted.

"I know. He came out of the café when we did, don't look back."

Roz sounded cool, but panic went through Jill as they tramped on. At last Roz said, "This won't do, he's gaining on us. We'll face him out."

"Oh, but Roz . . ."

"Keep calm," said Roz steadily. "It's the best thing to do. There isn't a soul on the road and we're half a mile from barracks. Oh – look . . ."

An Army car came haring down the hill but before she could run across the road it had disappeared.

"Bloody hell. So. Here goes."

She swivelled round and shouted to the figure behind them, "Want to speak to us?" adding "Jill, you do the talking, you're better at it. And don't be scared. There's two of us."

He came towards them. A big battered man wearing a beret nearly over one ear. His face was covered in bumps and scars from acne – it looked like a burnt-out volcano.

"*Alors*?" said Jill. Her heart pounded. Roz moved so that their shoulders touched.

"What were you doing in the Pierrot?" he said in a snarling voice. "That's what I'm asking."

"We can go where we like," interrupted Roz.

He took a step closer and showed his teeth like a dog.

"Why those questions? Eh? Eh?"

"We merely enquired . . ." began Jill, keeping her voice level but she was frightened and he knew it.

"You want to know about our enemies. Traitors. Dead or better dead. You women collabos, then? You're no better than the others."

"Collaborators!" burst out Roz. "We're part of the Allied armies taking part in the Liberation."

Seeing her white with anger the man gave a menacing grin.

"Allied armies, invaders more like. You listen to me. *You* listen," moving right up to Jill. "Your French is too good, how do we know who you are? And you ask questions about traitors. You look out or you'll be sorry you've been born. We'll find a way to shut your mouths, we've a lot of experience in that. *Comprends*? Or will this help?"

He put his hand inside his jacket and pulled out a gun. It was a German Luger.

"You're a murderer," hissed Roz, itching to snatch the gun and turn it on their tormentor.

"Roz, stop for God's sake. Yes, yes, we will ask no more questions," Jill was shaking from head to foot.

He was looking at the pistol, balancing its neat plain shape in one hand.

He lifted it and . . .

"Stop, stop!" yelled Roz, rushing straight into the middle of the road and narrowly escaping an Army jeep which had raced down the hill. It braked furiously.

As Jill stood transfixed, the man literally vanished. One moment he stood with a gun in his hand, the next – nothing. He must have rushed into a garden or jumped into a ditch, he moved so fast it was as if he'd evaporated. Roz was already by the jeep, gesticulating with the Army driver. She shouted, "Jill! It's Guy. He's taking us back to barracks."

Guy's pale high-bred face peered out.

"I should think I am," he said with deep disapproval. "What are you two girls doing out alone? As far as the Colonel is concerned, the curfew for you lasts all day. Jump in. Driver, back to barracks. Yes, I know it'll make us late. Too bad."

Jill climbed in beside Roz, the jeep swerved round and set off up the long hill towards the squat shapes of the barrack buildings.

"What did that fellow say to you?" enquired Guy, shaking his head at them. "Did he threaten you?"

Roz said, "No rape and pillage, if that's what you're thinking." Jill marvelled at her cool. "He didn't like our faces. Said the Allies were nothing but another gang of foreign invaders."

"And was about to bump off a couple of girls as a gesture?" Guy took the flippant tone. He was worried.

"Not as bad as that. Just a lot of grimaces and more cracks about the Allies."

"You're very quiet, Jill," remarked Guy. The jeep had entered the barrack yard.

"Jill's a softy. I expect she's sorry for the swine," said Roz, and Guy made a noise which could have been a laugh.

They thanked him for the lift and climbed out of the jeep, which swerved in yet another U turn and drove away.

The girls in silence went across the yard. Indoors, the unmistakable smell of NAAFI cooking was more pungent than usual but the place was blessedly warm. They went to Jill's room. Roz carefully shut the door.

"Narrow squeak."

"Do you think he'd have . . ."

"Killed us? Not sure. He wanted to. He'll certainly save us up. We must take the hint."

Jill sat down on her bed and unlaced her wet shoes. She felt sick.

"Hint," said Roz, doing the same, "is that we dam' well can't go out in this benighted dump alone. T'isn't safe. And a further hint. You may as well face up to it, Jill, you can't find out anything about your friend."

Jill looked at her.

"They know something, don't they?"

It was on the tip of Roz's tongue to tell her what the man at the Free French HQ had said, or not said. To add that she herself was sure François Ghilain was dead. Wouldn't it be better for Jill to know? But when she looked at the girl's face she couldn't add any more pain.

"Who are *they*," she said. "To quote poor old Captain Scott at the South Pole, 'Great God, this is an awful place'."

"Oh, Roz."

"Cheer up." Roz began to peel off wet khaki stockings. "You never in your heart believed you'd find your friend, surely? I certainly didn't."

It was clear to Roz that her friend's guileless plan for making a few enquiries resembled walking about with a primed hand grenade. François Ghilain had gone, there wasn't a trace and it would be lunacy to ask another single question. Roz was certain he had been a collaborator. Jill's description of the heroic figure in Free French uniform, the mysterious visit to the Kensington house, of her love and separation were true and not true. They were the vision, the memories of a romance, and as such were likely to be false. An undercover agent for the enemy, serving both masters, risking his life for what? Probably playing the patriot in secret while helping denounce Resistants who were later executed or dead under torture.

A life of lies and, it seemed, a death from the same things.

Roz lay awake for a long time. Jill, worn out, unhappy but still scarcely twenty years old, was deeply asleep. Roz could hear her regular breathing. She sat up, guiltily lit a cigarette, pushed the pillows more comfortably behind her head and lay thinking. The reason she had come to this country had been a phoney-noble gesture – all about Joanna who had been killed in the Blitz. Jo had been Roz's heel of Achilles; she'd loved her in every way, sworn to love her all her life. Poor Jo, it had been a short one. She'd had a face like a little pug dog, with a squashed nose and round eyes; she'd been confiding, funny, wondrously incompetent. Roz loved that too. When she'd returned to the basement flat and found Jo's shoe, she had stood in the wreckage and hadn't shed a tear. She remembered her thought – old songs said it all the time – I'll never love again.

Joanna's gentle ghost had brought her to France, to Bourg. But what was happening in France made Roz's grandiloquent vow, even her love, tame. This country's sick, she thought. I'll stay. Better try and do some good even in my footling way than try for a posting home. But I won't kid myself that people like that animal who threatened us are heroes. She thought – I've never understood the word bloodthirsty until now.

Next morning, dressed in well-pressed uniform, hair slicked with a wet comb, cap crammed on, not at the frivolous angle Jill sometimes used, Roz went off with her old pal, Dermot Brady, on what he called a 'recce' to ensure petrol supplies were safe. Dermot said he wouldn't put it past the Resistant lot to nick whatever they needed.

"OK, their cause is right but we're bigger than they are. Roz, I may need you. Some of the petrol's stored in farms on the road to Ambronay. You'll have to jabber some French for me."

The jeep was waiting and Roz, having breakfasted on her feet, swallowing down a mug of tea like ink, hopped in beside him. The weather hadn't changed a fraction. Sky a dull metal yellow. Snow hard as rock and along roads frequented by

Army vehicles, dirty and ploughed up. When they reached the country, it was a white landscape, the bare trees stretching for miles.

"The Ambronay Forest," said Dermot, studying his map. "Corporal, there's a farm down that track there according to my directions. On the right, that's it. Go carefully, we don't want to miss the turning and, in any case, it may be through a gate."

The driver slowed to a crawl.

Dermot sat staring at the woods. He said in an offhand voice which made Roz wary, "Guy tells me you and Jill had a spot of bother yesterday. Some ne'er do well in the town."

"Does the Colonel know?"

"What do you think?"

"What did he say?"

"Well. His language was colourful. The upshot is there's to be no gadding about by unaccompanied young females in future. You're to take a Sergeant with you. Preferably one who weighs sixteen stone."

Roz smiled slightly. She was relieved the verdict had not been worse.

They located the farm set back off the road down a track of snow. Dermot had visited it when the petrol had been dumped. The containers had been left in a series of barns at the back of the farm. The farmer, the epitome of the old French peasantry, physically large and strong, somehow menacing in his movements, had been well paid. He didn't bother to conceal that he detested the British.

Dermot and Roz, accompanied by the Corporal, went round the barns and checked every container to be sure it was still filled with petrol. It was obvious they suspected the farmer whose face showed what he thought. All he said was a savage "*Enfin*" when they finally agreed things were in order.

When they returned to the farm kitchen, the Corporal brought out the document and said, "Sign here, please."

The farmer grimaced, an indication he didn't understand a word.

"*Il faut signer*," said Roz.

With one of his looks – he had a repertoire – he signed his name. Dermot thanked him. No reply. He watched them from the door as they returned to the jeep.

"I wouldn't trust him as far as I could throw him," said Dermot. "Pity. There are many brave men around."

As the jeep moved away into the empty snow-bound landscape he began to talk about the Free French. "I have a lot of time for them." He knew a good deal about the movement and spoke with feeling – how they had suffered and thirsted for revenge.

"The trouble is that from the start the Allies have been wary of arming them on a large scale."

"Why, Dermot?"

"The French are a violent people. Too well armed they could start a revolution."

"Against the enemy. Surely that would be good?"

"And bring Nazi reinforcements just where we don't want them. The Colonel says arms to the Resistance have to be very very limited. And that drives the poor things crazy."

"You sound as if you agree with them."

"Of course I do. I'm no politico, Roz. No strategist either. I used to fence at school," he added irrelevantly. "I was appalling. No skill, no art. I just bashed away."

The jeep slowed at a sharp bend in a part of the road where the snow-heavy leafless woods reached right down to the road's edge. Suddenly there was a deafening volley of gunfire. Automatically, the driver put his foot on the brakes.

Dermot said, "Drive on."

"But sir . . ."

Dermot looked at the woods. Not a living soul. Not a bird.

Nothing. And then again the horrible sound of gunfire and a flock of crows rose up against the yellow sky.

"Drive on," repeated Dermot. He turned to Roz who had tensed.

"Nothing to worry about. Target practice, I shouldn't wonder."

Next morning at breakfast in the canteen Roz found herself sitting next to the Corporal who had driven Dermot and herself to the farm. He was attacking a large plate of baked beans.

"Heard the news, Miss?" he said. "Five bodies found in the woods last night. After – you know – what we heard."

"Corporal!"

"Shocking, isn't it? Just lying where they fell. Papers pinned on the poor sods. 'Terror for terror' – something like that."

Roz gave a shudder.

"Can't stop them, Miss. Bit of luck we didn't try, eh?"

Dermot told Jill and Roz that the Colonel had now ruled the girls were never to go into the town unless accompanied by a Sergeant. "And preferably not at all."

"An order, I'm afraid, is an order," Dermot added.

"Understood," said Roz laconically.

Jill went as white as a sheet. She'd told herself for weeks that coming here had been a total failure – she'd never truly believed it. Now it was over. She had not found a single sign that François had been in Bourg – except the frightening fact that when she had spoken his name in a café, a man had followed her with a gun.

She returned to her work alongside good friends with a death's head cheerfulness which Roz found harrowing. Jill hated the atmosphere in Bourg and it showed. She was chilled to the soul.

Her supportive and kind companion, her undeclared suitor, Peter, was around very little. The old problem of stolen army stores kept him away at all hours. Once, apologising that he couldn't meet her, he'd spoken about the thefts.

"Not ammunition. Food. I can't blame them, Jill. They're hungry. The Colonel blames them all right."

One evening when it looked as if he would get away, he asked her to have dinner with him. They arranged to meet at one of the two well-known black market restaurants. Exactly as in Lyon there were places where the food was miraculously good and enemies sat down at neighbouring tables as if a kind of temporary armistice had been declared in the kitchen.

Peter was late, a waiter brought Jill some wine and politely told her the dish of the day – Tripe *à la mode de Caen*. "A rarity," said Jill in a friendly way. He lingered, remarking on her good French, and polished a small corner of her table with his apron.

"More trouble tonight, M'selle. Evidently your people know it. Evidently they will not stop it. One of the horizontals. Now they are all smoked out," he used the French verb. "There were more than twenty. Ah. Listen."

At that moment the entire restaurant's clientele pushed back their chairs and moved towards the doors. Somebody pulled them open and shoved a chair against them. The waiter said, "We must look, M'selle. To see justice done."

Jill knew about the hounding of women who'd slept with the Nazis. She knew a mob was a horrible thing. But she couldn't stop herself from going with the crowd as it swept out of doors. Her waiter politely shielded her from being elbowed. She was in the centre of a crowd shouting with laughter, watching another crowd in the street, dancing and marching behind a figure in a white overall. The woman, accompanied by a single helmeted policeman, hadn't a hair on her head. She had been shaved bald, a swastika smeared on her forehead. To Catholic Jill it was eerily reminiscent of the sacred ashes put on the forehead by the priest on Ash Wednesday. The woman was cradling a tiny dark-haired baby in her arms, looking down all the time at the child in protective fear.

"Whore! *Putain*!"

The crowd in the street consisted almost entirely of women. There was relish, amusement, on every face. They could have been the same people who had greeted the Americans in Paris with necklaces of flowers.

"Still feel the warmth of the Nazi's bed?" screamed a respectable old woman. There were roars of laughter.

The prisoner marched on, the gendarme beside her. She still stared at the baby whom she'd wrapped in part of her overall. Somebody threw a stone which she dodged. The gendarme shouted, "Order!"

The policeman, the girl, the crowd, turned at the crossroads and disappeared. The shouting died away.

With a murmur of approval, an occasional "*Bien fait*!" the diners returned to their tables. The talk became animated. Jill thought she'd never seen these people look cheerful until now.

The waiter, pulling out her chair for her, saw her blanched face.

"She's alive, after all," he said.

Just then an English voice called out "Jill!" Peter hurried up.

"I'm so sorry to be late. My car couldn't get through."

"We saw."

The waiter respectfully filled a glass for the new arrival, presented a menu and left them.

"It upset you."

"It was nauseating."

"And you don't understand how they feel."

"Of course I do. But she had a tiny baby out in this freezing weather. I'm sure she thought somebody was going to kill it."

Beyond comfort, she said passionately, "I hate this place."

"You mean you hate what is happening. It must be worse

for you because you remember how it used to be. They're not all villains, Jill. There are good people too."

For no reason, for every reason, she remembered the little lady who lived above Philomène.

"I'm afraid we're saying goodbye to Bourg anyway. The Colonel told us we're being shunted back to Lyon, the supply contingent is badly needed and the main jobs here have been mopped up."

"You said the thefts have got worse!" burst out Jill. She didn't want to go.

He did not answer but took her unresisting hand and said gently, "You never talk about it but you badly wanted to come here. I've an idea what you've found has been a shock. Bourg meant a lot to you, didn't it?"

He spoke innocently and when she declared that after all she'd be glad to go, he wasn't sure he believed her.

The same journey in reverse. Hours in a jogging lorry squashed among soldiers with their bulky packs and great-coats. Roz used that gift of hers which Jill remembered during the trip from Calais: simply folded her arms, leaned her head against the shuddering side of the lorry's interior and slept.

"Some of us have all the luck," remarked little Corporal Powys, who'd become a friend of Jill's. They exchanged news in the canteen and he admired her. "Just my style," he used to say to his mates. He was in charge of the contingent of soldiers in the lorry and looked enviously at the unconscious Roz. "She's a one, isn't she?" In a fit of Welsh fervour, he praised the Almighty as they drove out of what he described as the dump called Bourg.

"The lads haven't had a bath for days. Sorry if we pong, Miss."

It had begun to rain by the time the straggling suburbs of

Lyon glowed in the gloom. Corporal Powys peered ahead. There was a narrow opening between the interior and the driver's seat. He could see wet streets.

"Now it'll thaw, sure as eggs. Floods next. Sloshing about up to the top of our boots we'll be. Probably above."

He sounded cheerful.

Peter's group was ahead of the convoy and he had told the driver of Jill and Roz's lorry to drop them at their lodgings, rue de Grand Sermon. The Corporal scrambled out first, having respectfully shaken Roz's shoulder to wake her. Not a yawn as she opened her eyes. Just a keen look round. She and Jill climbed down and the Corporal, a stickler for duty, marched up the steps thick with already melting snow, and rang the bell. The door gave its deafening click and opened slightly.

"Heard about that landlady of yours," said Powys, saluting them goodnight. "Talk is she's a heroine."

Jill and Roz climbed the familiar, stuffy stairs, knocked at the sitting-room door, and the deep American voice called, "Yeah, yeah, I know it's you. *Entrez*. So you're back. How was it?"

Philomène sat upright in her enormous chair. It looked as if she hadn't stirred for all the weeks they had been away.

"We're all right, Philomène," said Roz. "And you?"

"I don't exactly have the chance to travel around. What about Bourg? And don't say 'just fine' because it is not."

"No," from Roz, sitting down near her hostess. "It certainly isn't."

"Jill. Stop standing about, you make me fidgety. Roz, you know where the whisky is. I'll have a slug while you're about it."

Roz stood up with alacrity and went into the narrow kitchen which resembled a ship's galley. There was a noise of running water, a clink of glasses.

Jill met Philomène's probing gaze. The older woman stared at her for a long minute, then across at Roz who came back into the room.

"Ah. Scotch. I've been postponing this until you arrived."

She accepted the full glass which contained a minimum of water and was rich dark gold. She sipped. Then with her other hand tapped with her stick against her wooden leg. It was a hideous habit.

"Did you happen to catch sight of any of the horizontals getting their just due?"

"Jill did," said Roz. "It upset her."

Philomène again looked at Jill and remarked, "We've had three in Lyon this week."

"You don't approve, surely?" Roz's voice was sharp.

"A minor violence."

"It's no such thing."

"My dear Roz, there's a need for the people to let their feelings show. Their rage. Their bursting hearts. They've had to hide them for four years."

"How is it different from lynching in the States?"

"You would say that."

Philomène held out her glass for a refill; Roz had remembered to bring the bottle with her from the kitchen.

"Mobs are loathsome." Jill's voice was on the edge of hysteria. Philomène rubbed her chin and looked from one girl to the other.

"It hasn't occurred to either of you that a few whores dragged through the streets (and the barbers who shaved their heads) are instruments of salvation? So you scrawl a swastika on a woman's head. Throw mud at her. When you've had the satisfaction, orgasm if you like, you won't need to do any more, such as murdering the innocents as well as the blood-stained guilty. Or stringing up people, guilty and innocent, on lamp-posts."

Neither Roz nor Jill said anything. Philomène herself broke the silence, holding out her glass.

"Fill it up, Roz."

When Jill came in to say goodnight, Philomène put down her book and said casually, "There is someone who wants to meet you."

"Oh. Who?"

"You'll see later."

Next morning when Jill and Roz were collected long before daylight by Corporal Powys, the floods in Lyon had become worse. Moments after they were with him in the jeep they caught the first flash of water washing down a nearby street. The jeep had to turn and find another way to its destination. All morning it was like that, they were halted by water. Once they drove past a square so flooded that a woman was being rescued from a first floor window.

But Lyon was large and sprawling and the jeep made its way somehow. The girls spent hours interpreting demands from hard-pressed French officials to the British. When one problem was at least understood by the other side, back the girls would climb into the jeep to drive on. Before dark, they were both hoarse.

Pressure of work finally separated them, the Corporal drove Roz to an appointment north of the city and Jill, her job finished for the night, toiled home on foot. She had been set down not far from the rue de Grand Sermon. The streets were sloppy under foot, the air penetratingly cold.

As she climbed the stairs her mind was fixed on a hot bath. It floated in front of her like a vision. The apparition of Helen to Faustus could not have been more lusted after than Jill's desire for five inches of hot water.

"Which of you is that?" shouted Philomène.

Jill looked round the door.

"I hoped it was you. Come in."

"Philomène. I'm filthy and in a trance, frankly. Jabbering French to flood victims all day. I must go and clean up."

"Stay. Take off your shoes."

Jill was too tired to argue and wandered into the room. Philomène, leaning on her stick, regarded her with faint amusement. "I can see you've been giving them their dollar's worth. And no, you can't slope off and get into a robe. I have this visitor who's fixed to come and talk to you. Sit there. Pull your chair up to the fire, your nose has gone blue. Doubtless my guest will be even colder than you are, he's been travelling for two days. Yeah, yeah, you want to know what this is all about. Here's your answer. Captain de la Roche is a friend of mine. A remarkable man. The best we've got."

She sat thinking. Her face reminded Jill of the head of some Roman senator in bronze. Strong. Set. Pitiless in a way. The lines ran downwards from mouth to chin, from cheeks to mouth, and scored parallel on her forehead.

"De le Roche has no political axe to grind and he's never wanted power. Just to do the clean-up job. He's serious and he's just. Brother, he's that all right."

"What has that to do with me?"

"I'll tell you. I know why you persuaded that soft touch of a Peter Whittaker to fix it and bring you to France. Roz told me and don't glare like that. You yourself spoke to me about living in Bourg when you were a kid. What you didn't say was that you met up with some French guy in London whom you'd known in Bourg. And fell heavily for him."

"I don't want to talk about it."

"Christ, you British. You're about as cold as you look. For crying out loud what do you think I'm wasting my time for? And don't you dare hold it against Roz that she told me. I forced it out of her, I'm good at that. Any fool could see you'd come for something and secrets are my business. You didn't trace François Ghilain in Bourg, did you?"

"No."

"Of course not. He's scarcely a subject to chat about in that city. Which is why de la Roche wants to talk to you. Ah. The bell. Go down and let him in."

Jill obeyed. She thought – I must get through this somehow.

As she hurried down the stairs, a voice in her head said mockingly, "Off you go, *coquine*."

She pulled the latch sideways and opened the heavy door. A man in Free French uniform stood on the step hunched against the thin rain which had begun to fall again.

"Zelle," he said in the formal way. She stepped back and he entered the hall, gave her a nod and followed her up the stair.

"Didier?" shouted Philomène.

"Yes, here at last. My apologies for being late, the floods are incredible. I finally left my driver in the Place Saint Mathilde and walked," called de la Roche. He followed Jill into Philomène's room where the stove glowed red and the stuffy air smelled of Patou scent, cigarettes and Scotch.

De la Roche strode over and gave Philomène's hand a kiss of the kind Jill used to see when she was a teenager in Bourg. A gesture graceful, casual, natural, attractive. Philomène looked at him and smiled.

"Sit down. That chair where I can see you best."

"Not seating me with my battered old face under a floodlight?"

"Your battered old face is still handsome, Didier. You look well. It sure is a change to see somebody who doesn't look as if they've been through a hedge backwards."

"Yet I sleep in cars. Trucks."

"Hedges?"

They both laughed as if at an ancient joke.

Jill sat down and clasped her hands in her lap. She was angry. How dare these people with their secret history of whatever-it-was, their tough middle-aged faces, sit cosily here and keep her in suspense. De la Roche turned to her.

"I am sorry," he said. "You must forgive us."

The idea of forgiving Philomène anything, of Philomène herself admitting the least fault, almost made Jill's jaw drop. De la Roche went on, "It is a release in this work we do to be with a dear friend, to cease to be on guard every minute of the day. Forgive us."

"Don't make a song and dance about it, Didier."

"I do. Now, Mademoiselle St Clair."

"Sinclair."

"Yes, yes, but I am French," he said and his voice was kind. Jill's anger evaporated.

"You came here to look for the son of Jean Xavier Ghilain, did you not? I am sorry, Miss St Clair. Very sorry."

"You mean he is dead." She couldn't believe it after she'd spoken.

"Four months ago. In the forest outside Bourg."

The voice in her memory repeated, "Off you go, coquine." Jill said nothing. Philomène took out a cigarette and tapped it on the lid of her mother of pearl case. Was that a requiem?

"Philomène told me you came to France to try and trace Ghilain. As best you could. You were sure he was in Bourg."

"I had a letter," said Jill, whispering.

"How did you know it came from Bourg?"

"There was a sign."

"A 'B' perhaps?"

The man knew everything. She said miserably, "Perhaps you've got it wrong. A lot of the information we are given every day is wrong. Or lies."

"So it is. But I'm afraid this time there is no error, Mademoiselle. Ghilain was tried and the trial was fair. Many witnesses. He was working for the Milice."

"That can't be true! He was with the Free French. I was *there*."

"He was a double agent," said Philomène in her flat American drawl. "And he was not tortured. After the trial, which as Didier says was fair, he was condemned to execution."

"How do you know it was fair?" Jill suddenly shouted.

"Because Didier was the judge."

There was an awful silence. When she looked up, de la Roche was regarding her like a doctor.

"Ghilain worked for the Milice from the start. He went to Britain for information about the Resistance and was taken up by the SOE, they believed his story. He was good at what he did. He wasn't found guilty for working with the Germans, though God knows there was cause. It was for his collaboration with the Milice, carrying on his father's work after Jean Xavier was put to death."

They sat and looked at her. What they'd seen and suffered and been forced to join or to bear had hardened them. They had ceased to be kind.

"Don't disbelieve what Didier has told you, Jill," Philomène said at last. "You had to know."

Why did I? thought Jill wildly. She could not connect the man they spoke about with the lover in her body and her heart.

"I've seen the double game," de la Roche said. "Now and then we catch one of them, but not many. They're clever and very, very quick and they have a sense, an antenna, about danger. Your friend's didn't work the night we caught him. In the end, Mademoiselle, they pay with their lives. From one side or the other."

He leaned forward.

"Forget about him. You think now you never will. But you must banish him from your mind the way Philomène and I have banished scores of them. He fooled many more than just you. But in time his memory will fade. As the things happening in France now will fade. In the end."

Jill said nothing to Roz for an entire day. Apart from her work, she did not speak to a soul. She simply could not grasp the truth: that François was dead and, in a way, by his own hand. It had been his decision to betray. What she hadn't known before was that lies turn everything else rotten.

She was home very late that evening, Philomène was already in bed, the sitting-room in darkness. But there was a line of light under Roz's door. Drearily unlacing her wet shoes, Jill started to creep by but the floor creaked and Roz's door flew open. She stood framed against the dim light, wearing her old camel hair dressing gown and automatically tightening the belt.

"I want to speak to you."

She lowered her voice, Philomène's room was down the passage.

"Can't it wait?"

"No."

Ignoring the shoes Jill was carrying, ignoring the way she dragged unwillingly into the room, Roz silently shut the door after them, then pushed forward the only chair.

She lit a cigarette and stood looking at Jill, who bent and placed the wet shoes together on the floor.

"Tell me. And don't say 'what?' We know each other too well. Philomène won't say what happened. I asked her. I practically yelled at her. No good. Come on, *tell me* for Christ's sake."

Jill dumbly shook her head.

Roz knelt beside her and leaned forward to take Jill's freezing hand. The girl pulled away. Roz violently let go of the hand she'd managed to capture.

"Are you going to reject me because of what I told you

about Joanna? Do you think, now you know I'm a lesbian, you can't treat me as a friend, for fuck's sake? Stop screwing your head round in that ridiculous way. Look at me. That's better. I'm not after you. I swear it on whatever bible you like. The plain truth is I'm not after anybody. Sex has dried up for me in this awful country. But I *like* you, I'm fond of you, I demand to know what gave you such a shock last night. Did they tell you François Ghilain is dead? Ah. I see they did. Well, I knew that anyway."

Her cigarette had gone out. She lit it with a steady hand.

"I know, I know, I should have told you in Bourg and I didn't. When I talked to the Resistance lot I could see they knew something about him and it was bad. I felt he was dead. I didn't say because I knew nothing definite. But I was certain. So. What happened?"

Jill put her head down without covering her face and began to weep. She told the story slowly, broken with falterings and lapses and tears which started and stopped. She rocked to and fro as if with an excruciating stomach ache.

"How could he? How could he?"

When she did look up, Roz's eyes were brimming. The cigarette was out, she ground it into a battered metal ash tray.

"Poor girl. Poor, poor girl."

She put her arms round Jill and they rocked together in a harmony of sorrow.

"Will you take the plate upstairs to the canonised saint, Roz?"

It was Philomène next evening, pointing at a plate on which was one egg and a scraping of butter.

"Name's Massard. Second floor. I don't want her starving to death, do I?"

Roz climbed the stairs as Jill had once done. The squeaky voice answered the bell and the chair on the door was unloosed. Roz walked into the cavernous room.

Little Madame Massard, dressed in a black serge skirt to her ankles and a threadbare winter coat, was boiling water on her upturned electric fire. She carefully switched it off and said a gentle, "Good evening." When Roz gave her "a small gift from your friend downstairs", the little creature was, at first, almost speechless.

"*Ce n'est pas vrai*!" she exclaimed two or three times, looking at the egg. There followed a long sentence in flowery French in which Roz was begged to repeat her gratitude to Philomène whom she called Madame Au Premier.

Then the little lady looked up at Roz's tall figure.

"Forgive me, Madamoiselle. You are in grief, are you not?"

Roz started.

"You brought it with you. The food is magnificent and I thank you and all the people who have come to liberate France as well as my friend downstairs . . . but you are in grief."

"May I sit down?"

"Mademoiselle, you need not ask."

Roz sat by the upturned unlit fire and to her own disbelief – she never meant to do such a thing – told her. Madame Massard listened in sombre attention. When Roz finished she said, "You and your friend came here with pure motives. To help. To share, isn't that so?"

Roz couldn't answer. She knew very well her own vengeful reason and Jill's pitiful quest.

"To share," repeated Madame. "Now you must share the hardest thing of all. Learn to forgive, as France must do. Yes, yes, I am a silly old woman who prays too much, my friend Au Premier says, she sometimes teasingly calls me a saint. I am very far from that. All I do know is that we are forced to forgive or we are poisoned. I give you the antidote," she added dryly. "It tastes a little worse than the poison."

Part Two

Paula

1944

Eight

Throughout the war, people had been leaving London. At the very start, children with their names on cardboard labels tied with string to their lapels, filled train after train bound for the country. When the 1940 Blitz ended, many parents flouted government advice and brought their children back to their bombed and shattered city . . . Off the children had to go on the same country-bound trains in the February of 1944. The Blitz had started all over again.

But there was one young woman who travelled the other way, leaving the more-or-less safe city of Oxford for embattled London. She brought a cardboard suitcase and a widow's pension.

Thin as a rake, glassily pale, Paula Banks had lived in her home town since she was born. A constricted life, for she knew no academics, scarcely connected with the men who poured into the city for courses, training. She went to typing school and married, before she was eighteen, a boy from the wealthy part of the Banbury Road. Already in the Navy, he was posted to Scotland immediately after the wedding. And was dead four months later. Not killed at sea but in a stupid lorry crash in Glasgow.

Paula took the London train with one idea. To get away from Oxford, from the rich in-laws who would have nothing to do with her, and from her ineffectual mother. The Government did not force widows into uniform or factories and losing Freddy was Paula's only pitiful contribution to the war effort so far.

A mousy-haired girl with dark eyes, she stepped off the Paddington train without an idea of her destination. She had counted her meagre cash and took a taxi to the nearest YWCA.

She was accustomed to the blackout which had spread its dark cloak over Oxford for nearly five years. If you knew the district, the streets, you could walk easily in the dark and know where you were and Paula negotiated the suburban roads of north Oxford with confidence. But looking out of the cab window at the black void which was London, all she saw was obscurity, with an occasional dull gleam as a pedestrian shone his or her torch down on to the pavement. Where the hell was she?

"One and sixpence, lady," said the cab driver, drawing up at a large dim building. She climbed out, pulling down her battered suitcase, its metal handle half off.

"Don't do anything I wouldn't do," he added, seeing the pretty face or the indications of one. She giggled.

"Want to help wash up?" said a big-breasted woman at the Y after Paula had checked in.

"Must I?"

"Don't wear yourself out," said the woman, looking her up and down.

"I've got an important appointment for a job tomorrow, I have to get to bed early," said Paula.

"Please yourself." said the woman.

Upstairs she was given a bed in a dormitory of six. "Sorry it isn't the Savoy."

Daylight came, Paula washed in a basin in a line of other basins, studied herself severely ("you look awful") and, depositing her suitcase in the Left Luggage at Paddington, she walked down a road far more dilapidated than anywhere in Oxford. She was looking for an Employment Agency.

That morning she was offered five typing jobs and chose the one which paid two shillings more than the others. It was an organisation raising money for abandoned dogs. The office was behind the Law Courts.

There was a core of efficiency in Paula. She had rarely used it except to get Freddy Banks to marry her. He'd been sweet and manageable and deeply in love with her. She had persuaded him that it was only right after they'd slept together that he should make her his wife. His family were furious and refused to come to the wedding. Paula hated them.

She mourned Freddy. Still wore his ring. But instinct told her that a heartbroken widow in 1944 was a mistake. "I did love him," Paula said to her mother. She did not say "do".

With a new job settled and the prospect of a weekly pay cheque to add to her pension, Paula found some cheap digs, bought a sewing machine and began on a certain plan she'd worked out before leaving Oxford. She'd noticed – envied – the way the American troops looked at some of the Oxford girls. They never look at *me* like that, thought Paula.

Alone in her digs in Manchester Square with her clothes spread out on the bed and her new second-hand sewing machine rigged up on the dressing table, she began to make the first moves to crack open the chrysalis of the Oxford Paula Banks. She finally emerged, stretched wings creased from being folded inside the chrysalis – and set off for the office.

Her new boss, Henry Mitchell, was up to his neck in work. He was not raising money for one of the countless good causes – the wounded, the homeless, the widows. Henry had the unlikely job of money-raising for England's bombed-out dogs. It was Henry who had invented the brilliant slogan "Your friend *needs* you!" and Henry who had painted a bandage on to the dog's paw on the leaflet. (The medical board, at his call-up, had refused to take him because of what he described to Paula as a Dicky Lung.)

The plight of dogs emerging from wrecked homes was now his cause and he welcomed the arrival of an obliging girl called Banks. But that morning – Paula had been working for him for a month – when she walked into the office he jumped out of his skin.

She had turned into somebody else.

Her mousy hair was a pale silvery blonde, her eyes larger, with pale violet-coloured lids, her lashes starry with mascara. Her clothes were different, they fitted her narrow waist, they flared, the skirts wondrously short; Henry Mitchell hadn't known she had such beautiful legs.

This morning, the moonlight hair was neatly rolled round her head – tucked into a stocking. It would be released when the clock pointed to half past six. In the evenings a gold and silver curtain streamed down her shoulders and she became the sensual lass in every huge movie poster, enticing, entrancing and ogling the world.

She knew she had succeeded that first morning in the office, but she did not realise the extent of her success until evening came, when Paula's new appearance was recognised by every man in uniform – in the Underground, the bus, and walking down the Strand. There she was, the curvy girl who haunted their dreams. She winked at them when they opened their locker doors to pull out their jackets, pictures of her were pinned in tanks, in Flying Fortresses. Her double, her treble, wriggled on stage in night clubs, sang into mikes, leaned towards them in every Hollywood film. Her theme song was "Kiss the Boys Goodbye".

Slowly, quickly, she began to collect men and to forget Freddy. Her long dead father had been half-Irish and Paula inherited his charm; she was at home with men and learned about sex from those who briefly claimed her slender pearl-coloured body. She was a wild success.

For Paula, the right guy was the one today. She attracted men like gramophone needles stick to a magnet, as a man once described her. Paula thought this funny and liked to repeat it.

She did not fall in love but was what she described as "crazy" about this one or that. When they left London, as all the men did except the flyers, and were sent off to an unknown destination, Italy or the Far East perhaps, Paula was a little sad.

Except once, inevitably, with an American.

She met Philip Casey, called Flip, at a club round the corner from Harrods. Paula wouldn't wash up in the YWCA but she was willing to dry plates and wait tables, as the Americans called it, at the Hans Crescent Club. Where else could she meet Americans from all over the States, every one of them giving her the wolf whistle and the hopeful look?

Flip, big, rangy, with the rear gunner's sign of a single wing on the breast of his uniform, was Paula's choice.

She stopped, tray in hand, to joke with him. There were furious looks from a plainer girl who did more work.

"Let me take you dancing," said Flip. "You're just beautiful."

And dance they did. Paula had already learned the smoochy cheek-to-cheek; nobody danced like that when she'd gone to parties in Oxford with Freddy. Flip was very tall and bent nearly double to press his bony oily fragrant cheek against her own.

It was a girl's patriotic duty to have sex with the fighting forces. Flip came back every night of his leave to her digs. They made wild love until, when the dawn dragged him out of her arms and body, he left to return to his station. To what was called a mission.

The affair was so hot that Paula stopped using her head.

She found her work for the deserted dogs a bore, she could think of nobody but Flip.

He made plans. Howsabout they'd marry later?

"Not now. Don't want to make you a widow again."

"I wouldn't be a widow long," said Paula laughing.

"No you wouldn't. Not with that figure."

They planned for him to take her back to Ohio. He wrote to his parents and Paula received a parcel with two real silk shirts and some nylon stockings, her first. "Welcome to our family," wrote Mrs Casey. "We're so glad to know our dear Philip has somebody to care for him."

Paula could scarcely avoid the awful thought that every time Flip left her bed, he faced death. Two of his friends in the squadron had been killed recently. Flip had told her that in six words and then clammed up. He didn't talk about them and nor did she. Rear gunners had the worst of jobs, arse-end Charleys they were schoolboyishly called. There was nothing of the schoolboy in the job of sitting in the tail end of the plane, fingers on your gun, seeing ahead of you an ocean of bursting shells.

Paula began to avoid her other lovers. She saw Flip on every one of his leaves. Sometimes he could get to London, sometimes he had only a few hours off and she travelled down to the village near his station and put up at a country pub. She sat in the bar waiting for him, unaware (for the first time) of men's eyes. She sat wanting him. When he arrived at last and they hurried up to her room and made love, her joy and sexual pleasure were so violent she wanted to faint.

On a winter's day when they'd known each other three months, and he had forty-eight hours' leave and was due in London, he rang her at her office. He was stuck in barracks. With flu.

The squadron were on short leave and had gone to London "to have a ball" he said. "And I'm here, for God's sake, the

MO won't even let me get up until tomorrow. Christ, I've had it. It's so boring!" He missed his mates. He did not say he missed her and he was so self-pitying that he got on Paula's nerves.

She had always disliked grumbling, never grumbled herself, she called it moaning and it frightened her. As Flip continued to complain about the bad luck of being ill and the boredom of a squadron leader "thick as two planks and a Limey at that", who had come into his room to cheer him up "and dam' well did the opposite", Paula interrupted to say she must go.

"My desk is in such a mess, you can't imagine. And my coffee's got cold."

"You just get yourself a fresh one."

"Don't be cross, Flip. I only said . . ."

"I heard you first time, baby."

She tried to make a sexy joke and did manage to make him laugh. But when she rang off she was annoyed with both of them.

Not a call from Flip for a week. Paula never rang, it was a principle with her. She was going to bed, feeling depressed, when the telephone rang at last. She snatched it up in triumph.

It was the wing commander.

Flip had been killed the night before.

The shock was much worse than when she had lost her husband. With Flip she had been in love in the worst and best way. Crazy with sorrow, lying on her bed, hysterically sobbing, she wished she was dead.

With Flip dead, Paula's desperate longing was to forget him. She lay on her bed in the dreary Manchester Square digs, having rung her boss at the Dogs' Charity and said she had a migraine. It was a phrase she'd picked up from one of her pilots.

Henry Mitchell was full of sympathy.

"Of course, of course, you must rest. My wife has them. It is a sign of a sensitive nature, Mrs Banks. Just take the day off and have a good rest."

"I'll be better in the morning, Mr Mitchell."

"Let's hope," he said, the sirens were wailing over London, "our building is still standing."

He gave the courageous chuckle which was *de rigueur*.

Paula returned to her bed and lay, half asleep and half awake, with a pain in her breast which remained there no matter how much she fidgeted.

The telephone downstairs didn't ring. The landlady didn't tap and shout, "Phone for you, Missis." Paula indulged in an orgy of remembering Flip. It was her farewell, his epitaph. She remembered their sex, its bliss in this very bed. Her pillow was wet with tears.

And then it was late afternoon and she rose, dressed, made up her face – her eyes were red and took a good deal of painting. She put on her prettiest suit, her highest, thickest wedge heels. And went to the club by Harrods where she was whistled at from the moment she clumped into the crowded hall.

Carried trays. Smartly answered compliments. And later went to bed, in an expensive hotel in Basil Street, with a short ugly wisecracking New Yorker called Barney.

"Gonna be a one night stand, Lovely," said Barney, taking her into a stuffy and opulent bedroom. "We're posted tomorrow. Shouldn't be here at all but a buddy of mine lent me the joint. He's paid for tonight."

Sex did work for Paula. Afterwards she slept like a log, was passionately embraced goodbye in the morning and Barney gave her – "just to buy yourself sumpn' pretty" – fifty pounds.

I suppose I'm a whore, thought Paula.

It was funny how she didn't think about Flip that morning.

It was Sunday. With her companion of last night gone, she was at a loose end. She decided to go to Kensington to a movie – Paula's antidote, Paula's aspirins. There was a film at the big Odeon that she wanted to see. Conscious of the fifty pounds in her handbag, raying through the leather as if covered with phosphorous, she took a bus.

Almost immediately, while she settled down by the paper-latticed window with the consciousness that an American GI was eyeing her with a grin, Paula heard the air raid warning. Like everybody else in England, the rise and fall, the moaning sound, was familiar, alarming, boring, hateful.

"Anybody want to go to the shelter?" shouted the conductor, ringing his bell for the bus to stop. It was nearly dark. Five o'clock. One or two people shuffled off the bus and the GI, a thin boy who looked all of seventeen, said, "Better get down, lady. Safer in the shelter. You're too good-looking a dame to get blown sky high."

As they began to walk together in the dusky street past the Odeon cinema there was an earth-shattering shudder of an explosion – at a distance.

"We're OK," said her companion. "Name's Buzz, glad to know you. Going anywhere?"

"To a movie, actually."

He gave a guffaw. "I like 'actually'." Another explosion, closer, stopped them talking. For no reason at all they began to run. A third explosion was nearer still, followed by an ear-splitting sound, a kind of terrible scream. Her companion pushed her violently to the ground.

A terrifying, unbearable noise burst over them, followed by choking, blinding dust – then a strange silvery sound – breaking glass. Paula started to stagger to her feet but the GI gasped, "Don't get up. Maybe there's another."

And pulled her down on her face in the dirt.

But no new explosion burst over them and Paula thought

she heard the fading drone of a retreating plane. The aircraft guns thundered. And paused. After a minute or an hour, Paula managed to get to her feet, ears ringing. The GI had stood up too and when they turned to each other, both saw a figure from the inferno of the Somme, clothes blackened, face masks of dust in which the eyes glittered.

"Our name wasn't on that one," said Buzz. He moved towards her, his arms out. Paula, filthy and shivering, moved too, when a cracked voice yelled.

"*Private! Why aren't you in barracks*?"

As dirt-covered as they were but wearing his white helmet, an American military policeman appeared in the dark. He yelled at Buzz, ignoring the wreck of a girl standing beside him. Buzz gave her a helpless, imploring look.

"Sorry, Hon."

"What's your number, Private? What' you doing round here?"

The policeman's voice was loud and threatening and had fear in it. Paula heard both men march away, they made a crunching noise on the glass. With a shudder Paula began to pick her way across the great shards, lifting her feet like a water bird in an estuary. Once she stumbled over what she thought was a corpse in the gutter. It was a mink coat.

She began to run, legs weak, terror strong, when somebody – a woman this time – materialised and stopped her. "Ambulance," said the woman briskly. "Wounded, are you?"

"N-no. I don't think so."

"Mm. What you need's a cup of tea. Hospital check-up too, I shouldn't wonder."

"No. I'm not hurt."

Filthy, disorientated, she let herself be persuaded into a van full of huddled survivors. They were driven, bells clanging, to what looked like a school.

A round-faced elderly woman hurried up to receive them and they were taken into what had been the assembly hall where rows of camp beds had been set up.

"Want to wash your face? You can do it in there."

Still trembling, Paula wandered into the school lavatories. When she saw her reflection in the mirror above the basin, she came to her senses. Returning to the elderly woman, who was muffling an old man in a blanket, she asked if there was anywhere she could wash properly.

"Might find you a bucket."

"Bucket? Coming up."

Another woman, surely a schoolmistress who had worked in this place, bustled Paula back to the lavatories, disappeared and returned with an iron bucket, water and a sliver of yellow soap.

Paula took nearly an hour to clean up. Her favourite suit, it had been pale blue and she'd made it herself, was unrecognisable. Not only nearly black but with a jagged rent right across the skirt. When she looked down at her leg, she saw a graze and dried blood. Carrying what was left of her outer clothes, wearing a petticoat as dirty as the suit, she returned to the schoolroom.

"I must get home," she said helplessly to the schoolmistress. "Could I borrow . . ."

"Some clothes? Can't be done, I'm afraid. The Yankee sack will be here at eight tomorrow with luck."

Paula did not understand a word of that.

"You can doss down over there," added the woman, "but have some tea and a bun first. Do."

The night was surreal. All the refugees were given hot tea, plates of very stale Bath buns and a kindness which Paula was too shattered and dirty to notice. When she finally lay down on the camp bed, she still had fits of shaking. But at last drifted into a half-consciousness. She woke at six. And there was the schoolmistress squatting on the floor by a woman who was feeding a baby.

I ought to ring Mum, thought Paula. Quite suddenly she felt an intense pain. It was nothing to do with her shocked body, all in her heart. Apart from her mother safe in Oxford and knowing nothing about this, who would know or care if she had been killed?

She climbed out of bed and began to fold the blankets. The schoolmistress shouted cheerfully, "You're in luck. The Yankee bag's arrived. You don't know what I'm talking about, do you? It's Bundles for Britain, all those clothes they send us from the good old USA. At least you'll look respectable when you go home this morning. You'll find Colette doling them out in the old gym over there."

Paula trailed across the dormitory full of still sleeping people, with now and then a child climbing out to hop or play or sit clinging to its mother.

In the gym which still had parallel bars and a vaulting horse shoved in a corner, Paula saw a curious spectacle. On trestle tables there were piles of clothes. They were every colour of the rainbow, skirts, dresses, shoes, even hats. Crimson, yellow, vivid blue. There was a glint of sequins. A little woman in black, sorting and arranging them, caught sight of Paula and beckoned.

"My first customer. I'm the Yank Bag lady. Now, what can we find for you?"

She actually looked as if her war work was rather fun. She regarded Paula and said, "Very slim. I'm afraid some of my American matrons are on the broad side, bless them."

She picked up a purple satin skirt.

"How about that? No. Not really."

Paula said nothing and the lady grinned.

"I can see Bundles for Britain are new to you. The Americans are so generous. They keep sending us great sackfuls of the stuff . . . they go to a lot of parties, don't they?"

She wound a silver belt round her wrist. "Let's see what we can find for you which isn't too vast . . ."

She went through the heaps of clothes and finally brought out a full-length black taffeta skirt.

"This might do, what do you think?"

She held it up to Paula who stood there, meek and dirty.

"And a top," said the lady, "I noticed a blouse, sorry, it's a bit eye-catching."

The crimson satin blouse had enormous sleeves caught into wrist bands sewn with pearls. With the lady's help Paula struggled into the finery. The skirt fell off and had to be secured with a broad patent belt.

Men and women had begun to traipse into the gym and to cluster round the clothes. They gloomily examined the booty, fingering coats, suits, holding them up, letting them drop anyhow so that the neat piles soon turned into a chaotic mess.

"Is that all you've got?" said a middle-aged woman in bomb-rags.

"Can't do up them buttons," said an elderly man who had struggled into a jacket too small for him. He stood with his arms out, waiting for attention.

The Bundles for Britain lady was good tempered and helped here and there. Then she came over to Paula who was trying to hitch up the skirt again.

"Are you sure you're OK? You wouldn't like to pop along to the hospital? There's one down the road."

"Thanks. I'm all right. I wasn't hit or anything."

"I expect you just feel stunned. Everybody does for a bit. Are your family in London?"

"No. I'm on my own."

"Where do you live?"

"Digs in Manchester Square."

"You can't go all the way there!" exclaimed her companion, speaking as if it were a thousand miles. "Look, Patricia's just arrived, she's taking over from me. I live quite near. Why not come home with me and I'll rustle us up some breakfast."

Paula was, indeed, feeling stunned. Worse than last night. Her head was splitting and she had a feeling of unreality which frightened her.

"It's very kind . . ."

"Not kind at all. Glad to have you."

Ten minutes later her rescuer was letting them both into a flat off High Street Kensington. Oakwood Court.

"Good to be home," said the lady. "We haven't introduced ourselves. I'm Colette Ducane."

"Paula Banks."

"And we need breakfast." As Colette pushed open the front door there was a chorus of hysterical barks and she was engulfed by dogs. Paula had never liked dogs despite working for their welfare and was shattered by the attack of a large brown Airedale, a black and white mongrel who was half spaniel and a small yapping Sealyham. There was a great deal of noise and leaping and Colette shouted instructions and endearments. "Dear old boy, do stop!" "Binker. I've only been out an hour, don't be a pest."

She turned a sparkling face to Paula.

"Take no notice, they're ridiculous."

Having given her the essential welcome, the dogs surged slavishly round their mistress who bustled Paula into a high-windowed sitting-room, and settled her on a sofa.

Paula smiled a thank you and it was only then that she took in her rescuer. Colette Ducane was small, with a rakish lived-in face and hair carelessly dyed a gingery black. It was cut in a bob and she had a frizzy fringe like those worn by night club singers in Paris in the 1930's. She wore a siren suit, baggy black trousers and top and a good deal of make-up. Her manner was lively, actressy and matter-of-fact.

"You're so kind," said Paula, thinking – I sound like a refugee.

"My dear child, I'm glad to have you. Bob, Bill and Binker are dears, but their company is somewhat limited. Breakfast won't be a jiffy. Just relax, you need it."

She hurried out with her trio of admirers.

Paula, misery and shock slowly starting to fade, looked around. The flat seemed very big. Outside the sitting-room she'd seen a line of doors. Were they bedrooms? And the room where she was sitting was remarkably large and long and full of furniture which had surely come from some big country house. Great mahogany bookcases and chests of drawers, some heavily carved. There were a good many pictures, sentimental country scenes, muddy lanes, honey-coloured cows. The gilt frames were chipped. Everything looked as if it had once been rich; even the cushions had gold thread embroidery.

From the kitchen, she could hear Colette talking to the dogs.

"Greedy pig, lay off."

"Bill, it is *not* your turn."

She trotted in with a tray, a jug of something passing for coffee, toast and very little jam.

"Isn't that sofa awful? Like a rock. I'm afraid the cushions aren't much better but put one in your back. I covered them with my second husband's Masonic aprons."

Paula, whose elderly godfather in Oxford was a mason, said in hushed tones, "Weren't they furious?"

"I don't know any masons now," said Colette, pouring coffee and then lighting a cigarette. "Now, tell me about yourself. How are your digs in – did you say Manchester Square? OK?"

"I suppose so."

"Not too hot, mm? What about your job? Do forgive me for asking – don't answer if you'd rather not."

Paula was glad to. She mentioned working for the abandoned dogs and – Bob, Bill and Binker came surging in – earned a look of approval from Colette. Burying her nose in the hot and tasteless drink, Paula muttered that the flat was lovely and had Mrs Ducane lived there for long?

"Forever. Came here in the late 1930s with my third and last husband, Guy. He was killed in Tobruk, poor sweet. Nick – that's my son – is in the army on some fearful training course, very hush hush. Comes home sometimes but only for me to wash his beastly shirts."

She turned her insouciant grin on her visitor.

"People ask why I hang on in London. The poor old flat is none too clean, I'm afraid, but I loathe housework, always did. Imagine," she went on, "before the war I had two maids! Nick was a bit of a bore with them in the good old English tradition of nipping into their beds. I had one or two hysterical girls bursting into our bedroom. Guy used to get very shirty when he was woken up by sobbing women. He told me to hire plain girls. That did work better."

Thinking about the pre-war world of maids (the Bankses had had three), Paula said,

"The girls got called up, I suppose?"

"Not them. They volunteered. The morning it was announced that girls were needed in the ATS (I should think we'd been at war about a week) Alice and Annie left me. You never saw anything as fast as their exit. They had been happy too. They were great friends. I got them from some orphanage in North London, I always chose my girls from there and they came in pairs. Company for each other. I used to teach them to cook (one or two were brilliant after a few months). Eventually, of course, they got married from here. I'd give a reception. Those were the days."

She sighed.

"Alice and Annie hadn't even been with me a year. No wedding for them. The week war broke out they marched in when I was having breakfast in bed and said they were sorry, Mam, but they'd enlisted. I cried when I said goodbye. They were disgustingly pleased to be going and beamed all over their faces."

She fed Bob a crust of bread.

"Alice turned up here once. Smart as paint. An officer. Polite, of course, and brought me a present – her chocolate ration! But . . ." Colette reflected. "Distinctly patronising. I felt like saluting . . . I'm talking too much. Did you say you're not mad on those digs of yours?"

"They are a bit small. But it's hard to find anywhere else," Paula spoke lightly. She guessed and could not believe what might be coming.

"Why don't you move in here?" suggested Colette. "I used to have people billeted on me, rather fun, but not lately. The Army hasn't been in touch for months. Everything's in a turmoil and what with the Invasion talk and stuff . . . I rattle around here on my own. Do come. You can see what oodles of space I've got."

"Oh, Mrs Ducane, I couldn't put you to so much trouble!"

They both knew she didn't mean it.

Colette was pleased when her offer was breathlessly accepted. She'd taken a liking to the girl. First to the waif in the torn petticoat, then to the absurd creature sitting among Masonic cushions wearing American cocktail clothes.

Paula repeated, "*Are you sure*?"

Colette ran her a bath, five inches ("I've never believed that's all the King and Queen have, do you?"), sprinkled in bath salts and lent Paula a pair of her son's pre-war trousers, shirt and sweater.

The garishly dressed refugee vanished into the bathroom. The girl who finally emerged in too-large clothes was another matter.

"Goodness, how pretty you are. Just the stuff to give the troops," exclaimed Colette. "Now off you go to your digs and pack."

Two hours later Paula reappeared with the cardboard suitcase and some brown paper parcels tied with string. She had more clothes than when she'd left Oxford. Colette gave her the most spacious of the six bedrooms, decorated in faded chintz with a skirted dressing table, elaborate curtains (blackout linings coming unstitched) and Paula's first triple mirror.

Bliss indeed.

The unlikely duo settled down as if they were relatives. Paula, in her own clothes and her own beauty, took the bus and Underground every morning to work for the damaged dogs. The Blitz was intermittent but one morning she had to step – just as she'd done outside the Odeon – over pavements of broken glass. Surprisingly the gaunt Victorian office was not hit and her boss continued to brighten up when she arrived.

"There you are, Mrs Banks!"

As for Colette, like every other woman still surviving in London, she was busy. Time had to be spent in food queues during which the dogs were really bored. She worked for Bundles for Britain and friends in uniform, passing through the capital, telephoned and came to see her invariably bringing a bottle – or a half or a third of a bottle. One young officer brought her an egg wrapped in his handkerchief. An important part of Colette's life was her flirtation with the butcher. Without Colette's fading sex appeal, Bob, Bill and Binker would have starved to death.

Nine

It was a wet June and the invasion, at last, had begun. But to Colette and Paula and everybody in London, the atmosphere was flat and so were the uncommunicative bulletins on the radio. The newspapers compensated by showing maps of Normandy with thick arrows indicating the armies of the allies shooting ahead.

When the siren went that damp summer night, Colette and Paula groaned; they were just going to bed and, as usual, had taken the precaution of putting their clothes at the end of their beds.

"Don't forget your shoes," shouted Colette.

They never went to the basement shelters during a raid; Colette had once seen the spiders, "four times the size of ours up here."

They said goodnight, shut their doors and lay listening to the raid. Perhaps it would be a short one. It was not. All night long in uneasy sleep they heard explosions and muffled gunfire. At seven in the morning, when Colette looked in, Paula was wide awake.

"Isn't it peculiar? Still on. Shall we get dressed and see if we can find out what's happening?"

Dressing hurriedly they went down in the lift, out into a summer morning and deserted streets. Colette's three dogs on their leads pulled hard to get to the grassy patch in the middle of the square which had been a garden once.

Having waited for the dogs, they walked down the road until, "Look! There's a warden," exclaimed Colette. "He'll know something."

As they hurried towards the man, *he* seemed to be hurrying to get away from them. But Paula had long legs and caught him up. "What's happening, Warden? Have we missed the All-Clear?"

"Hasn't been one, Miss," grunted the man, still trying to get away. "You'd best go back to your shelter."

Colette, coming up, said firmly, "We haven't been near a shelter but why is the raid . . . ?" But before she had time to finish, he'd escaped, practically running down the street and round a corner.

She watched him go and said very loudly hoping he would hear, "Well, *really*!"

"Morning, Missis. Not much of a one, is it?"

Trying to talk to the warden, they hadn't noticed a small elderly man emerging from one of the further Oakwood Court buildings. He was the porter for the flats, well over seventy he had been a soldier in his youth. He gave them a salute.

"Mister Pierce," said Colette winningly, "we were trying to ask the Warden if he had any news – but he rushed off without telling us a thing."

"Wouldn't tell you because he can't," said Mr Pierce. "Not allowed to, see? This raid's a new sort, Missis." He lowered his voice in the deserted street. "Them planes haven't got no pilots."

"Robots!" shrieked Paula, fascinated and appalled.

"That's about the size of it. Gotter go. Might miss the *Mail*, shop only has about six of 'em."

With another salute, he, too, hurried off.

Colette and Paula looked at each other.

Everybody in London knew from the very first day that the things now droning overhead were not planes. They had flaming tails and made a noise like giant sewing machines. When the din stopped and the engine cut – that was when you had to throw yourself on the ground. People learned almost at once that they were safe as long as the engine went on making its awful buzzing. Intently listening they went to work, to shop, to queue for food or a bus. *Punch* had a cartoon of Londoners in the street, one ear had grown gigantic.

"I do think," said Paula when the buzz bombs had been on for a week, "it'd be maddening to go and get killed just after we've started to win."

Colette heartily agreed. A handful of days ago there had been the news of the Invasion – even that dangerous sentence "the war will be over by Christmas". Now Londoners talked about nothing but doodlebugs; they gave them cheerful names and loathed them.

Paula's admirers had virtually disappeared. The great floating mass of American troops hanging about in Piccadilly, whistling to passing girls, had melted away. The American service clubs were closed. There were still uniforms in the streets but "not the Yanks," said Paula to Colette. She missed them.

Fortunately for her morale, one or two RAF boys turned up. They had short leaves and – typically – came to embattled London "just for a bit of fun," said Hugh or David, telephoning Paula in her office.

Colette wondered how many worn address books in servicemen's pockets held Paula's scribbled telephone number. The boys (why were the RAF called boys? Well . . . most of them were about twenty-one) came to Oakwood Court to collect her, delighted as children given an expensive present. Watching Paula's welcome, her manner – as if the man tonight was the only one she'd been waiting to see – Colette was impressed.

At breakfast the morning after one of her dates, Paula was up to the minute with RAF news.

"The aircraft guns have all gone," she announced, coming into the kitchen, pale and yawning. "They've been moved to the south coast."

"Hell. I've noticed it's too quiet except for explosions."

Paula had the transparent look of too little sleep.

"Harry said the pilots are trying like hell to intercept the beastly things before they cross the coast. They go up after them all the time but, honestly, they hardly manage a prang. Boy, Colette, isn't it *hot*!"

"Sizzling," agreed Colette, her own forehead under the frizzy fringe was already sweating.

"I had to collapse on to my stomach in the Strand *again* yesterday evening," complained Paula. "The pavement was filthy."

"Where isn't?"

The poor city was battered indeed and, with no official information, rumours ran wild about the number of the dead. There were more roped-off streets than ever and ambulances constantly hurrying from one emergency to another. One morning Colette counted seven. The air – even at some distance from where a flying bomb had exploded – was suspended and foggy with brick dust especially since in the heatwave there was no wind. Roads once lined with green summer trees had a nightmarish look, the leaves had turned from fresh green to dirty yellow under coatings of cement powder.

Nothing was washed. Nothing repaired. The doodlebugs went on.

But during the day-and-night bombardments, London had no mass evacuation. Despite their miserable preoccupation with themselves, Londoners did listen to the radio, saying "Oh yes. We'll win. No doubt of that now."

But they were war-weary and it showed.

Not Paula; missing the Yanks and the whole caste of

international admirers in uniform, she began to notice some Free French still about. She won the usual admiring looks from them and smiled back. One morning on the top of the bus she sat with a mild little Frenchman who was overcome by her looks, but, "alas, Mademoiselle, tonight we leave London."

Colette told Paula why Kensington seemed to be an outpost for the French – one of their headquarters was in a cul-de-sac just off Kensington High Street.

"I used to know a lot of them before the Normandy landings. They came here in droves. Brought wine in beer bottles," Colette smiled reminiscently. "They talked each other down, arguing, paying me ridiculous compliments, then back to whatever argument was on that night. I remember a battle once about which of them spoke the best French, there were four each claiming theirs was perfect! One guy had a terrific Provençal accent." She said casually, "They'd have loved you."

"Do you think so?" said Paula without a trace of conceit.

She was in the relaxed mood which came over her on one of her sewing nights.

Paula never missed staying at home for two evenings a week, even when invitations came ringing on the telephone. She dedicated the time to her clothes. For a girl who looked as if she couldn't thread a needle, she sewed like a professional. She worked for hours, altering dresses snatched (by kind Colette) from the Bundles. She shortened skirts. Sewed pockets in the shape of hearts on tight-fitting jackets. To round off the evenings spent on her appearance, she washed her hair, did her ironing and patted lotions into her flawless skin. Colette approved of the dedication.

Tonight was a sewing night and after a scrappy evening meal during which she was nagged by the dogs, Paula went into the sitting-room, knelt down and spread out three yards of pale blue fabric she had recently bought with the usual black market coupons. She reached for her sewing scissors.

Colette was going out and went into the kitchen to tell Bob, Bill and Binker.

"I wish you'd pay attention. Mistress will be back before eleven and don't be pests and bore Paula."

The front door bell rang.

"It'll be for you," called Colette.

"It can't be." Paula was concentrating.

She heard the front door open and Colette laughed.

"Good grief. You!"

There was the low sound of a man's voice, then Colette, "My dear, I can't stop, I'm late for a delivery of Bundles for Britain, remember those? If I don't run, I'll lose our consignment. I'm dreadfully sorry, it's ages since I saw you. But there's a friend in the sitting-room, I know she'd love to look after you . . . Paula," in a shout, "here's a friend of mine. Sorry, both of you, got to fly!"

She slammed the front door.

The man went across the hall into the sitting-room.

"Hello," said Paula, not turning round.

All he saw was a slender back, yards of leg, a glimpse of silk knickers. She still did not look at him.

He gave a foreign bow.

"Laccombe. Alexandre."

"Sorry, I won't be a minute, this is a tricky bit. Do sit down."

He remained standing.

"That looks difficult, Mademoiselle."

"Not really if you're good at it."

"Could I help?"

"I'm sure you couldn't. Do sit down," she said again.

Vaguely aware of her hitched-up skirts, she was too interested in the cutting to bother.

"May I offer you a glass of wine?" said the visitor, "I brought some from our canteen."

"That'd be lovely. You'll find the glasses in the kitchen."

"Yes, yes. Often have I visited Madame Colette."

Paula had not the heart, much as she wanted to, to continue with her work. Regretfully she folded the fabric, put it away in a drawer, picked a lot of threads off the carpet, accepted the glass of wine and sat down.

She looked at the visitor with interest. He was not as tall as the men she was accustomed to – lanky Americans, Brits, Australians. He was short and burly and reminded her of a wrestler she'd seen in a movie – her references were always from films. His skin was olive, his hair black and wavy, his mouth thick-lipped and turning up at the corners. He wore the navy blue French battledress with the usual French panache. His smile gleamed with gold teeth.

"I have been here to visit Madame Colette but never had the good fortune to meet you."

Paula briefly explained about the bomb outside the Odeon.

"I was lucky," she finished. She guessed he was going to trot out the one about *him* being lucky she was around. That she'd been spared was the phrase used sometimes. Spared for whom?

He set down his glass, leaned across – he was sitting close – and took her hand. A pale hand, too pale for these wartime days, with rings and dark red varnish on long finger nails.

"I am the one with no luck. I see you are married."

"Not married any more, Lieutenant. A widow."

He put on a false expression of respect. It annoyed her. Who was this unattractive foreigner pretending to be grieved about poor Freddy?

But when she looked at him, the assumed expression left his face and there was admiration in his black eyes.

"Is Madame Colette due to return soon?"

Paula knew that one too. She hadn't decided whether to accept the date about to be offered. Colette, she said, wouldn't be back for quite a while.

"I am wondering – I am on leave for so short a time, Mademoiselle, a thousand pardons, Madame . . ."

"I prefer Paula."

"That is gracious. Paula, might I perhaps invite you to a cinema? And a little meal somewhere?"

She omitted to mention that she'd had supper. Anyway it had been dire.

"What about the raids?"

Experience had taught her there were lion-hearted men who hated them.

He gave her a bold look.

"The raids do not worry any man who has fought in the desert with Montgomery."

A pause.

"Yes, yes. I boast. It is my nature. But why should I not? To have been with the English general was an honour every soldier must envy."

Paula sipped her drink and considered. Her love of enjoyment for once outweighed her worship of good-looking men. None of Paula's conquests was plain like this man. They didn't brag either.

"I would like to hear about your adventures, Lieutenant."

"And I to tell them. How disgusting is this wine, is it not? I will take you to chez Prunier. Shall we brave the flying bombs, charming Paula?"

It was high summer and broad daylight. A bus lumbered up and Paula jumped on board followed by her new admirer. There was an Alert and the passengers had the listening look.

Alexandre paid their fares with a flourish, sat too close and began his story on the slow journey to Piccadilly.

Paula had heard many stories of the Eighth Army and

could not decide whether her companion had actually been at Alamein or not. She did not entirely disbelieve him. She vaguely remembered Colette saying the British Army had transferred some French troops to British regiments. A battalion or two of Free French had fought there. Certainly Alexandre Laccombe's admiration for Montgomery was unfeigned. He spoke of him as a priest of the Holy Father. Montgomery was, "the general above all generals. Even our de Gaulle cannot hold a candle . . ."

"He'd be furious to hear you say that."

"So he would."

Montgomery had addressed them "before the great battle, standing upon a tank and speaking like some hero of the past. I only wish," said Laccombe, as the bus stopped outside the Ritz and he put out his hand to help Paula jump down, "I only wish we French could claim him as our countryman. He would take his place beside our own General."

Paula wondered how Montgomery would enjoy that.

Chez Prunier – she had not been there before – was surprisingly full on an evening of danger. Calm reigned. Waiters did not hurry and orders were taken with reverence. When the wine arrived, it was twirled in silver ice buckets. Impossible to believe that any moment they could all be smithereens. There were one or two thumps. Far off.

Alexandre ate his sole heartily, picking it off the bone and offering to help Paula with hers. She accepted, liking to see things done skilfully. He returned the sole with perfect fillets lying on the plate and whipped off the long bone to put it on his side plate.

There was the long, uninterrupted sound of the All Clear. "Ah bon," said Alexandre, "We must eat well tonight. At least, I must. Who knows if I will ever meet my beautiful *copine* again?"

"What is *copine*?"

"Friend. Companion. Mate."

"I love mate," said Paula. "You call all your girls that, I bet."

A flash of golden teeth.

"I cannot deny it."

Good-natured as she was, Paula had no wish to hear about his sexual prowess. She supposed without vanity that her own would beat his hollow. She decided to talk about France.

She was aware that the subject was painful. She thought she'd risk it.

"I have never had a French friend before. Tell me where you come from, Alexandre. And before you start, I must warn you I'm hopeless about abroad. I gave up geography when I was fourteen."

Alexandre had no hang-ups. He came, he said, from la Bourgogne. The most beautiful of all the provinces and the richest. She had heard of Burgundy perhaps?

"I remember a song. To Hell with Burgundy."

That made him laugh. Yes, yes, that rubbish in a musical about François Villon, he had seen it ages ago in Paris. He returned to the subject of himself. He was a Burgundian of pure blood.

"I confess, Paula. I have a title."

"No!"

"Indeed, yes," pleased with her round eyes. "I am, in actual fact, *le Comte l'Accombe de la Vallière*, that is my full name and my estate . . ." he gestured, "is very large. Many hectares of the most beautiful and fertile land in France."

Her eyes were still round.

"Are you rich, Alexandre?"

"I cannot deny it."

The pudding arrived. Crême brulée. Paula had never eaten that dish before.

"When the war is over, you'll go back to Burgundy?"

"Ah, yes."

"Have you got a castle?"

"We call it a château." He flashed a golden smile. "God knows how things will be when we return. What will the Germans have done to the château? To my *vignobles*? Although they will have drunk the wine. But – my family, the servants . . ."

Looking at the girl facing him, he saw her dazzled.

He reached for the bottle and refilled their glasses. A hovering waiter darted forward, gave Alexandre a wounded look, took the bottle from him and added a few token drops to each glass.

"Naturally we French in London cannot forget our homes. We did not think of that when we answered the General's call and set out to cross the sea like good little heroes . . . If things were different, if I had a little time, instead of knowing I must go tomorrow I would pay court to you," he added thoughtfully.

"I like French compliments."

"It is not a compliment. You are beautiful. But your thoughts are not with me."

"Of course they are."

"You still wear that."

He touched her wedding ring.

She lifted her hand and studied the thick gold band.

"It reminds me of my husband, poor darling."

She twisted the ring. Above it was a diamond circle given her by Flip Casey. "A babe like you needs diamonds." On her charm bracelet were coins, naval crowns, little gold houses, wings. Sometimes she looked at each of them and remembered the givers. Not often though.

Alexandre beckoned for the bill and they walked out of the restaurant which was gradually emptying. Of course the Warning moaned out again. There was a not-distant-enough thud this time.

"Zut. I was going to say we would walk. Now I take you to the shelter."

"Don't let's. I hate them."

"You would hate more to have one leg only and such a pretty one."

The escalators at Green Park had stopped and streams of people were walking down towards the bowels of the earth. When Alexandre and Paula reached the packed platform, he put his arm round her shoulders to protect her. A few people had set up camp beds the way they used to do when Paula was still at school. But most had come from the street and stood about, tired and depressed. Cockney exuberance was long gone.

Alexandre managed to get them both through the press of people to lean against the wall.

"When the All Clear sounds I must take you home. But we will meet again."

Paula was accustomed to the look, men always wore it when they were with her. Alexandre's look was sexy, it was also self-assured. Paula had a moment of marvelling. France had been made a slave, the few Frenchmen (Colette had told her the numbers were small) who'd managed to come here were poor and dependent on Britain. Colette said they didn't really like us much. Why did they have such confidence?

"*Embrasse-moi.*"

They kissed. Nobody looked at them.

"Remember me when I am dead."

"Do stop!"

He had the grace to grin.

"OK. If I am alive I will pay court to you, charming Paula."

"Did he give you the spiel about vast acres in Burgundy?" asked Colette.

She had an ongoing goodwill to all Frenchmen, but Alexandre was not a special favourite.

"Do you think it is all made up?"

Colette, in the usual black trousers, darned black sweater and dyed black hair, gave a shrug.

"Every single Pole you meet is a prince."

"I've only been out with two."

"What a surprise."

"You're laughing at me."

"As a matter of fact I'm not. I like the way you make friends with everybody. I'm sure, for instance, you've had lots of American boyfriends."

Delicately put.

"One or two," admitted Paula absently.

"You'll be seeing Monsieur le Comte, as he calls himself, again soon," said Colette. The dogs were crowding keenly round her like a pack of wolves round a sled. "OK boys, yes I did wrench some disgusting bones from Mr Richards at the butcher's. I know you can smell them."

She put out a hand to stroke glossy brown and black heads. Tails lashed.

"What do you mean, Alexandre will be back soon? When he left last night he said he . . ."

"Would probably be killed. Of course. He's a courier and goes over and back again. Rather good at it apparently, he enjoys coaxing supplies out of his fellow countrymen, like me at the butcher's. Poor things, it's never very much, they feel the pinch as much as we do. Anyway, Paula, you'll be seeing your conquest again."

There was a lull in the flying bombs and dramatic news from the Continent was splashed all over the papers. In the sky too – Armadas of bombers roared over London – 175 in one morning. Colette and Paula ran out into the street to watch one Sunday morning.

They walked home in cheerful silence.

"Colette . . ." said Paula, as they entered the flat. "I want to ask you something. Is it true Alexandre is a count?"

Colette laughed slightly.

"I'm afraid so. Title's as old as God. They fought in the Burgundy wars. Actually, it wasn't Alexandre who told me, it was his CO one night when they popped in for a drink. Apparently the family's vineyards stretch for miles and miles; they're rich."

"You mean they used to be."

"Oh sure. Before the Nazis. But land's land, Paula, and vineyards mean money. I should say when he gets back to France, he'll be rolling."

"Oh goody."

The newspapers continued to carry maps of France on the front pages every morning and the thick arrows moved further and further into the heart of France.

Then the great day came. Paris was liberated.

"By her own people," proclaimed the General in a sort of incantation, listened to dubiously in England, "with the help of the armies of France, with the support of the whole of France. That is to say the fighting France, the true France, the eternal France."

Paula, now seeing a good deal of Alexandre, reported to Colette that he'd told her that when the recording of the General was repeated in the canteen there was a loud cheer.

Colette raised her eyebrows.

"The General doesn't seem to have noticed huge allied armies pouring into his country. Did he do it all by himself?"

"Oh, you know. The French are like that," said Paula, now the expert on Anglo-French relations.

Paris or no Paris, the buzz bombs went on. Constant sirens and the hated things like poisonous bees flying over very low with that familiar ominous noise were heard. On her way back from work one hot summer midday – she had done extra time on the previous Saturday – Paula decided to look at the damage in Mayfair. Like all Londoners she had a fascination for this form of sight-seeing. In Berkeley Street every window of every shop had been blown out and the contents scattered all over the pavement. Passers-by never even picked up a scarf, they simply stepped over the bright silks, veiled hats and real leather shoes.

Having gawped with the rest, Paula managed to get on a bus which worked its way past Knightsbridge, a district which gave her a stupid heartache. It was here that she'd worked at the Hans Crescent Club, where she'd met Flip, where Barney from New York had given her fifty pounds. How she missed the Yanks, sexy and generous and loose-limbed and funny, their crowded presence had been London to Paula. Now they were gone. The RAF boys too. Her new beau was the only bright spot right now.

She had arranged to meet Colette at a pub they'd nick-named the Hogarth; *Mariage à la mode* prints were hung round the bar and up the stairs.

Colette was on a window seat, the three dogs at her feet.

The place was empty.

"Sorry, darling, they can't rustle up anything else," said Colette, indicating two plates: dry bread and a raw tomato apiece.

"That's OK. I'll buy us a drink. Just been paid."

Paula went over to collect "all we've got, Miss" – two sweet sherries. Sitting down again she gave Colette one of her smiles. Paula's smiles were the youngest thing about her.

"I'm treating us to this lunch too, if you can call it lunch. There's something I want to ask you."

"And what is that?"

"Will you be my matron of honour?"

Colette burst out laughing. She really laughed, mopping her eyes; the airedale wagged his tail.

"Is this one of your long-distance plans? Goodness, girl, it's scarcely necessary. Anyway, when that happy day finally arrives, if you need a matron of honour you must ask your mother."

"Colette, you haven't met her. She'd die of nerves. Yeah, I know I should be given away by a guy but just tell me where I can find one? So – will you do it?"

"In the dim and distant. Of course."

"Not all that distant, actually. Today week."

Colette, who had picked up her sherry, put the glass down so roughly that it slopped.

"Aha. That took you back. Fact is, Alexandre popped the question. And I've said yes."

Colette stared.

"But *why?*"

"Why not? We're crazy about each other."

Colette let that one go. She said weakly, "You don't know anything about him."

"Of course I do. So do you. You said yourself you've known him over a year."

"Off and on. Mostly off. The odd drink sometimes."

"OK, the odd drink. But you're clever with people, you understand them. You understand *me*."

Paula leaned forward, pale and dark eyed, her little voice quite soft.

"Truly, I know all I need to know. He loves me. We're mad about each other. I've often said I wanted to marry again, haven't I? Alexandre has never been married and he says this is the *coup de foudre*. I agree. I feel the same. Stunned."

"But marriage . . ."

All round the bar hung grimacing, mocking sermons.

"Sure. Marriage," said Paula with a sigh of pleasure.

"Alexandre's managed to get a special licence, dunno how. The other evening he dragged me round to meet a priest. Nice old guy, ever so Irish. He asked if I was an RC and Alexandre said, 'Not yet, but she soon will be.' I'm sure he's right, I'll be like Alexandre. A Catholic. And imagine, I'll be his wife. At last, at last."

"You've been married before," Colette felt impelled to say.

"Isn't it awful, I scarcely remember poor Freddy."

She gave Colette another smile. The man behind the bar was looking at her. There was something sexy about Paula all the time.

"You will be specially nice to Alexandre, won't you? Now I've told you our big news."

Alexandre arrived too soon after that, bustling into the bar, short and considerable, to kiss Colette's hand with a flourish. He was like a character in a French farce. I've always quite liked him, though I don't know him at all well, thought Colette. There were other Frenchmen she had preferred.

But his delight in Paula was endearing. Two or three times he turned to Colette and said, "Am I not the most fortunate of men?" He had to add, "She is fortunate also," and it was only half a joke. He called her "my little Countess" too often, and monopolised the conversation, peppering it with news of the General and his own new job as a courier.

Paula listened enthralled, laughing at the feeble jokes and making kissing faces.

Colette and the dogs stood up to go.

Colette took the sudden wedding in her stride. She insisted on giving Paula all her coupons to buy the wedding dress, short white lace, a wreath of silk flowers and a stiffened veil. Paula had spent her ill-gotten coupons on underclothes. When the two women unpacked the box Paula pulled the dress over her head and stood in front of the long mirror fixed to the wall.

"I look all Hollywood."

Paula's dyed silvery blonde hair fell to her shoulders. She was still the girl whose picture the troops pinned inside their locker cupboards; but a bridal one this time.

Colette said after a moment, "Alexandre adores you."

"I do too."

Paula wriggled out of the dress.

"I want to say something, Paula."

"Shoot."

"Sure you feel strong enough?"

"I can be rather strong. Haven't you noticed?"

"I don't know you well, darling, but I like you very much. It's good to see you happy . . . but . . . hows about making up your mind to stick to your French husband? When he goes back to France this time."

"You mean stay faithful?"

"Something like that."

Paula put up her hands in prayer.

"I won't look at another man."

On the evening before the wedding, Alexandre, who had two days' leave, decided to take his future bride to the Ritz. Their last meal before she became his wife. They snuggled up in a cab which braved bombs and rockets for half-crowns.

"What did you and Colette talk about when you were trying on that dress I am not allowed to see?"

Paula decided she would say nothing of her past. Until Alexandre she had been quite frank with her lovers, saying merely that whoever it was was not her first, of course, and indicating that past sex had been precious, rare and tragic in its ending. Then she would obligingly fall into bed. She'd chosen another role with Alexandre. He was to be the one with the past; during their supper he touched on mistresses in Burgundy, a possible illegitimate child. "She may not have been mine, women tell fantasies, do they not, *Adorée*?" Paula smiled. Too smart to choose, as he did, the luxury of the confessional.

Paula's matron of honour wore pre-war navy blue and white silk and a little hat, the brim somewhat bent by being in the top of a cupboard for the duration. Paula, in frothing white, came up the aisle endearingly holding Colette's hand. Her mother, Mrs Cox, little and thin, had braved the three-hour journey from Oxford, bringing Paula's elderly and rarely-seen Uncle Sidney. The only other guest, apart from three nameless French pals of Alexandre's, was Colette's daily woman, Irish, and sobbing at the wedding. She loved them.

Colette thought the Catholic church a surprise. The real one had been hit by a flying bomb and a temporary one had been set up some days ago in part of a furniture shop. Hideous utility chests of drawers and chairs were on one side of the over-large place, a few pews and prie-dieus on the other. Not that Paula cared. She looked so wonderful that even the priest, in this meaningless shop supposed to be dedicated to God, cheered up.

He was invited with Mrs Cox, Uncle Sidney, the talkative Frenchmen in uniform and the fat old cleaner, back to Oakwood Court. It was a good party, helped by the inevitable Algerian beer-bottled wine and two bottles of champagne Colette had hidden in her wardrobe for the Peace. This, she thought, was a more immediate cause for celebration.

Paula had organised a wedding cake from Harrods. It was very handsome, white, three-tiered, with hooped swags of icing and silver bells, and made of cardboard. When they drank the bride's health, Paula removed the cardboard and inside was an eggless sponge.

There was no rice, no rose petals. No going away clothes. No honeymoon.

Kissing everybody, off went Paula with her new husband in a taxi. He'd saved just enough money for one night at the Ritz.

Winter Interlude
for Two Girls in Wartime
1945

Ten

In Lyon the snow didn't let up and the conditions, said Philomène, using the French phrase, were infernal. Jill looked as if she'd caught some kind of permanent flu. She went on working, to the irritated disapproval of both Philomène and Roz who tried, scores of times, to reason with her. Her changed appearance upset them and Peter even more: he felt desperate. She'd grown so thin her inform was too big for her – she simply tightened the belt.

In the end Philomène chose a morning when Jill was at the depot and safely out of the way to telephone Colonel Fisher.

"This is Philomène. We've met."

"Of course, of course," rasped the Colonel who knew everything about Philomène and sought to avoid her.

"Can you come round and see me, Colonel?"

"Can't be done, I'm afraid."

Philomène, unsurprised, made her second, planned move.

"Then I will say what I have to say on the telephone. It seems a pity. Easier to explain what I want in person."

"Just tell me and I'll see what can be done."

He sounded – was – cautious. What was the female up to?

Philomène let him have it. Did he know the interpreter Sinclair? Yes, of course he did. Was he aware that the girl was ill and it looked to Philomène as if, supposing the Colonel didn't take this matter into his own hands, the young woman would become a casualty any minute now.

"What I mean is, Colonel," said Philomène, drawling, "that she'll turn up her toes and die on us. Not a pretty prospect. There are enough deaths right now. Wouldn't you say?"

Fisher was annoyed. Of course he knew the girl and remembered, far more, her excellent French. With the Ardennes offensive going badly and supply problems worsening by the hour, the last thing he wanted to have was a French Resistant heroine (and a bitch at that) on at him about an English girl and her troubles.

"Has the MO seen her?" he barked. "You've laid that on, have you?"

He was rude because he couldn't spare five minutes more on this conversation.

"She won't see an MO."

"For God's sake, Madame – I mean Philomène – what do you expect me to do? Hold her hand?"

Philomène swallowed a desire to say that the sight of Colonel Fisher would probably finish Jill off. She explained, spelling it out, what she wanted. And the Colonel, with two couriers standing in the door of his office and one of the three field telephones ringing, snapped an agreement.

That evening he sent for Peter Whittaker.

There had been many new snow falls since December – it was as if a new Ice Age had arrived. Peter Whittaker stumped through the slippery streets to the rue de Grand Sermon. He was blue with cold and when he rang Philomène's door and heard the shouted "*Au premier*" he went into the house with relief. It was cold inside. But it didn't take the breath away.

Philomène's room, on the contrary, was steamy hot. She'd had the ancient electric fire on all night.

She sat, as always, in her throne of a chair. Grey hair coiled, her long odd-looking dress had the neatness of a certain kind of poverty. She nodded as he came into the room.

"Good morning, Peter. Sit down near me. I don't want to be overheard."

"Is there anybody else . . .?"

"No, but both girls might come back for a meal or a hot drink if they get an hour off. The canteen packed up last night."

"We're dealing with it."

She studied him for a moment.

"You know why I'm here, don't you?" Peter said.

"Sure. The Colonel's sending Jill home."

The young man nodded. He leaned on his knee and gazed at the ancient electric fire, its elements – at some time or other – had twisted. But it was still red and glowing.

"She won't like it," he said in a low voice.

"She has no choice."

"Philomène, Jill's driving me mad – not seeing the doctor, dragging round looking so awful. What kind of bug is it, for God's sake? She hasn't got a temperature. I forced her to take it the other evening. It was subnormal."

Philomène regarded him in silence. For a hard woman, her heart filled up with pity. She saw that this man, young and what the French called *affairé*, in love with one young girl in this great mess of so-called liberated France, hadn't an idea in hell what ailed her. It was love that was killing her and poor Peter Whittaker thought it was a bug.

Philomène had asked her, on the day when de la Roche told her the truth about Ghilain, if Whittaker knew why she had come to France.

"No. He doesn't."

Philomène had thought – you should have told him. And then – how could you? Sharp as a needle in ways of fighting for her adopted country, the anguish of the heart was something Philomène had forgotten. She couldn't remember the pain of love, it was unreal to her. But Jill was real enough.

"What do you say to a girl who's sick and won't admit it?" he said. "What do I tell her about being sent home? It'll make her worse."

"Well, of course, we must lie," said Philomène with simplicity.

Jill scarcely remembered her journey back to England. Her parting with Peter and Roz. The long solitary journeys.

She continued to feel ill but it was true that when she was out of France, faintly, faintly, she was conscious that one particular part of her disease was gone. The French language. When she finally climbed out of the train at Newcastle station after a journey of thirty-six hours and saw her father waiting for her, her eyes filled with tears of weakness. He looked well. Strong. Real.

She ran over and he took her in his arms.

"My dear child."

Privately, he was horrified. He'd known she "wasn't well" as she had written in her dutiful weekly letters. "Some kind of flu," she had said. But the sight of the girl, her khaki uniform hanging off her, great black rings under her eyes and a strange difference in her face, the rounded girlish cheeks seemed to have fallen in, frightened him. For a terrible moment, as he took her bag and they went out into the wet station yard to his car – Clement typically had managed to obtain enough petrol to drive her home – he thought Jill was dying.

"What you need is feeding up," he said and tucked a rug ludicrously round her uniformed skirt and poor thin legs.

He admired her mother for not showing any shock when he and Jill arrived. She hurried forward in the shadowy hall, blackout curtains drawn across the front door, to give her daughter a kiss.

Lucy was all brightness and welcome, giving her little upward-trilling laugh.

"What a long time it's been. Come and sit by the fire. Clemmie's promised to make us some sandwiches."

It was a sentence Jill had heard on Sunday evenings right through her childhood. Clement had inherited from his French father a talent in the kitchen. When he cut sandwiches they were wafer thin. He did nothing fast, everything with artistic care.

"Ah yes, I will get started, I'm sure Jill must be hungry after that long journey." He paused at the kitchen door to add, "Good to have you home, sweetheart."

Jill's eyes brimmed all over again.

The evening was not easy. It was full of love and concern from her parents and helplessness from Jill. Should she tell them? Could she bear to? There was something else, the very strangeness of finding herself in civilian life. For months her world had been one of uniforms, orders, bustle, urgency, jokes and the bitter cold. The townspeople in Bourg, in Lyon, were poor and if they looked at you, it was with resentment. You rarely saw a smile. Her parents smiled. And looked strangely prosperous. Lucy's clothes might be old but they were handsome, a twinset the colour of caramel, the pretty two rows of pearls Clement had bought her long ago on their honeymoon in Paris. Jill wondered if soldiers back from the trenches during the Great War had felt as she did. Distanced by the world they had come from, no longer able to relate to home. How can I compare myself to men who suffered the way they did, she thought. Death was all round them, they lived in a sort of hell. The only dying for me was the death of love.

Yet the pain in her breast made her feel very ill. She could put her hand exactly on where it ached but it wasn't a physical pain. It was as if misery itself had taken up its abode inside her. Her soul ached. Was this what people called a broken heart?

Surrounded now by affection, comfort, safety, and yet Jill's other life seemed sometimes more real than the small comfortable house and her parents' voices. She thought of Roz crying that night – Roz who prided herself on being strong. She saw Philomène upright in her chair and heard the hideous noise as she banged her wooden leg with her stick. She remembered the hour upon hour of work and her nearly frostbitten fingers. And all the time, the beautiful cruel French language.

Jill knew she must tell her parents. She dreaded doing so – not only because of its effect upon them.

Her father was intensely busy, the factory he'd bought on returning from France in 1939 had been turned over from peacetime furnishings to RAF supplies. Great sackfuls of sheepskin-lined jackets were needed to protect the pilots from the icy cold of night flying. Recently, Lucy told Jill, there was a new demand from the Army – this time for garments lined with fleece destined for the troops in the Ardennes.

The newspapers carried stories of that winter campaign. It was going badly – and Peter was there.

When she read the brief news bulletins, Jill was anxious and guilty. But misery had made her selfish and she did not worry about her friend for very long.

To some degree, her strength returned; Clement knew this was entirely due to her mother's spoiling. There was nothing Lucy would not do for her daughter. Jill's day was threaded with Lucy's bright but gentle, "What can I do to make you comfortable?"

Some daughters would have found such concern stifling but not Jill. Not now. All she thought, watching her mother's trim and busy figure round the house, was how little she'd come home to them during the war, how often she had chosen to spend her (admittedly brief) leaves in London. She'd written faithfully. But she hadn't telephoned much . . .

One evening Clement was home earlier than usual, he had

called on one of his contacts in an Army camp outside Hexham and had brought home some booty, a sackful of logs from the Army stores.

"The Major was insistent because we kept the delivery date," he said, on his knees piling the logs on the fire. They blazed up – bone dry – when the family gathered round the fire after supper.

Sitting with her parents that evening, Jill noticed a certain quality about them, something she'd selfishly forgotten until now. When she talked, about French HQ in London or about Lyon, they listened so intently. They sat so still. And she knew just then it was time to speak.

"Something happened when I was in France," she began.

At the start of the story Clement and Lucy were intrigued and surprised at the idea of somebody they'd known in Bourg actually turning up in London.

"I suppose it isn't all that astounding," Clement said. "Didn't you say the HQ was a clearing house for Frenchmen who escaped to England?"

"The Mayor's son, Clemmie! Isn't it strange? I remember him. You and he had a lot of jokes about French grammar . . ."

"The subjunctive," said Clement absently. "What news of his father? I thought about him during the Fall of France. I'm afraid I had my doubts."

Jill gave a shuddering sigh.

She told them the whole story briefly, with many euphemisms. She used "fond" for love, she never said she and François had been to bed together, or how desperately she'd tried to get to France after she had received the letter. Just that she had been anxious to see him. Just that.

"As you know, I managed to become an interpreter. Took the exams and all that."

"But how did you possibly get to *Bourg*?" asked her father.

It was through Peter Whittaker, she said. She was billeted, remember? With his mother.

"Peter pulled strings for me."

She made the story so short. In a way she herself didn't understand, she hated herself for telling them what François was. How could you be disloyal to treachery? She remembered a poem about honour rooted in dishonour.

When she finished, her parents were shocked and silent. Finally Clement said, "And you believed that man, Captain de la Roche? Believed what he told you?"

"Dad. He was at the trial. Philomène said he was the judge."

"You said just now some of their trials are a farce. Not justice. Revenge."

"That's what people said."

"And this so-called court condemned Ghilain to death?"

"He was shot."

Lucy folded her arms tightly across her breasts as if she was cold. Clement continued to smoke.

"Oh, I'm so sorry!" Jill suddenly burst out.

"What do you mean, sweetheart?"

"I'm sorry for dumping myself and my miserable story on you. Forgive me. I don't know why I can't pull myself together."

"Because you are grieving," said Clement. "People have to. When somebody they care for is dead."

"But how can I still care for him? He's a Judas."

Clement said nothing. Those words, he thought, those verdicts. We need them in times like these. And they're killers.

"Try not to brood too much," said Lucy, breaking her own silence. And then in a change of tone, "Didn't you say you were expecting a letter from the Army?"

"It came this morning. I forgot to say. I have to go back to French HQ next week."

"Are you quite well enough? asked Lucy. "You don't look it."

Lucy turned out to be right, for two days later Jill, at last, caught the flu. She was in bed with a high fever for more than three weeks.

Being married didn't make a pin of difference to Paula, now the Comtesse l'Accombe. She still lived with Colette and worked for the abandoned dogs. Christmas had gone by. Everybody drank the same toast, "Here's to the last wartime Christmas." Somehow nobody believed it.

The snow seemed permanent and, its beauty long gone, the slush grew dirtier, lying on flower beds and grass and in gutters covered with London smuts. Paula went to work in three sweaters. When she told Colette she was usually freezing in bed, Colette said, "Borrow one of the dogs. All three sleep on my bed now. They're better than hot water bottles." Colette, cradling chilled hands round her breakfast mug, wore an extraordinary hairy red garment fastened by a long wavering zip. It was made by a dressmaker friend from a blanket. "No coupons for blankets."

"I suppose I could borrow Binker," said Paula vaguely. "Either of the other two would squash me flat like Mickey Mouse after a truck goes over him." But she wasn't mad on dogs, despite her war work.

It was a Sunday morning and Colette was in the kitchen for company. She put on the popping, low-burning gas for warmth. Outside, it was freezing hard. But Paula was bathed and dressed and smelled of scent. She looked perfect except for her short nose which was blue.

"Where are you off to, child?"

"I thought I'd call in to French HQ. You know. Might pick up some news . . ."

"But you said the French women on the desk are a pain."

"Old witches. But there's always some guy or other in uniform around and you never know, I just might get news of Alexandre . . ."

It was three weeks since she had had a letter from her husband and the letter had been five weeks old.

Paula was not over-nervous about Alexandre. Like everybody else, she could sniff victory in the air. Widowed, remarried, with a string of past lovers, many of whom had been killed, Paula religiously believed in her own luck. She was not even phased, a word of Flip's, by a new danger – the V2s. Rockets had begun to fall on London. The rockets fell fast with a horrible rolling explosion and somebody told Colette he'd seen one and it was coated with ice. But overhead the allied bombers thundered, fleet upon fleet. "It's their turn now, not ours," said Londoners watching the sky full of Flying Fortresses.

What preoccupied people far more was the cold. "The worst winter for fifty years," gleefully announced the *Daily Mail.*

Pulling on fur-topped boots – Paula had smartly taken possession of a pair from yet another Bundle for Britain consignment – she said she'd be back soon. "Wish me luck . . ."

Outside, the cold took her breath away. She huddled into her sheepskin coat and picked her way through the frozen snow. She did long for news (even the least snippet) of her husband. Being married wasn't much fun when you were on your own. She crossed Kensington High Street. Not a car or a bus went by; she saw only the long whitish road marked by trees. At the French HQ, down a cul-de-sac, nobody had cleared away the snow in the garden or the paths for weeks. In places it was up to the ankles of her boots. Alexandre had taken her there to the canteen. "It is not allowed, *Chère*, but we will have apple flan. You will enjoy that."

Paula had been interested in the place and, since Alexandre's last leave, she had called in. But Paula's friendly questions were given an overtly rude reception by the two French girls on duty. It didn't occur to Paula that the French girls disliked her for her looks.

She entered French HQ through the double doors.

Sure enough her enemies were sitting idly at the table in the hall.

There followed a farce. Paula sweetly asked for news of Alexandre. The dark-haired young women mimed incomprehension before treating her to streams of fast-spoken French.

Paula stood her ground, refusing to be unnerved, "I am Madame l'Accombe." She was too smart to add the Countess bit.

More mimed incomprehension and contemptuous shrugs.

Just then a young woman in khaki crossed the entrance hall, giving Paula a brief look.

"I suppose *you* don't speak English as well as French, do you?" exclaimed Paula.

The young woman stopped.

"Of course. I'm English. Can I help?"

"Oh, what a relief. Could you just explain . . ."

The young woman translated Paula's enquiry into French that was swift as that of the receptionists. There was a to and fro and finally the English girl said, "Yes, they know Alexandre l'Accombe. Of course they do since he was stationed here for months before the Invasion. No recent news of his unit, but I may be able to help you next week, there are a lot of reports due in. I could ring you if you'll give me your name?"

With contempt rayed towards them from the French girls, Paula and her new friend moved away.

"Come into my office," said the girl. "I'll just make certain there isn't any news from last week . . ."

She led the way down a narrow corridor into an office which made Paula's office for the damaged dogs look like a palace. The girl's desk was neat enough, but everywhere else was so heaped with paper that it looked as if there could have been a bombardment.

"A mess. Sorry," said the girl.

Paula was invited to sit down, the girl went carefully through some bursting files, found a few words about Alexandre's unit, to Paula's gratitude, then said, "Shall we go to the canteen and have a coffee? You look as cold as I feel."

"I'd love it. But is it allowed?"

"Oh, people take visitors in these days. Nothing's the way it was. And French coffee is so much better than anything we'd get at the Corner House."

It was only when they were seated at a table in a canteen which smelled more inviting than any café Paula had ever visited that they exchanged names.

"L'Accombe" said Paula brightly. "I used to be Paula Banks."

Her companion goggled.

"Paula *Banks*? Didn't you live in Oxford? And your husband was in the Navy . . ."

It was Paula's turn to stare.

"My first husband. Freddy Banks! But I don't understand . . ."

"I had a feeling we'd met before," said Jill. "Don't you remember? You were going up to Scotland to see your husband and I was on my way to Newcastle, my parents live there. We were on that train for hours . . . I often wondered where you were . . ."

There followed exclamations, interest, more surprise.

It was Jill who had had the larger shock. When Paula had sat with her in that stuffy compartment, when they'd shared sandwiches and confidences and boredom, when the company of each other, two girls of much the same age, had helped to pass an unending wartime journey, Paula Banks had been a mouse. A mousy little thing you wouldn't look at twice. The stylish fair beauty facing her across the table was totally unrecognisable.

"I suppose I didn't know you because you're blonde now," said Jill.

"Do you like it?" said Paula without vanity. "It brightens up my face, I think. But I ought to have recognised you, after all you were in uniform."

"But it's such ages ago."

"It is, isn't it? I know I've changed. And I'm married to a Frenchman now!" Gossiping to Jill in her friendly way, Paula had a very different shock. She remembered the pretty bouncy companion on the train. Jill Sinclair now looked terrible. She wasn't thin but scrawny. Any good looks had disappeared. There was a haunted look about her and it seemed to Paula that when she smiled, she did so with difficulty.

Worn-out, no longer ill but still poisoned by sorrow, Jill at least had a flicker of curiosity and interest when she met Alexandre l'Accombe's glamorous wife.

A friendship began between Jill and Paula that snowy winter. Now Colette had two girls to care for. She was glad to welcome Jill who, billeted with Peter Whittaker's snobbish mother, found Oakwood Court a second happier home. Colette became fond of Jill, so quiet and gentle. Inward-looking. Surely there was a sorrow she never talked about – someone she loved must be dead, thought Colette.

And Jill found Paula comforting too. She was so pretty and frivolous and laughed easily. She was very up to date, always knowing the newest fashion and beauty ideas. "Six glasses of water daily. It does miracles with the skin. Have you noticed mine this week?" She brushed her eyelashes with castor oil. "Look! Definitely an inch longer."

At weekends they sometimes had a sparse lunch (food worse than ever) at the Hogarth. Paula added sparkle.

"A tomato. Goody. They're crammed full of vitamins."

Now and then Jill managed to get some kind of news of Alexandre's division and, Paula listening intently, would say, "You *do* think he's OK."

"Of course I do. I'd know if the news was bad."

"You're the tops."

She asked if Jill remembered Alexandre. "I'm sure you met him so I don't need to describe him."

"Oh please do, I can scarcely say I know him. I should think I've said hello about three times." Jill recalled a short burly Frenchman with gold teeth. She wondered how the man, definitely not attractive, could have married this stunner.

"Did you know he's a real-life Count, Jill?"

"Well, I heard rumours. But some people . . ."

"Shoot a line? Sure. I thought Alexandre was doing that. But it turns out to be true. A title. A terrific lot of land, vineyards you know. Even," Paula said laughing, "a château."

Jill murmured, "Wonderful." But the word brought back an image of Bourg and she shivered slightly.

"You're cold," exclaimed Paula. "Have my coat, wearing it is like being as warm as one of Colette's dam' great dogs, look . . ." she stood up, pulled off the sheepskin, wrapping it round Jill's shoulders. The gesture brought Jill slightly back to life.

Paula began to fiddle with her charm bracelet.

"I suppose knowing that Alexandre is rich is rather marvellous. I've never really known anyone who *was*. My first husband, poor Freddy, had a revolting family who were rolling but the boy never saw a red cent of it. And the guys I used to play around with were loaded but it was only because they splashed all their pay on me. They used to finish without a dime. I expect it's the same with *you.*"

"I don't play around. I wish I did."

Paula registered amusement and surprise. So far, Jill had told her very little about herself. Her teenage years in France, of course. And being sent to Lyon as an interpreter. Bare facts. She also mentioned Peter Whittaker – "He wants to marry me, but hasn't exactly said."

"Shall you say yes?"

"I don't expect so."

"You ought to have a guy or two about," said Paula, meaning something else. "Of course now I'm married I've given up all that. But it's different for you. There must be loads of guys who'd jump at the chance of being with you."

Sex was the cure, according to Paula. For whatever was wrong with Jill.

"I couldn't," said Jill, looking at the worn carpet.

"I have an idea you don't sort of *think* of men in that way any more," said Paula very kindly.

It was true. Sexual thoughts, the consciousness of men, the desire to be admired, even the simple pleasure of male company, were gone. Mentally Jill was still afflicted. Her parents had done all they could. During the long drawn-out flu, her mother had nursed her with devotion and when Jill was up again, weak and thinner than ever, her father had taken them both out to dinner two or three times and had bought her an expensive dress. Alone with him one afternoon, Jill asked him not to speak about François Ghilain again.

"Of course. I understand," he said.

He had his own thoughts about the country of his father, the land where he and his wife and daughter had been happy, the land which had cruelly wounded his only child. When he thought of Bourg and Les Lys it was in sepia. An old tattered photograph.

Against both her parents' wishes, Jill had obtained the necessary medical certificates and was re-posted to London and to French HQ. The place was short-staffed now, Captain Gautier was long gone and Jill's new boss was a kind and gloomy man who actually thanked her for working for him.

Peter Whittaker fixed for her to be billeted again on his mother in Markham Square. Clarissa's reserve, coldness, absorption in her own affairs, brusque no-conversation, were a relief to Jill. She was grateful to be spared living in French barracks. Peter wrote to her often. The letters said little, but began "Darlingest", and she felt guilty because it was an effort to reply. He had one short leave, was welcomed radiantly by Clarissa, took Jill dancing, kissed her warmly and chastely at the door of her bedroom. Jill did try to be human, but after they'd kissed she saw in his face a misery not unlike her own.

He returned to France and soon the Ardennes offensive had begun and the Allied suffered sharp reverses. That was the only thing which penetrated Jill's selfish misery. She did actually worry about him.

And she was grateful to be with Paula, bright and busy and optimistic and sometimes concerned about her.

"You're a Mystery Woman. I hope you've noticed I haven't wheedled to know the story."

"It's not a bit interesting. Dreary, actually."

"That's the last thing you are!" declared encouraging Paula. "Shall we do something different with your hair tonight?"

Jill smiled. Oh, she was tired. Worn out with pain, really. Overhead in the sky, day and night, thundered the allied bombers in formation, the great Flying Fortresses loaded with the weapons of death. At night Jill heard them in her dreams. And sometimes she heard François's voice.

Part Three
Knots of Peace
1946

Eleven

It was sunny. Peacetime. An extraordinary thought, reflected Colette. Such an anti-climax. Months ago, those crazy celebrations, drunken pilots on the top of streetlamps, strangers shouting, "Come and join us!" from every crammed taxi. And now this.

Making up her face, she hunted in her dressing table drawer for her lipstick, finding it only to exclaim, "My God," when she saw it was down to the metal rim. She painted her lips, grimacing, when the front door bell rang. There was a moment, shoved aside, of joy. Her son was thousands of miles away in Australia.

"Pull yourself together, Ducane," she said aloud and went out to the front door followed by her dogs. She opened it without interest.

"Paula!"

Colette, amazed, put out both arms and gave the girl a strong hug; Bob, the biggest of the dogs, jumped up to join in. Paula laughed weakly.

"He remembers me."

"Of course he does. Give me your case, come into the sitting room. My dear child, you look worn out."

"Wooden seats in French third class."

"My dear child!" repeated Colette. "Surely you could manage second."

"Not a hope. I just scraped enough dough for my ticket by

selling my bracelet. Funny when you think of it." Paula sat down and yawned. "I sold poor Freddy's watch that other time to get to London."

Colette and the dogs bustled out to make coffee. When she returned to the long bright room, the sunshine was lighting Paula's figure. It cruelly showed her shabby clothes and scuffed shoes. Where was her beauty and her panache? She was creased and travel-stained, the familiar wedge shoes sagged, the shimmering hair blonde no longer but growing back to indeterminate brown.

Colette sat down beside her. "Drink up and then tell me the news. Where's Alexandre?"

"In Passy l'Eglise."

"So you decided to pop over and see me. I take that kindly."

"No, Colette. I didn't pop. I've left him."

With three marriages in her own past, Colette did not exclaim; she offered her guest a biscuit.

"You look half starved. It can't be as bad as all that in France."

"They had food. I wasn't in the mood to eat."

Colette waited in interested silence. The news wasn't going to be good. Paula's face was changed. There were two little lines, quite new, one on either side of her mouth.

"I know I look a wreck. Isn't my hair a mess? I haven't a franc, I mean a bob. I suppose I could try and tint it myself."

"Paula, stop wittering. Tell me what's happened. All I've heard since you went to France over a year ago is one card saying 'I'm OK'."

"How could I write when it all turned out to be rubbish."

"The vineyards?"

"Oh, they're there. But they don't belong to the l'Accombes."

"And Alexandre isn't a Count after all."

"That bit's true," said Paula indifferently. "He's a Count all right. Le Comte l'Accombe de la Vallière. And I'm the Countess. His family's as old as God and that's about it. He hasn't a bean and nor have they. When we got to France he didn't have the guts to tell me what I was in for. Then literally the evening we arrived at a big dreary old house in a poverty-stricken village at the other end of nowhere out it came."

She began to talk. She poured out the whole story in a voice totally lacking vivacity. Colette knew she was hearing the same tale many parents in peacetime England now had to listen to – from daughters who'd trailed home from the United States. Starry-eyed GI brides, in tears over their misjudgements. Or their passionate credulity.

"All that guff he filled us up with, about the château and the family money and vineyards producing famous wines – the Pinot Noir which makes all the great red wines and the servants in the château – well. The vineyards did belong to them ages ago but Boy! they don't now. We had to live with his parents who haven't a sou. *And* they're ghastly."

"How ghastly?"

"Like those characters in the *New Yorker*, what are they called?"

Colette managed to laugh.

"You don't mean the Addams family. The vampires?"

"That's them. Spooking about in a freezing house that hasn't got a carpet. Nosing through my luggage. The old mother did that, you can guess what she was looking for. Cash. Tell you something else, Colette. They obviously believe I used to be some kind of successful prostitute."

"That can't be true."

"Oh yes it can. The thing is they'd never clapped eyes on somebody like me before. They gawped as if I'd arrived from another planet and it was the same in the village. Boy, how they stared! And Alexandre sucks up to his parents all the time. Pathetic. No, it's isn't, it's sickening. He's afraid of them. Doesn't seem possible, does it? He calls his father *Papa*."

She stared into space.

"He has the idea that they're not as stony broke as they pretend and there is some cash somewhere or other (of course they swear blind there isn't). But if there is, Alexandre wants his share of it.

"His father is an old pig. He used to be rich. The stuff Alexandre dished out was true once, I suppose they were very grand. But he gambled the lot away, I mean he was off his head with gambling like a loony. Sold everything – the vineyards – you name it. During the war he was too old to be dragged off to Germany like most of the guys in the village. He and Thérèse, the hideous old wife, managed somehow. The locals are all snobs and the title and an enormous family crest (you should see it, you'd die laughing) and the château which is falling to pieces, it was used by the Germans, impresses the village still. But Alexandre. You wouldn't know it's the same man. He can't cope with his parents loathing me. All he used to do was tell me to try and understand. Understand what? That he'd brought me over to a dump where I was treated like a retired whore."

"Don't exaggerate."

"I just wish I was. Alexandre can't cope . . ." she repeated. "With me. With not having a bean. With his parents. With anything. I once mentioned getting a job to that old devil of a mother-in-law. She obviously thought I meant going back on the streets. You should have seen her face."

Paula looked at her weather-worn shoes.

Colette gave a little sigh and Bob put a whiskery face on her knee.

"And you don't love Alexandre any more?"

"I dunno. No, I guess. How can you love somebody

creeping and crawling to mean-faced old parents? He's afraid of them."

And of you as well, thought Colette.

There was a pause.

"Are you going back to Oxford to your mother?"

Paula shook her head with its burden of two-coloured hair.

"I know I ought to but I can't. Colette, I suppose I'm a bitch but I just couldn't drag off back to Oxford and pretend it's the way it used to be. I can't. The Bankses are still living in that bloody great house, I'd have to walk past it to get the bus. I'd meet them sure as eggs. And although Mum's a dear, I couldn't. I can't live with her again."

"Want to come back to me, then?"

The start Paula gave was genuine.

"But I couldn't take advantage."

Colette did laugh at that.

"I'd like to have you back, Paula."

"But there's your son."

"He's come and gone. First a long leave. Then demobbed. Of course, I hoped he'd stay, but post-war England got on his nerves. He kept saying Europe had had it, and what the hell did we fight six years for? And it was as bad as in 1940 with austerity this and austerity that and queues for food. Poor love, he was fed up to the back teeth. He's in Australia living the life of Riley."

Sadder than she would admit, Colette had survived. But the reappearance of Paula, even a Paula wrecked like debris washed up on the shore after a storm, was a welcome distraction.

"So that's settled," she said. "No thank yous, please. Go and have a bath and use my French soap. Nick bought it for me when his regiment went through Paris. He found a shop which he said was out of this world."

"My train went all round Paris but we didn't go right in."
Paula picked up her suitcase.

Colette was glad to have Paula there. She had few young friends now that the Free French and the Americans were history, though she lacked company. Paula, arriving with her changed and desolate face, her case full of worn-out clothes in the taste of two years ago, was Colette's new cause.

It was clear that the first thing was to help her back to those lovely lost good looks. Colette's obliging cleaning woman (the one who had wept at Paula's wedding) sold them books full of clothing coupons and Colette was still working occasionally for Bundles for Britain. When a consignment arrived she took Paula with her to cut open the sacks and Paula, entranced, bagged the first and best. Another coup was to find the girl a part-time job. Colette went to a dress shop in Kensington High Street and talked the owner into hiring Paula in the mornings. "You'll find she's an asset. Oh, by the way, if she buys things, can you give her ten per cent off?"

It did not take Paula long to start, with Colette's support, the fascinating task of transforming herself all over again. She went to the hairdresser and was restored to former glory. She crawled around on the drawing room floor as she'd done in the old days and altered the American clothes to look like pictures in this month's *Vogue*. The metamorphosis was completed when the girl began to eat and sleep well.

But life in London lacked excitement. The uniformed figures had vanished, the American vitality was gone as well as the excitement, sex heightened by fear, during blitzes. Rationing and shortages were if anything rather worse. When Paula took her shoes to be mended it was six weeks before she got them back.

Colette sometimes saw a particular look in the girl's beautiful face. Paula was brooding about what Colette privately called the French Fiasco. The girl detested failure and was no different from any other disillusioned young wife dragging miserably home from Denver or Ohio. Something had happened to Paula when she met Alexandre l'Accombe. She'd fallen out of love with her naive vision of Hollywood and straight into love with France. She learned to speak the language with unexpected ease, the very name La Bourgogne stirred her. Poor exiled Alexandre created in her imagination a land of castles and rivers, of mountains and hazy distances and the loveliest cities in the world.

Although her beauty had returned, Paula was still deeply affected by what had happened. Travelling on the bus to the Kensington shop she did not look forward – always her strong suit – but back. Colette, in the days before the hasty marriage, had tried to warn Paula not to be crazily optimistic, but Paula had just laughed. And when Alexandre had feebly attempted to play down his former claims, Paula had not heard a thing.

She recalled her first meeting with her parents-in-law. Alexandre's father was old enough to be his grandfather, a weather-beaten nutcracker face, – he looked like an unkempt priest. As for Alexandre's mother, she was dressed in gloomy black mourning. Alexandre explained later it was for a cousin, and women in France wore mourning for six months. The entire year Paula was in Passy, Madame l'Accombe was dressed from head to foot in rusty black. Even to a hat and veil.

At first Paula tried to talk to her naturally, even to make a joke. All she was given in reply was, "*Tiens*". Once she tried to help her to lift a heavy and antiquated vacuum cleaner. Madame gave her a violent push, seized the cleaner and staggered off down the corridor.

What a cow, thought Paula. The classic battle settled down to one word on either side. *Putain* from Madame. Cow from Paula.

Paula knew Alexandre hadn't a hope of improving anything. She began to despise him. Knowing of his wife's growing contempt for him, his sex with her withered away completely. Paula had needed it, loved and enjoyed it; in England he had been a passionate lover who satisfied her and made her blossom. Without the sex, in a dark house with no future and parents-in-law who detested her, in the end Paula's solution was to sell her charm bracelet.

She finally took action on a day when Alexandre and his father had gone to the local wine co-operative and Madame, as usual, was somewhere in the huge house, at work mending sheets with the help of a little spinster in pince-nez, the only French female who ever smiled at Paula.

Trudging through the ancient village, Paula did not bother to look at the beautiful ancient buildings – the stone houses which the sun had turned the colour of walnuts, the church the tint of cinnamon. Jackdaws wheeled round the square tower where the bells rang a quarter of an hour before Sunday Mass to call the congregation together.

The bus journey into Beaune was slow but Paula did not mind. She was excited. Imagine, she thought, being excited by such a crummy little expedition. She had spent two hours the previous evening (Alexandre was out drinking with pre-war friends at a club where "women are not permitted") cleaning her bracelet. She'd sat in their bedroom and cleaned and polished every jangling charm. Crept down to the deserted dining room and stolen a glass of brandy (she knew where Madame hid the key) to clean the diamonds set in a little gold heart. Brandy made them gleam.

And here she was in Beaune at last.

The sun shone on the girl in her 1940s oh-so-English clothes and blonde hair. One or two men gave her the speculative look she was used to, but Paula wasn't interested. She was searching for a jeweller's shop. Ah, there was one.

As she went in, a bell rang.

A man appeared from a back office and gave her a pleased and respectful bow. His expression changed when she said she wished to sell something.

She took the bundle from her handbag. It was wrapped in a lace handkerchief. Paula undid the folds and spilled the bracelet on to the counter.

There it lay. It was her favourite piece of jewellery, she wore it all the time; Colette had said it was Paula's personal collection of scalps outside her Red Indian tent. "Another scalp" Paula had once shouted, returning to Oakwood Court with a gold anchor from Asprey's.

The bracelet was so crammed that it positively bulged. The shopman, with a "*Permettez*", picked it up and examined the richer of the baubles, a diamond-decorated heart, a Cross of Lorraine in 22 carat gold, Alexandre's wedding present, a bunch of cultured pearls from Flip . . . other things.

"It is interesting."

"I know. But what would you give me for it?"

"In the trade we call this a specialist object. I could not offer much, Madame."

"You could take some of the little things, the diamond, the pearls, and sell them separately."

"That is possible."

It was obvious that was what he was going to do.

They bargained. In the end he gave her what she knew was a disgraceful price. She had no choice but to accept.

She took the money and politely thanked him; one thing she'd picked up from her time in France was a certain formality. The man, carefully placing the bracelet in a small tissue-lined box, muttered, "*Plaisir*". Paula left the shop to a second jangle of bells.

Behind her, packed away until they made their new owner money, were the tributes of young men she had nearly forgotten. Men who had possessed her for a night or two, called her Honey or Babe, sometimes given her American dollars, "Buy yourself sump'n pretty". There was music somewhere in her bracelet, old dance tunes, laughter, such a lot of love-making. And some, though not all, of the hands which had cut off their uniform buttons for her, had been the hands of heroes.

Like a patient who wakes one morning to realise the illness, a possessing demon, has gone at last, Jill was herself again. She began to think about her future life. Like most young women when the war was over, she knew she couldn't simply go home. Independence mattered. So, curiously enough, did London. If she could find a reasonable job, she'd stay. Secretaries just then were in startlingly short supply, and the first job that came up, working for a solicitor in the Temple, was offered and accepted.

She telephoned her parents who were unsurprised and, if sorry, weren't going to say so. "Just make sure you come up to see us sometime," said her father, typically adding, "I'll send your fare."

Peter Whittaker, still with the RASC, solved the problem of where Jill would live – why not in her old digs with his mother in Markham Square? Jill was pleased and so, in her brief manner, was Clarissa who disliked Jill slightly less than her son's previous girlfriends. As Clarissa remarked to a bridge-playing friend, "At least she's quiet."

It was a summer of heatwaves. Hot, hot July. It was extraordinary for Jill to feel relaxed again. She enjoyed her Temple work, walked slowly homeward in the evenings to the Square in the breathless heat. She liked blessedly dull evenings, listening to the wireless, reading, preparing a solitary supper. Clarissa was often out. Jill was glad of that too.

One sunny Sunday morning Clarissa was away, having

been invited for the weekend to the country. "To some people I know." She never said their names and it amused Jill to think they all had titles.

She was alone in the shabby old house, reading Clarissa's *Sunday Times*, when the front door bell rang.

"It'll be for Clarissa, it always is," she thought, picking up a pad of paper and a pencil. She was meticulous about messages, an old Army habit.

There was an elegant figure in dark blue linen on the front step.

"*Roz!*"

"*Jill!*"

They both burst out laughing.

"I took you by surprise. I phoned two or three times, no luck, and took a chance today that you might be in – Peter Whittaker gave me the address, we met at one of those regimental parties in Paris . . ."

"Come in, come in, how terrific to see you."

Jill took her visitor upstairs to the drawing room, jumped up to say, "Coffee," and sat down again when Roz exclaimed, "Hey. Give me time to get my breath and take a look at you."

She leaned back and regarded Jill closely.

"You're better. I can see."

"Oh yes, yes."

"Peter said you were. I mean, I said you'd been under the weather and he was very nice and concerned and said you were quite recovered."

"Stupid, wasn't I?" Jill thought – all that heartbreak.

"Of course you weren't stupid. You'd had a blow. May I smoke? Oh good."

Roz lit a cigarette with the old neat flick of the lighter. Jill remembered the lighter too, battered and made of a sort of gunmetal.

After a moment's pause Roz said, "Did you get my letter?"

Jill was taken aback.

"No. When did you write?"

"Soon after you went back to England."

"Roz, I'm so sorry. I wish I'd received it. I ought to have written too, I did try, but the letter was so gloomy I tore it up."

"You didn't miss much with mine. Just a lot of regimental gossip. I was moved soon afterwards, we were sent to the South. It was sheer chance I met Peter recently in Paris, I nearly didn't go to the awful party but Dermot persuaded me. Jill, it is *very* good to see you. A different person."

"And you're just the same."

"Not sure that's a compliment."

Roz stayed to a scrappy lunch and they talked of their wartime life in France and the times and places they had shared. They wondered, in unison, what had happened to Philomène. "She'll have been plastered with De Gaulle decorations," said Roz. They talked of the RASC, recalled the Colonel, the Sergeant deputed to accompany them like a sheepdog. And came – at last – to the name they had avoided.

After lunch they went out into the courtyard garden at the back of the house and sat under thick shady trees. It was very quiet on Sundays.

Roz said, "Did you ever hear any more – about François? Does it upset you to talk about him? If so, forget I asked."

"No, it doesn't. And no, I never heard any more. Or wanted to, actually, Roz. Isn't it strange how you forget? I was so certain I never would."

"I thought the same. But we don't forget, Jill, what we do is heal. The scar is still there, but the skin of scars is thick."

And Roz lit another cigarette.

She said, smiling and changing the subject, "I'm glad I managed to track you down at last. It would have been nice if we could have met in London, wouldn't it? But the reason I risked today is because it's my last chance. I'm off to Ireland tomorrow. May not be back for months . . . even longer. No, no," she read Jill's face, "I haven't fallen for an Irish colleen. I've taken a job working for Dermot. You remember him?"

"Of course. Your friend who bought us lovely drinks in the canteen and made you laugh."

Jill added ruefully, "I was hopeless at getting his jokes, but he was very nice."

"He's very desperate," said Roz drily. "His father died and Dermot's inherited a dam' great house in County Clare, and land and horses and debts (of course) and God knows what else. I'm to be his agent. That means I shall run the place and Dermot will breed horses, a dream he's had since he was six years old. I shall take on everything else. We went over together last month. Fantastic Georgian house falling to pieces."

She spoke with relish.

"I've told him I'll work for him until he marries, (Dermot's pathetically susceptible). Then some brave young woman can take him on and I'll move back to London."

"And see me?"

"You'll be first on the list. Mind you, write if you move on from here. And maybe Dermot and I can tempt you to come over and stay in the crumbling ruin sometime? Here's the address."

Later Roz said she must go, "Haven't finished packing," and Jill walked with her down the King's Road to the Underground in Sloane Square. When they said goodbye Roz took both her hands.

"A joy to see you better."

"And a joy to see *you*," Jill was slightly shy. "Lots and lots of luck in Ireland."

"Sure and I'll be needing every scrap of it."

* * *

Not long after Roz's visit, Peter Whittaker came to London on a very short leave. When his mother, the evening he arrived, finally dragged herself away from her son's company and went to bed, Peter said to Jill that he wanted "a serious talk" with her. He sat her down facing him, poured her a drink, and said, "Darlingest? What are your plans?"

"Plans? I dunno. To squeeze a rise out of my solicitor boss, he's on the mean side. And get some new clothes."

She smiled easily. But why did she feel breathless?

He was silent for a long minute. Then, "I suppose you wouldn't consider marrying me?"

She couldn't help laughing as she threw her arms round him.

"Of course I will, you mad fool. Why haven't you asked me sooner?"

He did not say – because you used to be so sad. He didn't say a thing but held her and gave her – to Jill – a too chaste kiss.

They broke the news to Clarissa during breakfast. Jill was quite sorry for her future mother-in-law who pretended to be pleased. But Peter hugged his mother and said, "You'll have a daughter now!" and laughed at Clarissa saying, "You've messed up my hair." She brightened when Peter said, "Of course we can't marry just yet, there's a mile of work in the regiment and so many things to fix."

Jill went to Newcastle the following weekend with the news. Clement and Lucy were glad and relieved. It was the best news for their daughter since she had grown up.

"She's back to her old self," said Lucy, after they had seen her off on the London train, her lively face at the window, a wildly waving hand.

"She's certainly happy." Clement was thoughtful.

That summer in London was a time of reunions. Jill telephoned Colette – she had meant to do that for months.

"Jill! Yes, we're still here. The dogs. Me. And what's more a friend of yours is staying. Guess who? Paula!"

Remembering Paula's beauty and glamour, Jill took special trouble when she was dressing for dinner at Oakwood Court. A silky blue and black dress, lattice-work black suede shoes (they had been Lucy's). The best feature was a square-cut aquamarine engagement ring. A whopper. It had cost Peter far too much and Clarissa had not been all that enthusiastic, but Jill thought it the loveliest ring she had seen in her life.

It was fun returning to Oakwood Court, the greeting of the dogs surging round her as if she'd been there yesterday was as warm as Colette's hug. And there was glamorous Paula. Jill did not know that the re-made clothes were all created out of Bundles for Britain; to Jill, Paula was totally unchanged. If she was a little harder than the girl who had sat with her in the Hogarth, Jill did not notice.

But Colette noticed that neither of them spoke about the past. Paula didn't mention Alexandre except, when they first met, saying casually, "He's still in France. I'm over here for a bit." A bright blonde smile. Jill accepted this with the same vagueness and she in her turn said nothing about France or the last winter of war. All her talk was of Peter, wedding plans, her parents in Northumberland, her job. Things like that.

Inviting Jill round to supper or to Sunday lunch became a habit of Colette's again. She had the impression the girl had few London friends and Jill was frank about Peter Whittaker's mother. "She only knows people if they're called the Honourable Mrs Thing."

Colette liked to see the young women, enjoyed the sound of their voices and the almost (not quite) lively atmosphere. Colette thought, Paula is recovering too. Both young women were war casualties, in a way.

It was still hot, hot July and London sizzled. Every window of the flat was wide open but the breeze blowing through it was hot too. The trio sat with long glasses clinking with ice – Jill had brought some rum, Colette had added lime. When the telephone rang, Colette said, "It's almost too hot to get up," as the three dogs trotted out to answer it.

"Shall I go?" But Paula was not expecting a call, and had put up her feet on one of the sofas. She looked relaxed.

"No, no, I'll get it," sighed Colette, "I'll take my drink with me."

After she'd left the room, Jill and Paula were silent for a moment, they could hear Colette speaking in the hall. Her voice was suddenly so loud that Paula gave a comical look across the room to Jill and whispered, "What do you bet, it's her ex-husband. The first. She said he does turn up occasionally. When he does he gets on her nerves."

She listened openly.

"*Who* did you say?" Colette's voice was still loud; then, "I'm sorry, I can't exactly make out – could you spell it?"

A giggle from Paula.

"She's forgotten his name!"

Less interested, Jill swirled her drink round so that the ice knocked against the sides of the glass.

"Yes, I remember you," said Colette not very positively. There was a pause, then, "That's odd. Yes I do know where she is. As a matter of fact she's here this evening. Do you want to speak to her? Sorry, could you spell the name again – bloody hell, he's been cut off!"

She came back into the sitting room.

"A man asking for you, Jill. He rang French HQ which, of course, is closed. Found me in the book. His name's Ghilain, François Ghilain . . ."

Both she and Paula looked across at Jill. The girl had gone an extraordinary colour, a kind of greenish white. She rocked slightly, then collapsed on the floor in a dead faint.

* * *

"I don't get it," said Paula for the third time.

She was sitting in Colette's bedroom with the door shut. Jill, stammering something as Colette had helped her to her feet, had staggered out of the room and down the passage; they heard her being violently sick.

Colette hurried after her and took her into one of the bedrooms, slamming the door. Paula heard muffled voices, for what seemed a long time. At last Colette returned.

"Shock. I wanted her to have some tea but she said she'd be sick again."

"What's *happened?*"

"Come into my room."

Bemused, Paula followed her and sat down on the bed, exclaiming, "I don't get it. Is it some Frenchman she used to know?"

"Yes."

"*But why faint!*"

Paula had literally never seen anybody lose consciousness before. It was very dramatic. Colette hunched down in a chair.

"She was in love with him."

"Colette! That's – that's ridiculous. I mean, she's OK, isn't she? Getting married to that Whittaker guy. So what's with fainting all over the place about another man?"

"I told you. Shock."

Paula took it in.

"So she went to bed with him. And they split afterwards?"

"No. He was sent to France. Something about the secret service. Anyway, she didn't know where he was. That's why she got herself transferred to France."

"She thought she'd find out where he was or something?"

"Of course. But didn't. Later she was told he was dead."

Paula remembered the thud as Jill fell to the floor.

"So that was why . . ."

"She fainted. You can imagine. She was certain he was

dead. All that time when she used to come here, she mourned him. Remember how she looked? So haggard and unhappy?"

Paula sat trying to grasp the idea of somebody – say Flip Casey, say poor Freddy – coming back from the dead. The idea was out of the confines of her imagination. She gave up.

"How did he find *you*?"

"I don't know," Colette was impatient. "He did come here once or twice, everybody from HQ did. My name must have stayed in his head."

Paula began to study her long, dark red fingernails.

"I suppose he's in London?"

"No, he isn't, Paula, didn't you take it in? He's stuck in Dover."

"*Dover!*"

"Apparently his papers are dodgy. For the moment they've put him in a Detention Centre."

Paula did look up then. Her eyes were enormous.

"A prison! She *can't* trek off down there and see him."

"Wouldn't you?"

Silence fell. It was broken by the dogs who objected to being ignored and began to jostle annoyingly round their mistress.

"No. I wouldn't go," Paula said.

"She was in love."

Paula sighed. "Yeah, sure, but who wasn't? It was like that all the time. You know it was, Colette. Now she's engaged to a guy who sounds just right for her. Then suddenly this man turns up . . ."

"Whom she thought was dead."

Silence washed back. Burned-out passion, sorrow, the very war itself seemed to fill the room.

When Paula looked up again, Colette's expression hit her with such force that she burst out. "You think I'm tough. Yes, you do, but I'm not. She's OK now. That's done with, she's going to be married and . . ." relapsing into American "it's just fine. Of course she shouldn't go."

"Are you sure?"

"Colette, don't! All this talk is like the movies, real life isn't like that. Nor are Frenchmen."

"Like what?"

"Oh, you know. The way we thought they were. Look at what happened to me."

Later the telephone shrilled and Colette gave a start. She looked so anxious that Paula said, "I'll get it. Don't worry, Colette, it may be for me."

She went out into the passage – to come face to face with a ghost.

Impulsively she ran up to Jill, put her arms round her and kissed the ashen cheek. She couldn't think of a thing to say and was still holding her when Colette came up to them.

Colette took Jill's unresisting hand and led her into her bedroom – she could hear Paula's voice answering the telephone. "She's out right now. Can I take a message?"

Jill was silent. Colette shut the door and said quietly, "Shall I ring Mrs Whittaker? I could say you're staying here tonight."

"Would you?"

"Right away. Then you can go to bed. Would you like a sleeping pill? I've got some knockouts."

"I don't think so, thank you," said the polite child of despair.

Colette forced her to sit down, saying in a natural voice, "So. Shall you go to Dover?"

Jill let the question wait for a moment.

"He did say *Dover*, didn't he?"

"Yes. He'd just docked and there had been trouble with his papers, which was why they've taken him to the Detention Centre."

Jill nodded and said nothing. Ever since she'd spoken to him, Colette had been searching and searching through her memory to try and recapture François Ghilain. So many figures in French uniform, men standing at her front door with those beer bottles of Algerian wine, the smiling foreign faces, accented voices . . . faintly she half recalled François Ghilain; he'd been one of the self-possessed kind.

When Jill raised her eyes there was a heart's history in her look.

"I haven't told you what really happened."

"Why should you? It's often worse to tell."

"Yes. It is. I did love him. Horribly much. When I was in France we got sent to Bourg where my father had his hotel."

"I remember."

"It was there that I found out. François was shot by the Resistance. As a traitor."

"*My dear child.*"

"I've got over it now."

She certainly had not.

Colette waited for Jill to say more. Then half understood that Jill on her side, waited; she began to feel the need for common sense and said in a practical voice, "I'll ring Victoria and find out the time of trains."

She did not fully deserve the look of total gratitude that Jill gave her.

Twelve

François hadn't spoken English for two years and was surprised to find the language still in his head like a dog asleep from boredom. He woke it up and there it was, obliging and alert. He needed its company. The first thing he asked for was a cigarette. Which was given to him.

What he'd forgotten was the lethargy of the British, the painstaking way they filled in forms, asking the same question three times and writing as slowly as children learning their letters. As he watched, François knew he must not flash out at them. They had treated him from the start with heavy suspicion. He managed to keep cool and control his temper when they confiscated his passport. It was more difficult when he was marched off to a car and driven to this godforsaken little police station.

He was given a room (clean), allowed a bath (half cold) and a mug of tea (disgusting). Then locked up like a felon.

He sat by the barred window which overlooked a deserted street. I will never find her.

Displaced was the word for the world now. Masses of humans trudging stateless across Europe to be shepherded or herded by overworked officials. People lost. Grieving. Parents. Penniless. Sometimes starving.

François thought, I am displaced from choice.

The sight of the English cliffs when the ferry made its slow way into the harbour had given him a surge of painful joy. He longed for her. Optimism breathed on him. He was here. In Jill's little country. He stepped ashore light-footed. But not for long.

"Could we have a word, sir?"

Merde, thought François. And knew he'd underestimated them. Coming from the chaos of France, how could he have guessed?

There followed hours of frustration and Gallic astonishment at the lumbering slowness and adamant grip of English law. They Sir'd him now and then. Said they would make enquiries. They wrote down Jill's name and the address of French HQ. And politely locked him up in this place like a bedroom in some fifth-rate boarding home. A sergeant returned, after François's desperate request, with twenty Senior Service and a box of matches.

Smoking and sitting on the lumpy bed with his arms round his knees, François saw the hours limp by. The same sergeant, a big man with a red complexion and a wheezing voice, brought him a four-page English newspaper which François was too tense and yet too bored to read.

The man returned hours later with news.

"That address you gave us in London. Free French Headquarters in Kensington. Number unobtainable."

François stared.

"You mean there's no way of finding out if someone . . ."

The sergeant was sorry for him. Hell, he was sorry for the whole boiling of gimcrack foreigners washed up on Dover beach. Different in wartime. Heroes then.

"You're still allowed one phone call, Sir. But I have to tell you, London sustained a great deal of bomb damage. So . . ."

Do I ring the dead, thought François. Do I speak to a Jill blown to pieces two years ago? But the shock wore off fast, he was practised at that and he smoked four cigarettes while he searched his mind for a single remaining London name.

Later the sergeant reappeared.

"That second address you gave us in order. Occupant answered. You can step down to the office."

François did not notice that the sergeant stood close, ready if the prisoner made a dash for it.

He picked up the telephone.

"Madame Ducane? I 'ope you remember me . . ."

There followed an unsatisfactory conversation, the trouble with his name and the heart-stopping news that Jill was *there* . . . then the line went dead.

She's alive, he thought. He did not know why it scared him.

Leaving Victoria in the mid-morning, Jill spent the entire journey to Dover concentrating on nothing to do with François.

She couldn't bear to imagine what lay ahead. She bought the *Daily Mail* at the station and determined to read it right through. Nearly quarter of a million tulip bulbs had been given to Britain by the grateful Dutch; they were being planted in Kew to bloom next April. Queues of recently demobbed men (pictures of cheerful faces) waited overnight to leave Britain: the most popular choice – Australia. One indignant *Mail* story highlighted a new racket, charging people what was called key money for London flats. A pilot just out of the RAF was lucky enough to get a £2 a week room in Chelsea. Key money, £1,500.

Jill read on. She finished the newspaper and turned back to the beginning. Maybe she'd missed something. It wasn't until she took a taxi at Dover station that she faced up to what was unbelievable. The thought made her so ill that she stopped thinking about it and looked out of the taxi window at the sunny town and the shabby people.

The police station in a quiet side street faced a severe Wesleyan chapel. There was a sergeant on duty behind a polished counter. Jill said in what sounded to her own ears an unnecessarily loud voice, "My name is Sinclair. I rang your duty officer last night. About Monsieur Ghilain."

The sergeant nodded calmly. She thought – did I expect a dramatic start?

"I was told he is in your Detention Centre and it would be in order for me to see him, officer."

"Quite in order, Miss." The sergeant was actually the one dealing with François. "Would you sign here, please, and then come with me."

Jill did not read the form placed in front of her.

The Detention Centre was at the back of the station in a kind of annexe, a few rooms up and down a flight of stairs. Jill was left in what looked like a schoolroom except for the bars at the window. She couldn't stop swallowing nervously.

The door opened.

"Sorry to lock you in, Miss. Got to be done."

Somebody came into the room; at the same time the door behind him gave a loud click.

They both stood.

Jill stared with feverish intensity at the man who had owned her body and her imagination, whom she'd worshipped, slept with, grieved for, shamed over. What *he* saw was no longer the girl of two years before. She was altered from the sweet, lost lover on Victoria station. Older. Elegant in something yellow and a straw hat.

The shock was Jill's. His face was wasted, beneath the cheekbones were hollows which made his eyes look strangely large. His suit was old-fashioned and creased as if it had dried after a storm of rain. A healed scar of shiny silver tissue stretched across one cheek.

She forgot everything else.

"You've been wounded!"

He put his hand up automatically.

"I was in a fire."

Then, with curiosity, "Were you really with Colette Ducane last night?"

"When you rang. Yes."

"I tried to get hold of the Kensington HQ."

"They closed some months ago."

"I see."

But he didn't and neither did she.

They sat down on chairs like those in school. She heard the awful social politeness in her own voice.

"I'm sorry you're stuck here. Will it be long?"

He searched her face, half frowning and said in a voice of infinite sadness, "Oh, Jill."

She wished she could cry. At being here with this man from whom she'd fiercely cut herself free.

"François."

"*Coquine?*"

She flinched.

"Don't call me that."

"No. It is not true any more. Tell me. Did you think I was dead?"

"Yes. They told me in Lyon."

He looked for a moment astonished.

"What in 'ell were you doing there?"

"I was with the RASC."

He made a grimace she remembered.

"But why *there*?"

She was sure he guessed why she'd gone to France, wanted her to say it. She wouldn't. François felt for a packet of cigarettes, automatically offering her one, was refused and lit a cigarette. With one arm clasping his shoulders he smoked in silence.

Oh, why did I come, thought Jill. It was better when you were dead. I've made a new life. I've learned to forget what you did. But I did love you. I loved you so.

She caught his probing look through the smoke.

"You've changed, *coquine*."

"*You* didn't."

"What does that mean?"

"You stayed the same. You betrayed us."

He did not even blink but looked at her calmly. She was horrified at herself.

"Us?" he repeated. "Do you mean you?"

Jill said recklessly, "I mean the people who fought and died to free France. You betrayed them all."

"*Ça alors*."

"Yes. *Ça*!"

"*Dieu*, Jill, how can you be so naive? The Allies fought for themselves."

She wanted to put her hands over her ears. She burst out, "I won't listen to you making brave things hateful. You came here to spy. You worked for Pétain."

He gave a graveyard grin.

"Pétain. Poor doddering old man."

"I must go. I should never have come." She didn't move.

"Ah. But you owe me that."

"What can I possibly owe *you*?"

"I came here because of you. I am in this absurd place because of you. A wasted journey, mm?"

She felt like dying. He was the same and not the same. His voice, with those intonations which turned English into French, his manner never treating her quite seriously, a look of certainty, a mockery, were still somewhere in this composed, damaged man. How do you rise from the dead unless you are Jesus Christ?

"I see your love is gone, *coquine*. Poor thing, did you cut its throat? What is that ring on your finger?"

She looked down; the aquamarine seemed twice its size.

"I am engaged to be married."

"Why did I not think of that? Of course you are. And what does the engaged man think of you coming to see a criminal?"

She said, looking away, that he didn't know.

François leaned back in his chair and pulled another one towards him. It shuddered across the splintered floor. He put his feet up. She saw the heels of his shoes.

"Listen for a moment. And stop looking at me in that way, so sad, so accusing. Would it be better if I told you the whole melodrama? It is stale now. There are hundreds, maybe thousands of Resistants who do not think that about their own stories. I do. Don't look at the floor, look at me."

Jill, not wanting to, obeyed.

"The English make good spies," he said. "They know so much. They knew everything about my stupid father. *Lâche. Lâche*. Dead now. They wanted information and decided that I was the one to get it for them. Vichy had begun to crack, my connections at Bourg could be useful and so on. They sent me on a course which was like a *roman policier*. Then I was dropped near Bourg with my pianist."

"Your *what?*"

He smiled slightly. "You don't know the word? It is the name the SOE gave their secret radio operators. Mine was Philippe. *Brave homme*. 'Igh-minded, is that the English word? We did much useful work. But then the invasion, the Germans started to retreat and the Milice were mad with fear, up to their necks in blood. My poor Philippe was murdered and I . . ." he paused and said with a different kind of smile, "I was taken to one of their Resistant courts."

He put out his cigarette in an old, cracked saucer on the table.

"You don't believe any of this, do you?"

Her body longed to, but common sense reminded her what Philomène had said. People in danger stole other lives, other proofs to clear themselves. What he was telling her could have happened to many other Frenchmen.

"I don't know. I don't know," she said, struck and stammering.

Just then he showed the first real emotion since she had come into the room. He widened his enormous eyes.

"Almighty Christ, have I come here for this? To be stuck in this foolish English prison and told I'm lying *by you.* The Resistants knew I worked for the Germans. Of course I did for God's sake. The whole plan was secrecy." He spoke as if to a child. "Secrecy is a poison. Without Philippe who could prove me innocent? The Milice strangled my poor friend. When the Resistants found him they did not discover his secret radio. Maybe they did not bother. So. I was tried."

"They found you guilty. Captain de la Roche told me."

His face changed again. He looked at her very curiously.

"The judge? How did you see my judge? I understand nothing of this."

"I told you. I was in the Army in Lyon."

I'll never tell you why, never, she thought.

"You should not have gone to France. Better in London."

There was a pause. then, "He said you'd been . . ."

"Executed? Oh yes, they believed it."

"How did you escape?"

She thought, he's going to tell me another melodrama and how shall I know what's true and what's fake? In her head she repeated with a trembling sigh the words he used to her. Oh, François.

He said in a low detached voice, as if thinking aloud, "I didn't escape, Jill. There was another prisoner, a German doctor, Dettmar. They condemned us both and we were driven into the woods to be shot. The Milice saw the car and gave chase. That was our good fortune. They and our captors drove like devils out of hell, the forest was swimming in mud and slush, the cars collided and caught fire. Dettmar and I were thrown out. I was burned."

She listened in misery.

"Dettmar nursed me like a mother. He knew about burns, he is a brilliant doctor. The good Nazi," he added with a strange smile. "After weeks, months, and much much trouble, we got to Spain. And I, yesterday, to England."

He saw that she had begun to cry.

He put out his hand and touched hers for the first time.

A look of desire was in his face.

"Oh, François. Oh, François."

"*Ma pauvre.*"

He regarded her with pity. He still held her hand and when she took it away did not resist.

"Poor love. Poor Jill. All those people who taught you their simplicities. Fight the good fight, mm? As if there is anything good about the struggle. It is debasing and debased. You don't know where you are now, do you? Or what you believe."

She couldn't answer.

"So," he said, in almost the old teasing voice, "you are to be married. To an Englishman of course. *Allons-y.* And I must get back to Bourg."

"To Bourg!"

"Indeed. When your people get some sense into their heads, or somebody of higher rank than a sergeant in a Dover police station takes charge, I will go back. They will be glad of that. And there are many things in Bourg to settle, including men who will be sorry to see me again. Don't be sad, *coquine.*"

There was a noise, it seemed deafening, of a door unlocking and the sergeant's not unkind face looked in. "Sorry, Miss. Can't let you stay any longer. Sorry."

He disappeared, this time leaving the door unlocked. They stood up. She searched in her bag for a handkerchief.

"I'm such a fool."

"You are not a fool. You're instinctive and beautiful and *toute brouillée*. I don't blame you for thinking me a traitor. What a word. Already it sounds a hundred years old. It is I who am the fool."

"For coming to England."

"For loving you, I daresay. For not being the good French realist. Go back to that fiancé of yours. Be happy."

"Don't! Please don't!"

"*Ça alors*," he said and laughed a little.

Thirteen

Jill was gone next morning when Paula appeared for breakfast.

"*What happened*?"

"She's gone to Dover."

"I wish she hadn't," said Paula with feeling.

"Nobody could have stopped her." The two women, one worn and thin with her *Moulin Rouge* fringe, the other an odd beauty no longer touched by illusion, looked at each other. Colette made strong tea.

When she left with the dogs, Paula was relieved to be alone. She felt disturbed. She didn't *want* to be miserable about Jill. Heartache, heartbreak, frightened her. She was glad when the telephone rang.

"Kensington 6058."

"Paula? Is that you?"

"Hello, Mum."

Paula fidgeted, waiting for the unwelcome suggestion that she should go to Oxford. I know I'm horrible, I can't help it, she thought. Mum's OK, but when we talk she only tells me it's my duty to go back to Alexandre. What does she know about anything?

"I'm so glad you're in. Since you got that job I never know when I can ring."

"Afternoons and evenings, Mum. What is it?"

Hell, that sounds sharp she thought. I really must be nice. I am nice. Aren't I?

"Well, dear, the fact is you'll have to come to Oxford as soon as you can arrange it. Will your employer give you time off?"

Worse and worse.

"Mum," patiently, "I can't just ask for time off. What's the matter? Are you ill?"

She doesn't sound ill.

"Ill? Of course not, dear. It's the solicitor, Mr Clachan. He says there's a paper to sign . . ."

Paula felt a thrill of fear but her head sternly told her not to be an idiot. The name Clachan rang a bell. Hadn't Freddy, in the past which she never thought about and sometimes believed hadn't happened, mentioned him?

"Mr Banks has passed on, Paula."

And out it came. Freddy's father, the at-the-time hated wealthy businessman who had tried to stop Freddy from marrying her, had died suddenly of a heart attack. "Such a shock," went on Mrs Cox (who'd never liked him). Mr Clachan had telephoned to say it was most important Paula should come to his office.

"What on earth for, Mum?"

"He wouldn't say exactly. Something to do with poor Freddy."

Paula's mother never spoke of him without the preliminary adjective. She almost ran it into one word. Poor-Freddy.

"You'd best ring him, dear, very insistent he was and I don't want him to think I haven't been in touch with you."

"He could've rung me himself."

"He particularly said it would be best if I spoke. As your mother."

Paula was perplexed. But considerably brighter, now it didn't look as if she'd have to go to Oxford only to see her mother who (Paula's phrase to herself) was "perfectly OK".

Mr Clachan was a new element. She agreed to come the following day, rang her boss, a snappish woman whose temper, as business did not improve, grew worse and wrung out her permission to be away for the day. The Oxford train, Paula knew, would get her back by early evening.

Then she telephoned the number her mother had given her.

A secretary answered.

"Ah. Mrs Banks."

Paula let that go.

"Mr Clachan will speak to you," said the girl with a touch of reverence. "I'll put you through."

A voice Paula instantly put a face to, a sonorous yet prissy vowel-picking voice, answered.

"Ah, Mrs Banks." Secretary and boss were a double act.

"I am the Comtesse l'Accombe de la Vallière, actually, Mr Clachan. Did you want me?"

The weeping widow of 1944, the tear-smudged seventeen-year-old, was avenged.

Mr Clachan was taken aback.

He rallied.

"Ah. Yes. There is a matter we need to discuss with you, Countess . . . hm . . . I'm afraid it will be necessary for you to visit this office. If you could inform me of the day. Next week, perhaps?"

"Tomorrow would be fine."

For a dignified moment he debated whether or not to accept the woman's sudden offer.

Grudgingly, with a number of "rearrangements to my schedule," he agreed to see her the following afternoon.

When Paula returned from work that evening she duly enquired after Jill, and Colette, whose good temper had returned, answered that she'd heard nothing.

"She'll ring in her own good time, poor lass."

No more was said and Paula, bursting with her own news,

told her about the solicitor's call. Colette chuckled.

"Sounds as if you've been left some money."

"Come off it! I told you those Bankses are as mean as muck. I can guess just what this is – poor Freddy's gold cigarette case."

"Surely they gave that to you when he was killed?"

"Not them. I got nothing. They wouldn't even let me call at their beastly house."

Colette thought it no wonder that this sexy vision, with her dyed hair and flawless face, had two sets of in-laws who loathed her.

"The case would be nice," said Paula. Neither of them said, but both thought, and if it's real gold it'll fetch a good price.

Paula's journey to Oxford was as bad as any during the war. The compartment was gritty under Paula's American wedge shoes. The train was packed and all the passengers except Paula produced greasy packets of food which they shared or exchanged – camaraderie still existed. The train stopped now and then without reason in a countryside drenched in hot sunshine.

Paula looked at the passing cows and sheep and thought of vineyards and the little crooked shrub-things you'd never imagine would produce a leaf, let alone grapes. During their first week in Burgundy Alexandre had taken her on a muddy tour.

Oxford at last.

Her mother had arranged to meet her in a tea shop she and Paula used to visit years back. There it was – Sally's. Unchanged, with dishes of cakes in the window. But, as Paula pushed open the glass front door she saw with amusement they were made of china. Little china cakes, pink, yellow and chocolate colour.

Her mother was at a table by the wall, gesturing and smiling.

Paula hurried over to kiss her. It was well over a year since she'd seen her, but Mrs Cox's welcome was un-reproachful. The little woman beamed, noting as she'd always done how people stared at her daughter. Paula thought her mother older and crossly dismissed guilt from her thoughts, as she gave her a scented kiss.

"It's been ages," they chorused.

Paula's appointment at the solicitor's ("I chose Sally's because Mr Clachan's office is round the corner") was at four and there was time for tea and for her mother to repeat everything she'd said on the telephone, to interrupt herself with local stories of people Paula did not know, and to ask Paula whether she was thinking of a divorce.

The question took the girl by surprise.

"Not sure. Haven't thought about it."

"But you must. Has Alex mentioned it?"

Mrs Cox always called him that.

"Alexandre's written twice. He wants me back."

"Then why not?"

"Mum, it's no go. I can't."

"Best find out about divorce then."

Mrs Cox fidgeted with her gloves and said, looking at her, "You'll be sure to marry again."

She laughed when Paula laughed, but did not think it funny. When tea was over Paula looked at the clock on the wall and said she must go. "No, Mum, I'll pay. Wage earner now, aren't I? See you soon. Got to dash for my train after I've faced Clachan in his den, but I'll ring tonight. Promise."

She kissed her, left too much money for the small bill and darted out.

"That's my daughter," said Mrs Cox to the waitress.

The Clachan office was in one of Oxford's cobbled alleyways, a narrow entrance up narrow stairs into a suite of rooms unchanged from the 1920s. The secretary who worked a small switchboard sprang up to usher Paula into an office, which was the biggest room in the place.

Clachan rose as she came into the room.

The solicitor was enormously tall, six foot three, broad of shoulder and long of arm. He would have looked good on a stage. He had a long pale face, thin hair, rimless spectacles. He went in for sweeping gestures with his impressive arms.

"Good afternoon, Countess. That is the correct way of addressing you, I believe?"

The hearty laugh was received by Paula with a blank stare.

"Yes. I am a countess. How do you do, Mr Clachan."

"We've met before, met before. Please be seated."

He pulled a chair up for her and waited, stooping from his height, for her to settle.

Then returned to his desk.

While he looked through his papers, she regarded him coldly. If it is poor Freddy's cigarette case, he could easily bring it out from a desk drawer and plonk it on the table. Why the palaver? Because it makes him feel important. That pathetic secretary. How can she stick him?

"You are the widow of Rating Frederick Silverton Banks, is that right? Married 29 June 1942."

Paula nodded and pulled a lock of hair straight. She had returned to wearing it down, having seen a film recently starring a girl called Hayworth.

Clachan put down the documents.

"You have heard from your mother, of course, that your father-in-law is recently deceased?"

"Yes."

She did not bother to sound respectful or say she was sorry. She'd thought poor Freddy's father a rich old toad. What was different because he was dead?

"It seems," said Clachan, meaning "it is", "there is a matter of inheritance."

Big deal, thought Paula, that's a big word for a little thing.

"You mean my first husband's gold cigarette case?"

Clachan could not have been more astounded if the carpet had reared up and spoken to him in a muffled voice. I am the carpet. Stop treading on me. Pay attention.

"Mrs . . ."

"Countess."

"I beg your pardon, Countess. What is this about a cigarette case?"

"Mister Clachan. My husband had a gold cigarette case, a nice one, rather large and old and his parents told him he mustn't take it when he was posted to Scotland. It belonged to Freddy's grandfather. You opened it . . ." said Paula, as she remembered, "by sliding it sideways. Mr Banks kept the case after Freddy died. I gather you will now return it to me."

The man on the other side of the desk recovered his composure. He gave a smile which even Paula, looking forward to a case she could turn into ready money, saw was patronising. She thought – hell – I'm not going to get it.

"Countess, certainly your late husband's cigarette case will be among various possessions (at present at the Banks residence in the Banbury Road) which will soon be in your possession. The family wish it. However, this is not a matter I am here to discuss with you, it is a bequest from your late husband's godmother, a Mrs Elizabeth Ludgate. Curiously enough, she died within a week of your late father-in-law. And left you, her godson's widow, the beneficiary of – let me see . . ." consulting his papers, "twenty thousand pounds."

Describing the story both to her mother and later to Colette, Paula said, "I nearly fell right off the chair."

Signing her name with a flourish half a dozen times, she scarcely listened to Clachan who, in command again, droned on about the money and when she would get it and added that all her late husbands "goods" would be insured and registered and delivered to the London address she gave.

In answer to her question, Clachan informed her that it would not be necessary for her to visit the Bankses' home. He did not say that the stout and beady widow of the late Mr Banks had told him she "didn't want to set her eyes on that baggage". Clachan presented the fact as if he had pulled off a coup.

The Countess, whose title had become a third presence in the room, said goodbye.

Money. Sitting in the train, and later travelling back to Oakwood Court by taxi (the bus not to be considered) Paula felt drunk. She stared at the figure Clachan had named. A sensation of triumph came to her as if she'd achieved some near-impossible goal, as if she had won by courage, even by genius. I always knew I'd make it, she thought. She was deafened by the sound of falling coins.

When she let herself into the flat, she heard Colette's voice. Shaggy Bob and the small white Sealyham both rushed out to welcome her, but Paula was in no mood for dogs and waded through them.

Colette was standing at the telephone, raised her hand to greet Paula and went on speaking.

"Poor Jill. Yes, I do understand. You will let me know what happens, won't you. And try to get a good night's sleep."

The sort of thing we always say, thought Paula, when you're miserable, when you're in some awful mess. How can you *try*?

When Colette rang off, Paula followed her, clip-clopping on her high wedge shoes into the sitting-room. Colette was thoughtful.

"As you may have gathered, she saw him. It sounds as if it was all pretty painful."

"I guess it was. That'll be it, I suppose?"

Something in Paula's voice, perfectly practical about sorrow, her own and other people's, made Colette smile.

"Shall we have a drink? I definitely need one."

"Good idea."

Paula came back with the remains of the rum they'd drunk the day before. She poured out two glasses. The two exchanged amiable looks.

"I've got some news!" said Paula.

When Colette was in bed that night, she lay for a long time wide awake, thinking about the two girls. Would Jill decline into that wreck she used to be? She found herself cruelly wishing the Frenchman had never returned, so to speak, from the grave. When she asked if François Ghilain had explained what had happened to him. Jill's voice had been ragged.

"Yes, he did. But how can I believe him?"

What a tangle. She thought of the French Fiasco, the down-at-heel girl in the third-class compartment, Paula's bitter return. Such a frivolous fashionable creature she used to be. And full of hope. Well, thought Colette, we all were, but maybe Paula most of all because she knew her power. Beauty had given it to her. She'd married Alexandre serenely sure of her future and set off for France believing in it. A château. A title. The ordered acres of vineyards. A future etched on an old-fashioned wine label. The sense of being conned and a hatred of her in-laws had done their worst.

Now an heiress was asleep down the corridor – out of nowhere she had money. Power was back with a vengeance.

Fourteen

"Is that the Countess I'Accombe?"

The solicitor on the telephone used the title with a flourish.

Paula, standing in the hall at Oakwood Court and until that moment in a mood to match the fine weather, had a thrill of alarm.

"Hello, Mr Clachan."

Was he going to say the money, or part of it, was not hers after all?

"Good morning, Countess, and how are you?"

Oh get on with it, thought Paula in agony. Something's happened.

"Is anything the matter, Mr Clachan?"

She felt as if a tight elastic band was round her heart.

"No, no, everything is in order."

Zing went the band, released.

Mr Clachan went on to explain that "the lady who was your mother-in-law before your second marriage, that is Mrs Banks" had decided to leave Broadoaks, the family home in the Banbury Road.

"I remember it, Mr Clachan."

Hearty laugh. "Of course you do. Maybe had your wedding reception there? Old history now, eh?"

Paula had inherited from her mother a suspicion of officials, specially those who made jokes.

"Yes?" she said, in a voice which told him she was waiting for him to come to the point.

Clachan hastened to do so. It seemed Mrs Banks would be glad if Paula could "call round to Broadoaks" some time soon.

"Why?" Paula was still suspicious.

"Only a small matter. Small matter. There are one or two items connected with your first husband, nothing of value (those will be registered to you in due course). But Mrs Banks feels there may be something else you would prefer to keep. Could you manage to come to Oxford, Countess?"

He'd grown attached to the title.

The idea of swanning into Broadoaks took Paula's fancy just then. She had always been afraid of the overblown house; it smelled of the condescension, the dislike she'd met in the faces of Freddy's relations. She and her mother didn't know a soul who was even reasonably well off and the Bankses were filthy rich. Mrs Cox and Paula hadn't known academics either, why would they? Nobody but neighbours and Paula's pals from school.

In her sudden way she said she'd come tomorrow. Good, good, said the solicitor, chalking up the time spent, to be put on Mrs Banks's mounting bill.

Paula took a first-class ticket. Before the train started she sat looking at the shifting crowds on the platforms. Few uniforms now. She noticed a huge bronze sculpture, a soldier in a great-coat, old-fashioned tin helmet pushed back, long knitted scarf, reading a letter. Doesn't look a bit like the boys I remember, she thought. The train drew out from the platform, passing the immobile figure eternally reading his letter from home.

At Oxford she walked up to a waiting taxi, said she wanted to be driven to the Banbury Road, and would he wait for her.

"Not sure I can do that, Miss. Needed at the station."

"Suppose I say I'll double your fare."

How could he resist?

With the new sensation of winning, Paula climbed into the taxi. The journey was not long and he soon slowed down at the open gate of Broadoaks. There was the house, set back among flower beds and lawns.

The driver opened the car door for her, but did not betray his private satisfaction as he said, "See you later." When Paula left him, he reached for his folded copy of the *Oxford Mail*.

The sun shone down on a house which now did not look so large. Pink roses smothered the front and drooped over the porch. The leaded windows which Paula had once thought so artistic were small and dark, although the entire front of the house was nothing but a line of windows.

She rang the bell. The door was opened, not by a maid, the Bankses always had at least two, but by Mrs Banks herself.

"Oh. It's you. Come in."

Paula said a bland good morning to her old enemy. Leah Banks had always been fat, bonny and fat, now she lumbered like an elephant. Her expensive clothes were of the kind called Matronly, to allow space for her hips, bottom and huge shapeless bosom. Paula saw with faint interest that she wore that dated accessory, a rope of pearls.

She made her slow way ahead of Paula into the drawing-room. Paula had only been in the room twice when the family had been away. She and Freddy had sat on the floor and cuddled and drunk his father's gin. Glancing round the lattice-windowed darkish room, it looked exactly the same as when she and Freddy had crept in here. Grand piano with the usual photographs, all old. Awful paintings in gold frames. Bulky Chinese vases on black stands and Persian rugs which slipped on the parquet. Mrs Banks's Pekingese, surely it couldn't be the same one, came in, feathery tail erect as he slithered on the floor.

"Sit down. Coffee's coming," said Mrs Banks.

Her once mother-in-law did not look too cheerful but brightened up when a young woman, presumably a maid but not an apron in sight, came in with a tray.

"That will be all, Cissy."

Neither presumed-maid or mistress thanked each other.

While Paula drank her coffee, Leah Banks unbent as far as to ask what the journey had been like.

"The trains are always late. Did you get the bus from the station all right?"

"I came by cab. He's waiting. Mr Clachan said he didn't think this would take long."

She wondered why this shapeless lump of late middle-age had bothered to send for her. And why did she ask me about a bus. Had she forgotten my money?

Oh no she hadn't.

"Quite a windfall you had, didn't you?" said Leah Banks. "A sizeable bit. Surprise to us in the family, never guessed she was so comfortable. Always a fool over Freddy." A sigh. "Nice for you," she astoundingly added and drank her coffee to give her strength.

As with Mr Clachan, Paula somehow indicated that she was waiting for her hostess to come to the point. Her silence was unmistakable as she crossed her beautiful legs.

Leah Banks stood up, wincing at the effort, and went slowly, in shoes that looked too tight, across to the piano. She picked up an office folder and came back.

"We thought you might like to take a look at these. Well. Keep them if you want. I've got albums full."

She placed the file on Paula's lap, said she'd just pop into the kitchen and left the room.

Paula opened the folder. And there, on the top of a pile of photographs, was one of Freddy she had never seen. He wore his matelot's uniform, tight jacket, big blue and white collar, stupid little cap on one side of his head. He grinned mischievously. There were many other photographs in the file. School groups with Freddy putting on a respectful face. Freddy playing school cricket, garden cricket. Freddy on the loggia of the house, bending down to lace his plimsolls.

She leafed through them. And then came back to the large picture of him in sailor's uniform.

She had such a pain in her heart.

Oh, she remembered him sharply just then. She heard his voice. "Poppet," he always called her. "Poppet, you're so lovely. Give me another of those special kisses." "Poppet, let me look at you. Come here."

The voice was quite real and so was he. All the fun we had, she thought. Jokes. Lovemaking. Her big mascara eyes brimmed.

When Leah Banks lumbered back, Paula gave her a smile and said it was good of her to spare the pictures, could she keep them all? Mrs Banks looked quite pleased.

"Good. I'll fetch an envelope. Expect there'll be one in Harold's old desk."

She came to the door to see Paula off, catching sight at the end of the drive of the extravagantly waiting taxi.

"Well. Goodbye, Paula. Glad you like the photos."

"Oh I do."

Leah half turned and looked up at the roses.

"Take a few to London, why don't you?"

She went to fetch some scissors.

All the way home in the train, frail petals fell round Paula's feet on the floor of the carriage.

The next morning dawned hot and still and Paula was up and about early. Very brisk.

"Going to give in your notice at the shop?" Misery never

stayed long with Colette and Paula's fortune had begun to amuse her.

"Sure. This morning. She won't be too pleased, I was very good at selling."

"Of course you were."

"Colette, the thing is that I must see my lawyer. And start the divorce."

Colette, sitting down in her favourite seat at the kitchen table, made a face.

"Isn't that a bit sudden? After all, now you can afford it you and Alexandre might make a success of that remaining vineyard, mightn't you? You're so quick at learning, Paula. Look at your French. You could have rather fun, I should have said, a whole new life and a challenge . . . you could turn up your nose at the dreary in-laws."

As she talked, Colette was busy mixing handfuls of dog biscuits hammered small into some sinister grey mince she had coaxed from the butcher. Bob, Bill and Binker sat at her feet like statues.

"Don't you think, Paula, it would be a good idea if you went to France for a few days?"

"What for?"

"To see Alexandre, of course."

"Why?"

"Have a heart, woman. He is your husband. You can't get that divorce you keep talking about by post."

"Yes you can." Paula had acquired her own solicitor, the first she'd had in her life. Smooth. Fiftyish. Good looking. Office in Cavendish Square. She liked to quote him, "Mr Ransome says it takes time but it can all be done by post. I'm prepared to wait."

"Bugger Mr Ransome. What's he? A solicitor wanting to make a buck. Have a heart."

She pushed her fringe out of her eyes.

Paula, in a white cotton off-the-shoulder blouse, was perched on the kitchen table clasping her legs. It was uncanny how the way the girl sat, walked, repeated images of glamour.

Colette bent down and placed three bowls carefully apart. Then stood watching. Bill was a thief and ate fast.

Paula worried her. Did unexpected money have to bring out the worst in people? She loved the girl. She wished for the umpteenth time that Paula's mother was not a twittering fool – it was impossible to have a sensible conversation with the woman. And God knew what had happened to Jill since that telephone call.

"No. Bill, lay off and don't be a pest."

She caught hold of the thief's collar. He reared up, but then surrendered and stood fixing Binker's half-full bowl with burning brown eyes.

"You haven't answered about Alexandre. You waved his letter at me yesterday but you never said what was in it."

"He wants me back."

"And?"

"What do you think?"

Binker had finally finished his dinner and began to lick the empty bowl, pushing it about with his nose. Colette released Bill who dashed over uselessly to join in.

"Listen, Paula. Pay attention. Since you ask, I will tell you what I think. You loved that man when you married him. Don't bother to invent some cock and bull story about being sorry for the guy, I can see that's coming and it's rubbish. You were as in love with him as he was, doubtless still is, with you. Your marriage was a war casualty. But so is he. You've suddenly got a lot of money which I might point out you haven't earned, or deserved come to that. It's only come to you because that poor kid Freddy had wealthy connections. You've had a stroke of luck that happens once in a lifetime. It doesn't mean it's

OK to behave like a dog to Alexandre. Badly put. Dogs behave rather well."

Paula scowled and used a phrase Colette had heard before.

"I don't get it. Why should I pander to a man who told me a pack of lies?"

"Because he's a child. Because while the war was on he started to believe that stuff. He was an exile without a bean, fighting for his country which crawled with the enemy. And I bet he believed when he married you that you were strong enough to see his parents off. He thought you were wonderful. Once he said to me "*c'est une femme remarquable*."

She looked at Paula for a moment.

"You don't love him, do you?"

Paula shook her head, the bright hair swung.

"What are you saying, Colette? You can't imagine I'd go back to that hellhole."

"I am saying you've got to see him face to face. At least break the news kindly."

"I refuse to set foot in Passy again."

"Oh, have some sense. Spend some of that money. You remember the BBC man who came for a drink last week?"

Colette had tenuous connections with Broadcasting House.

"Yeah," said Paula absently.

"He's just back from Paris. He says it's fun. Shabby, of course, but never bombed and definitely more fun than here. People give big parties and some of the best restaurants are packed. Of course there's still fake coffee and the girls still wear shoes with wooden soles."

"I don't know anybody in Paris." Paula's voice had changed.

"With your money? Everything would be different. Gorgeous clothes to buy, Chanel or Heim, you'll only have to ask around. Some of the hotels are very smart, because of the Americans. Stay at the Crillon. That's where I spent my first honeymoon. Meet Alexandre in Paris."

Silence.

Paula spoke at last.

"But how could Alexandre possibly afford a ticket to Paris?" And then, before Colette could reply, "I suppose I could send him the fare."

Fifteen

"Colette, can I see you?"

"Of course. When? Now?"

Colette had been waiting for that call and just that tone of voice. She felt part of the French story. Of Paula's. Of Jill's. The girl had rung on returning from Dover but only to tell her she was going back to Markham Square and would be in touch.

So Colette had waited. Now here it was.

When she arrived, Jill did not seem any better than two days before after she'd recovered from a dead faint. She tried to smile but the attempt was a failure and Colette's heart sank. In the sitting-room the sunbeams slanting through the high windows were shrivelling the furniture. Colette vaguely noticed a square of inlay curling up on a table which stood right in the glare.

She didn't bother to move it into the shade.

They sat down and Colette lit a cigarette, lifting her eyebrows in a question.

Jill said, "You did say you wanted to know what happened."

"Indeed. You saw François?"

"At the Detention Centre."

"How was he?"

How pinched and pale *you* look, Colette thought. Both of you, I suppose.

"So thin. And a big scar across his face, he was in a fire. That was when he and a German both escaped."

Colette nodded as if the idea was ordinary enough. Jill appeared to be suffering from a traumatic shock worse than two days ago. Because the Frenchman had risen from the dead? But what about poor Peter Whittaker? Colette had never met Jill's fiancé, he was still in France with his regiment, but he had come into Jill's conversation a great deal. Like a promise.

"François said he's innocent. Said he was working for the secret service. He told me how he escaped. You can imagine. One of those far-fetched stories you read in the newspapers."

"Sometimes they are true."

"Oh, I know." She was not listening.

"Jill," Colette spoke her name severely. "You sound as if you don't believe what Ghilain told you."

"I don't. Oh God, I don't know."

"Do you want to?"

"Yes. No."

Colette said nothing and Jill burst out, "There's Peter."

Ah, thought Colette, looking fixedly at the poor damaged girl sitting opposite her. Jill sat, turning her engagement ring round and round on her finger. It was badly balanced and the great square jewel kept slipping to the inside of her hand.

"You'll never settle until you find out for sure if François Ghilain is speaking the truth," Colette said, thinking – she's afraid that it's all lies. Yet, wouldn't it be simpler if that's what she's dealing with?

"Who could possibly tell me?" said Jill, still looking down at her ring.

Colette said patiently.

"Use your nut. Didn't you tell me the other night some odd story about going to a house round here with François during the war. M15 stuff."

"I've thought of that."

"And?"

"And I did go there. Ages ago when the war was still on and before I got sent to France. I thought I might see that man, whoever he was. Ask about François or something. I walked round to the house. It was all shut up."

"Why not try again?" said Colette.

Jill walked slowly down Wright's Lane passing a man selling flowers from a barrow. Red and yellow roses. In the square where the Armenian church still stood – the bombs had spared it – the traffic diminished. The day was sunny, dusty. At the bottom of the street she turned right.

She knew the house at once. Early Victorian, differing from its neighbours by two cherry trees growing in the front garden. When she had been taken there by the Free French driver the trees had been bare. Now they were in full leaf.

She rang the bell.

Nobody answered. Despite the thick curtains and a look of occupancy in a city where many dwellings were deserted, Jill was unsurprised. Why should she imagine the same people lived here? She was about to turn away when the door opened.

She knew the woman at once. Her dark hair was coiled in a chignon, she was as conventional as Peter's mother but far more handsome. And had a calm presence.

"Yes?"

Jill was speechless and the woman said in a relaxed voice, "Is it my husband you have come to see?"

Jill murmured something and the woman smiled.

"We can't talk on the doorstep. Do come in."

Jill recognised the interior of the house. The curved staircase in the distance. Hooks on which were hung raincoats and tweed caps. A sprout of walking sticks. A gilt mirror. There was an open door on the left leading to a drawing-room overlooking the street. The very room.

"You want a word with my husband?"

"Could I? I did come here once before. Please forgive me for bothering you. My name is Sinclair."

"And I am Mary Ward. My husband is John Ward. I expect when you came here last time he didn't tell you who he was. It was like that then. There are still a lot of people who need to see him. Do sit down, Miss Sinclair. I'll get him. Can I offer you some tea?"

Colette had done that twenty minutes before. People only take one look at me and they start offering me hot drinks, thought Jill. You'd think I'd been in an accident. I suppose I have.

She sat down on the sofa and glanced round, wondering if spies still came to this house. There was a white and gilt clock on the mantelpiece, a dark painting of a castle and the usual wartime photograph in a silver frame, a bride in borrowed white, a groom in uniform. The man was a Naval lieutenant, the girl very like Mary Ward who now reappeared, just like Colette, with a tray.

"He'll be with you directly. I hope you don't dislike your tea strong? John likes his positively red. I enjoy mine dish-water weak."

Before leaving, she turned at the door.

"Don't be nervous. John has a gruff manner but his heart's in the right place. At least," she added dryly, "I like to think so."

Jill sat looking at the silver teapot, recently cleaned. Everything in the house was spotless. She was still trying to cope with nerves when John Ward came in. She remembered him. Burly, broad, an olive tint to his thick skin, a bullet-shaped head with black-grey hair combed back. Thick glasses. Thin lips.

He strode in with a swinging gait, nodded to her, and sat down facing her in a high-backed chair. Like Philomène.

"Miss Sinclair? You want a word, I believe. Mary's a treasure. Tea already. Good show."

John Ward looked enquiring.

"Shall I pour? Or are you good at it?"

When Jill gave a feeble laugh and said "not very", he picked up the silver pot, and poured out. He offered her a biscuit which Jill refused. She was sure it would choke her.

But her heart had begun to slow down. Like his wife, John Ward had a parental air which had certainly been absent when she'd met him last. In the recent, oh so distant, war.

"Tell me the trouble," he said, biting a biscuit and regarding her through his thick glasses.

She tried to keep the story brief. François Ghilain had come to this house two years ago. John Ward had interviewed him.

"Ghilain? Ghilain? Let me think. Ah yes, I remember. Son of the Mayor of Bourg-en-Bresse . . ." he spoke almost to himself and then looked up, staring keenly at her. "Don't I also remember you, Miss Sinclair? You were here with him. Posed as his interpreter. His idea, no doubt."

"I did become an interpreter later. I was sent to France with the RASC."

"Were you indeed? And when you were in France, what did you find out about him? I don't doubt you tried to make enquiries. I have an idea," he used the fatherly tone, "you discovered something which upset you."

"I heard in Lyon that he had been shot as a collaborator. The man who told me was the judge at the trial."

"Trial," repeated John Ward. "That's a glorified name for the things they did. So. Young Ghilain is dead, is he?"

Jill almost shouted.

"No! He's alive. In Dover. I saw him this morning, they're keeping him in a detention centre."

John Ward poured more tea but did not drink it. He reflected for a moment.

"I take it you are here because you want to know which of the stories, the one in Lyon or the one the young man has apparently told you, is the truth?"

"Yes."

He rubbed his chin for a moment or two. Like many swarthy men, however well shaved, the skin was faintly dark on his heavy jowls. She noticed his signet ring and remembered Peter's Colonel. These men in command. When he turned to look at her, his spectacles made his eyes as large as François's had been. He didn't blink.

"Doesn't your feminine intuition, something I respect and about which I've had a good deal of experience, provide the answer?"

She said nothing.

"That's a pity. Are you certain you didn't feel something like that when you saw him? Talked to him? Think carefully."

Jill burst out. "I'm sorry. Sorry to waste your time, sorry to barge in here. I haven't any intuition about François, I'm out of my depth. I don't understand anything. I just want to know if the stuff he told me . . ."

"Stuff?"

"It was so melodramatic. Like a film."

"Truth often is. Worse than."

"Mr Ward."

Her angry eyes seemed to please him.

"Pity about the intuition. Going to marry him, are you?"

She went scarlet and shook her head.

"Ah. I thought perhaps the ring. The world is a sad place, Miss Sinclair, and at present a great many of us are bent on making it sadder. In your friend's country this purge is still happening. Purification, they call it. Inevitable and intolerable. De Gaulle won't have it and it's being stamped out."

She scarcely heard what he was saying, until he added, "As for Ghilain, certainly I briefed him. Agents are queer customers. Wholly self-reliant. Patient as Job. Inured to the most terrifying setbacks, ready to pounce on any chance, however fleeting, to harm the enemy. What a dog's life, eh? Responsive. Aggressive. Subtle. False. A damned odd mixture."

He held up his hand.

"You must not ask me any more. I'm not at liberty to tell you and even this discussion is out of order. But yes I briefed him here in this house and," he maddeningly added, "I think perhaps you may believe him."

"The Resistance found him guilty!"

He stood up and gave her the driest smile.

"Do you imagine in that chaos they made no mistakes? The Liberation published lists of the accused. Some were guilty. But they lumped the guilty, half-guilty and innocent all together. Many good men, women too, were killed. They died for nothing."

He sighed.

"Yes, I think you can believe your unfortunate friend."

He walked with her to the front door and shook her hand.

"Kipling said truth is at the bottom of a well."

It was despicable to trust somebody because you'd been told it was safe to do so. Knowing François was innocent – the word, like "traitor", seemed 100 years out of date – Jill loathed her own weakness. What's love if you can't trust? She attached no blame to those figures from the past, de la Roche, Philomène. They were players in a game of survival for their country, ruthless because if you weren't ruthless you were dead. But I failed, she thought. No wonder François was sorry for me. Now there's another test ahead of me, almost as bad. Peter. How do I know, when it's over, that I shan't have lost both of them?

She wondered how she was going to get through the next few hours, and sat on a bus taking her to Chelsea in a kind of trance. Last night Peter had telephoned her and his mother in Markham Square. His voice on the Army line had been so small that Clarissa scarcely heard him and shouted gaily, "Darling! Speak up, did I understand you're due home?" while Jill stood, not knowing whether to go or to stay. Clarissa frowned and gestured her to remain, knowing her son would ask for Jill at once. He did.

"Darlingest? With luck I may be with you around six tomorrow. Can't wait!"

It was hot evening when Jill walked slowly home down the King's Road. Markham Square was quiet, the houses half asleep in a deepening golden light. How dirty they are, she thought. Five years of dirt and no paint, you'd never think they were once white. She put her key in the front door and hadn't opened it wide before she heard Clarissa calling, "Darling, is that you?"

"No, Clarissa. It's me."

When she went into the drawing-room, disappointment hadn't quite left Clarissa's face. Jill was accustomed to Clarissa's coldness towards her and to the eager love Clarissa felt for her son. But this evening she felt a wave of envy for Clarissa's happiness, that breathless waiting, that overt tender joy-to-come.

"I expect the train's late," was Jill's dutiful offering. Clarissa agreed but continued, like a lover, like a dog, to listen for the front door.

The woman who until less than two days ago had been her future mother-in-law had been pretty once. The only trace now was the startling blue of her eyes, Peter had inherited those. Living with her was satisfactory enough. Clarissa was polite in her cold way, even occasionally thoughtful. If she produced pretty awful meals, who didn't? It isn't her fault she doesn't like me, thought Jill. She dismissed from her thoughts the idea that Clarissa disliked any girl whom Peter took out for a drink. And if she does, so what, thought Jill. Love's like that. Selfish.

They sat in silence for a while and Jill, every moment more tense so that her stomach was aching, was about to go and fetch a book when there was the noise Clarissa was waiting for. A taxi drew up outside the house and a door slammed.

Clarissa sprang up without a word and ran out.

"Ma! There you are. And Jill . . . both my girls, but Ma's pipped you to the post!" exclaimed Peter as his mother reached the bottom of the stairs. He put both arms round her and lifted her right off her feet, swinging her round like a child.

Clarissa exclaimed and laughed and demanded to be put down.

"You are such a fool, still in short trousers."

"That's what you like, Ma. A great lout of ten years old."

"Don't call me Ma."

"Sorry, Ma."

He set her neatly down and with a soft "Darlingest!" came over to hug Jill. He pressed her so close and so tightly that she could scarcely breathe.

"You look beautiful, doesn't she, Ma? Now – shall we all have drinks?"

"What about tea?"

"Good grief, Ma, is that the way you celebrate the hero's return? Wait till you see what I've brought this time."

He bent to unstrap his Army holdall and fished out a bottle.

"Now this, both of you, is the real thing, something we haven't seen for a century. Real vintage French champagne. The man I bought it from swears it was hidden from the Germans, and I must believe him – it's 1932! Come along, we'll drink to each other."

Reflecting his mother's radiant face, Peter was in a mood for celebration. Up in the drawing-room he opened the champagne by the open window, the cork shot out on to the balcony and was retrieved by Clarissa.

"Do you know, Jill, my mother is quite capable of mounting this cork in silver!" He filled their glasses, sprawled in an easy chair and launched into talk about France.

"God, it's changed. It's so much better than when you were with us, darling. Believe it or not, some of the French are actually pleased to see us now. Even hospitable. The other evening the Colonel and the rest of us were invited out to dinner. A huge old château, Ma, you remember the sort of thing when you went to France before the war? The family now live in one corner of it but the way the invitations were given was very grand. The Colonel said he thought we were in for a feast.

"Our hostess was a little fat lady, a duchess or something (they have oodles of those, though they cut their heads off in the French Revolution). She was dressed up to the nines and so were her husband and a young daughter. We had *port* before dinner! Then we all trooped into a huge dining-room and our hostess said, 'We have a special rarity for our distinguished visitors." Guess what we got? Baked Beans and peanut butter!"

He roared with laughter, Jill smiled, Clarissa shuddered.

"I suppose the Americans dumped that stuff on them because the poor things haven't enough to eat."

"Not true, Ma. The château's grounds are teeming with game. The Colonel counted four pheasants in the drive. No, it's the new thing in France – they're in love with the Yanks."

He sprang up to refill their glasses. He repeated thoughtfully, "God, it's changed. Jill and I saw the worst of it, didn't we, darling?"

Jill did her best to sound natural and to join in. A settled terror had come over her. She felt like a woman watching an innocent animal at play, while behind her back she held a knife to cut its throat. They say animals can smell death. But Peter went on talking and joking and later said, "Got a little surprise for you both," and bustled out, to return with a larger holdall. He dumped it on the floor.

"First you, Ma. The regiment spent a day in Paris. I couldn't find a thing for you but then I had a stroke of luck. Dermot introduced me to a dubious chap in the black market. So. *Voilà*!"

"The black market. I'm shocked," said Clarissa girlishly, opening a parcel. Inside was a magnificent bottle of scent.

For once she was awed.

"Good gracious! It must have cost a fortune."

Peter helped her to take out the elaborate stopper. The room immediately smelled expensive and foreign.

"Now your turn, darling."

Jill's present, also packed in cheap brown paper, contained two small ivory figures, one of a naked girl standing four-square on pale ivory legs, the other, bare-bosomed and Indian, was a dancer.

"Peter, they are beautiful."

"I'm so glad you like them. I discovered them in a dusty old antique shop in the Rue de Seine. I couldn't resist them. They remind me of you somehow."

He threw a laughing look from Jill to his mother, but she was too busy anointing her wrists to notice.

Jill's room in Markham Square was across the landing from the one which had been Peter's since his parents bought the house when he was fourteen years old. Both rooms were a floor higher than his mother's big double bedroom which had remained unchanged since Peter's father's death.

Clarissa did not know if her son and Jill slept together. She didn't want to. She avoided the thought of sex and had always been sexually cold. Her husband's sex life was something she'd also known nothing about.

Neither his mother's prudery nor his father's hidden sex drive, whatever form that had taken, were inherited by Peter. He worshipped and wanted Jill. Jill had expected sex after they became engaged and had been willing, almost eager to go to bed with him. All Peter did was kiss her. Once when they'd been out to a film and had come in late, he wandered into her room and kissed her with surprising passion, quickly taking his caresses further before suddenly breaking off. To her astonishment he whispered, "Darlingest. We mustn't fall from grace."

This evening they went upstairs to change for dinner, something Clarissa insisted on. Peter tapped at Jill's door. She felt quite frightened when he sat down on the bed and pulled her on to his knee.

"Why are you so pretty?"

"There's a question."

"When I'm away you are always with me. In my heart. Darlingest. Do you think I ought to leave the Army? I'm sure Army life isn't you, really. The wives and the pecking order and the funny old rules and customs. We must talk about it. Our future, I mean."

The bed was close to the dressing table, and as she sat with his arms round her she saw her own blank face in the glass, Peter's unscarred cheek against hers. And thought of the knife behind her back.

"Have I time for a bath, darlingest? Mustn't be late for Ma's welcome home dinner."

Jill went to his room very early next morning, long before Clarissa was awake. He was deeply asleep and she bent and touched his shoulder. Peter woke at once and, conscious of her standing there, was alarmed. He got out of bed. He was a man always elegant in uniform and when Jill saw him in his pyjamas it made everything worse. When she told him, he didn't make a sound. The horrible part was that somehow he seemed to expect it.

"I understand."

Of course he didn't.

His eyes filled with tears and he turned away. Jill put her arms round him but he shook her off. She couldn't say she was sorry. How could she say that?

She went back to her room and packed nothing but a nightdress and underclothes in her old Army gas mask case. And her passport. When she turned round, he was standing in the doorway. He said an awful thing.

"Why couldn't you love me?"

In the stuffy telephone box, Jill spoke to Colette who said at once, "*What's happened?*"

"I told Peter. About François."

"Did you break the engagement?"

Jill whispered, "Yes. He cried. I've never seen a man cry before."

"It's awful, isn't it?" said Colette. And sighed. There was a pause. She stood filled with pity – as much for Peter Whittaker whom she didn't know as for the desperate girl talking to her. Knowing the answer, she asked, "Did you see that man in Kensington?"

"Yes. He told me – he told me I can believe in François."

"Thank God. So you and François . . ."

"Colette, *I don't know*. How can he forgive me? I didn't believe in him."

"Where are you?"

"Victoria station."

Of course you are, thought Colette. She longed passionately for things to be righted, for the girl she had mothered to be happy. She said suddenly, "Have you got any money?"

Jill gave a sobbing kind of laugh. "Lots. I went to the bank."

She didn't say she had her passport with her.

"Don't ring off," Colette said, "I want you to promise me something."

"What?"

"Don't you dare be cautious, for God's sake! Promise me that whatever happens, whatever you decide, you'll get in touch with your parents. And with me."

Jill was ashamed at that. Why hadn't she rung her parents? She couldn't bear to.

"I promise. I do promise."

Again she noticed nothing on the train journey to Dover. Just stared out with blind eyes at the yellow grass in suburban gardens and shorn fields after the harvest. Pitiful arguments went on in her head. What will happen if he doesn't want me? He still loves me, doesn't he? He never said so. Her thoughts, thrashing back and forth, returned to Peter's sorrowful face. She faintly remembered Paula saying long ago that she brought bad luck to people. She'd meant the boys who left her bed and flew to their deaths. Who had said the stupidest words in the English language were "poor me"?

When the train drew into Dover station and Jill got out into dazzling sun, she was hit by a strong wind. It was the first for weeks. It blew fragments of dust into her face and in the sky overhead the clouds had begun to rush and race. Giving up her ticket, Jill raced too, through the town towards the police station. She was out of breath when she arrived and pushed open the old-fashioned door.

The same sergeant was at the same counter. He was dealing with a woman who held a wriggling child in her arms, a small boy who sucked his thumb and kicked his legs.

"Do stop, Eric," she said, shifting him.

The sergeant was patient.

"Just give me the details, Mrs Thompson, what date did you lose your handbag at the shop?"

Jill stood in a fever. She couldn't interrupt but stood, mentally gabbling, "Oh please, oh please." At last the woman thanked him, repeated all over again her dismay at finding she'd left her bag somewhere, "I feel sure it was at the Co-op but they say . . ." She finally left, the little boy was still loudly sucking.

"I've come to see Monsieur Ghilain, sergeant. It's urgent, may I see him at once?"

"'Fraid not."

From intensity, even terror, she nearly fainted for a second time.

"The fact is, Miss, he has gone."

"*Gone*?!"

Wild ideas of escape, of the SOE with their practised now-useless skills, came to her.

"Why yes, he went about . . ." he looked at the clock on the wall, "Half an hour ago."

"Did he say . . ."

"Returning to France, Miss, and glad to go if you ask me. All that trouble's been settled. Misunderstanding apparently. Things like that happen nowadays. 'Tisn't like in wartime. Tell you what, you might just catch him at the harbour. Boat doesn't go for, let's see, another ten minutes. Better hurry though," he called. But the station door had already slammed.

The wind blew harder. Waves slapped the harbour walls and showed their teeth in the sharp sunlight. With desperate haste Jill bought a return ticket to Calais and, carrying nothing but her old gas mask case slung over her shoulder, hurried up the gangplank on to the ship.

Less than three minutes later the ship began to move.

Is this crazy, she thought, watching the harbour begin to get slowly smaller. Am I doing something mad? But the thought of François vanishing to France, lost to her for a second time, that was insanity. Still staring across the widening gap of water, she thought, why, why did he go without trying to see me again? Because I didn't trust. Because I'm not the one he used to love.

When the ship, the *Pride of Kent*, came into the open sea, the weather was rough indeed. The ship began to heave and climb and slide down. Many of the cheerful passengers soon vanished to the lavatories. Others, who had remained on deck, were sick over the side.

Jill was too distraught to feel the heaving of the ship as she began to search high and low. There was no sign of him. The ship was quite crowded and people huddled together ashen-faced. A woman steward carried a pea-green child off to the Ladies. One or two men who had sea legs drank at a small bar and laughed as the ship rose and fell. Jill hung about in the bar for a while, eyes on the swinging door, then she stumbled out again, half reeling, all through the ship until at last she knew he wasn't on board. Returning to the bar she sat down and closed her eyes. I've lost him. I don't know how or where. I do know why. How like François simply to go.

As she sat there, the idiocy of boarding a Channel boat in the hope of finding him did strike her. She thought – what would my parents think if they saw me, with no luggage, chasing after a man I know now I'll never see again?

For a moment or two, as she imagined her conventional mother's incredulity, her practical father's disapproval, she was free from pain.

Then back swept misery with the noise of waves breaking over the decks.

"There it is, mate!"

A man and his friend at the bar went over to a porthole. Jill followed. The last time she'd seen that low-lying coast, the war had been on and terrible hope lay ahead of her.

Rising, falling, the engine throbbing, the steamer made its careful way into the harbour. Jill crept up on deck to watch the ship dock. She remembered how once François had called his country *La Belle France*. On this grey, blowy noon, amidst the still-unrepaired bomb damage of Calais, it did not live up to its ancient adoring name.

I suppose I will just take the next boat home, she thought. She realised with a sense of shock that she couldn't go back to Markham Square; that part of her life was finished. She had no home there now and no future either. I'll go to my parents. Poor Mum, she'll hate all this, it will embarrass her and she won't understand. Dad will. Because half of him is French? Maybe. But he'll never say what he truly thinks . . .

When the passengers were all ashore, Jill spoke to the man at the passport counter in her beautiful French and asked when the next ship would be leaving for Dover. "Not for four hours, Mademoiselle," he gave her a look of curiosity.

She was at the end of the queue and thought, I shall just sit here and wait.

A voice said, "*Mignonne*."

She started so violently that people nearby gaped. François, as green as the most seasick child on the *Pride of Kent* stood beside her.

"But I looked for you. All over the ship!"

"My ship?"

"Yes, yes, that one . . ." she wildly pointed at the door of the office.

"I took a cabin. *Dieu*, Jill, we French hate your accursed Channel."

"*François, I'm here*."

"So I see."

The crowds began to troop out towards a waiting train. François and Jill stood in the empty office. He was beginning to revive slightly.

"Why didn't you wait?" she repeated, moving closer.

Saying nothing he put both arms round her, pulled her to him and pressed his face to hers.

"Why didn't you wait?" she repeated, moving closer.

"Why didn't you believe me?"

"Don't. Don't."

"Perhaps I thought you did not love me."

"Oh, I do. I do."

He pushed her at arm's length then and looked at her with a faint smile.

"Somebody told you about me."

"Oh François. I should have trusted you. I'm so ashamed."

Ignoring the beseeching voice and face, he regarded her thoughtfully.

"You shouldn't button up the neck of that dress. It's better like this," undoing it. "You have a pretty neck."

"You drive me mad!"

"Of course, *coquine*. Of course."